# VLAD THE PALER

## MALTHEA

**Dreamspinner Press**

Published by
Dreamspinner Press
382 NE 191st Street #88329
Miami, FL 33179-3899, USA
http://www.dreamspinnerpress.com/

Vlad

Cover Art by Catt Ford

ISBN: 978-1-61372-244-2

Printed in the United States of America
First Edition
December 2011

eBook edition available
eBook ISBN: 978-1-61372-245-9

To all the Draculas of book, stage, and screen
who have meant so much to me.

# PROLOGUE

CALL me Vlad until I can think of something more righteous. And cut me some slack, okay? I was just Turned like a biscuit ago, and I haven't had a lot of time for things like pondering the ultimate *nom de noir*. If that makes me sound gay, it's probably because my mother made me learn French, or more probably because I *am* gay. If you're a hater, then you can just fuck off forever. Right now would be a good time.

So I'm a little touchy about the whole homo thing, but you tell me. Why the hell can't people just mind their own damned business? What I do in bed is no one's affair but mine and my lover's. If I *had* a lover anyway. Looking for one is what got me into this sitch.

Before you ask, I can't go by my birth name, which is Cyrus Lloyd Gae. Seriously. I'm not making it up. You can call and ask my mom, who's a very weird white woman from a very weird family in deepest, reddest Florida. When she was eighteen, she married a Korean tourist—with one of the least common surnames in a country where they only have like five to share among the entire population—who was dying to live anywhere else. The divorce was final before I was delivered. Dad went to work as a chef at Disney World and paid child support, but passive-aggressively resisted ever seeing me or Mom. Maybe his rejection is what made me gay. Who knows? It is what it is, and I'm cool with it. Anyone who isn't can.... Shit! Almost started another rant.

I don't want you to think I do nothing but bitch all the time. Even though you're an imaginary audience listening to the talk radio show of my life, my death, and my undeath. No, wait; that's not right. You weren't there for my death—my death at the hands of a jackhole that doesn't deserve the name "vampire." There was nothing darkly romantic about it, believe me.

All right, so I *did* swoon, but that was from shock and blood loss. Here, let me tell you how it went down.

Basically, this super-hot guy picked me up at Don Tay's Inferno, owned by gay ex-Miami Dolphins fullback Donovar Tay. Super-hot guy goes with me into the alley out back—the default hookup spot for the club—but instead of the mutual hand job I'm looking forward to, he slams me against the wall and tears my throat open. After he drinks his fill, he does kiss me, but it was a definite afterthought, bet on it. I taste blood in my mouth as he drops me behind a dumpster. I'm so weak I can't move. Then the world starts pulsing with my heartbeat, blinking in and out, slower and slower. Everything grows a misty halo that gets brighter and bigger until there's nothing but white. And then nothing at all.

But then I wake up. My head is still wedged between metal and brick, and the vile reek of dumpster-water is up my nose. My neck has the mother of all kinks in it and hurts like blue hell no matter which way I turn it.

Then I remembered... I remembered my date *du heure* attacking me, and I knew why I felt so strange. There's no other explanation. Super-hot guy was a real vampire, and I'm now a creature of the night, as I'd often fantasized. I just wish it had been a *little* more like my fantasies, you know?

In my daydream of a vampire lover, *he* wears a long coat with a big fur collar over a dark suit tailored just for his tall, lean-muscled body. He sweeps into the club, puts his arm around me, and steers me away from my flabbergasted friends—who are paralyzed by envy for several minutes before they even think about trying to get a phone picture, and failing that, Tweet everyone they know, so I'm a Facebook legend inside an hour.

We slide into his limo that has windows tinted as dark as a Goth's outlook on life. He leans over me, putting his gorgeous face right up in mine, taking a long smell of me. After telling me that my scent is intoxicating, he kisses me, whether I want to be kissed or not. I want, of course, and offer my neck to him. Touched by my gift, he bites me, and I get off like six times while he sucks my blood. Then he takes me away to be his hellish studmuffin, and we travel around the world in a glamorous jet wearing really cool clothes and being really snarky to mortals who don't know their place before stealing their boyfriends for a hot suck and fuck. Need I point out that the word suck is a double entendre here? Didn't think so.

So, you can easily see the disparity between my fantasy and the reality. It totally pissed me off. It still does. I mean, would it have killed him to use a little finesse? Or at least leave me somewhere that didn't have the aforementioned puke-inducing dumpster-water stench? What the eff? Am I a piece of squirty-gum to be spit out when the flavor's gone? Oh, hell no.

If it's the last thing I do—and I assume I have plenty of time now—I'm going to find this butt-munch and thank him in my own unique way.

# CHAPTER ONE

I HAVEN'T talked to you since I declared vendetta last night, so here's what happened between then and now, *plus ou moins*.

I go back into the Inferno and look around, but I don't see Mr. Tall, Dark, and Dickless, who I know only as Troy. I see several guys in black leather jackets, but none of them are as hot as the guy I went into the alley with. None of them have red hair so dark it looks maroon. Maybe he dyes it, but I have a pretty good eye for that kind of thing, and it looked natural to me. This is really starting to sound like the beginning of a Harlequin romance. You know the kind where the heroine is poor but honest and deceptively beautiful. Her job has unexpectedly taken her to an exotic land where she meets the hero, a square-shouldered, dedicated-doctor type with wavy auburn hair and slate-colored eyes like storm clouds over the ocean. Really lame, right? But Troy's eyes really are slate-colored—kind of like blueberries, inky blue with a foggy surface. I've never seen anyone who looks like him in the Inferno before—probably because the Inferno is where the geekier Goths hang. The coke-whore staff isn't exactly strict when it comes to proper ID, so you get a lot of underage kids in there vogueing for each other, taking about a zillion pix with their candy-flake Droids and sending them to dweebs who are even bigger losers for not getting in the door.

I skirt a school of Lolitas and Lolitos near the unisex bathrooms, witchy marionette girls and sulking naughty schoolboys. They give me the once-over through the sneeze guards of their bangs, and I see something that rocks me, yes, me, the most blasé guy on my shift at Metro Media. The little cynics are *impressed*, which hasn't happened in like *ever*. Figuring I'm misreading their Kabuki faces, I go into the bathrooms and look around.

When I come out, I hear something I haven't heard since like high school, before I crawled from the sucking primordial ooze of public education. Just to clarify, I was home-schooled until I was fifteen and begged my mom to let me go to public school. Another fantasy that ended badly, but I digress....

"SyFy," yells some chick who sounds like she just inhaled an entire party balloon of helium.

The underage clotheshorses are bounced aside by a pair of boobs that would make the Goodyear blimp weep with envy at their size, buoyancy, and excellent torpedo shape. I recognize these land leviathans, though they were somewhat smaller the last time I saw them. What are the odds? The one time I *don't* want to be recognized and it's turning into a class reunion up in here. Such is what passes for my luck.

"Vinnie!" I greet the owner of the large-breed sweater puppies.

Her name's Lavinia Testardo. Yeah, I know. Sucky name for a kid to be stuck with. She got teased a lot at recess, but she's a counter-puncher and schoolyard bullies tire quickly. When the prey doesn't dissolve into mucus and salt water right away, they tend to lose interest—not always, but usually. Me and Vinnie hung out almost exclusively my senior year, skipping class, swiping makeup from Walgreens drug store, and having face parties. She was not only cool with my gayness, she thought it rocked balls. Which I guess it does. *Literally.*

"Where you been, SyFy?" Vinnie says as she looks me up and down. "Whoa! You are *so* rockin' that look. Have you been living in a basement? That's a beyond awesome moon-tan."

*Huh*? Understand, I've always wanted to be as pale as new-fallen snow on a gravestone, but due to my Asian genes, I have skin as smooth as honey and roughly the same color. I want to run back into the bathroom and look in the mirror, but then I remember. I'm a *vampire*. No *reflection*. *Shit!*

"Uh, thanks," I respond a bit lamely because of my sudden, crushingly disappointing revelation. "I love your Rainbow Brite vibe."

Vinnie preens a little, fluffing her brassy ringlets and flipping a hip so I get a glimpse of the petticoats under her short blue-velvet dress. "When I found these rainbow socks at the thrift store, I was inspired. They have toes," she says, as though informing me she's won the lottery.

I nod. "Cool," I say. I've fallen into a pit of lameness, and I can't get up. What's next? A comment on the nice weather we're having?

"*You* look amazing," Vinnie says, getting my attention back. "You're as white as your shirt." Her eyes go down to my tuxedo shirt. "Is that *blood*?"

"Not real blood. It's a sort of a, you know, fashion statement kind of thing."

"Bullshit." Vinnie hustles me back into the hall where the light's brighter. "That's blood," she says triumphantly. "Real blood starts to turn brown once it's not in your veins anymore."

"And you're an expert because…?"

"I'm a nurse, or I'm going to be when I graduate."

"I thought you were a theater major or some such."

"Keeping tabs on me?" Vinnie flirts automatically even though she knows I'm gay. I've been out since I was nine—yes, nine. You wouldn't believe some of the things I made my superhero action figures do.

"My mom heard from someone else's mom that you were in Liquordale at a performing arts school." Liquordale is Fort Lauderdale, but I'm too cool to call it that. Every year at Spring Break, college students from all over America converge there to consume all local supplies of beer, stack the empties in humongous pyramids, and fall off the balconies of their beachfront hotels. They go home sunburned and hungover, bitching about how they didn't get any.

"Oh yeah, no," Vinnie says. "I was at the Ringling School of Art and Design for a while, but then I met this totally hot guy from Canada on Spring Break and went home with him. I had to break up with him, though. Despite his hotness, Canada remains lukewarm on the Testardo scale of fun and games."

I'd forgotten how much I enjoy Vinnie's company. She's never anything but herself and has a boundless, incongruously innocent curiosity about almost everything. It seems she hasn't changed a stitch. Except for those dirigibles on her chest.

"I see the girls are all grown up," I say suavely.

"I had 'em done when I was dancing my way through school," she says in the common euphemism for "I had surgery to make my boobs bigger because I take off my clothes in a sleazy bar for tips from drunken letches."

"I didn't know you were actually on the stage." My suaveness amazes even me.

"Aren't you sweet?" Vinnie gives me what can only be described as a calculating look. Her big blue eyes go all squinty until she looks like a big cat with Grand Canyon-scale cleavage.

"Why are you looking at me like that?" I back up a step even though I'm technically one of the undead, and she should be the one cringing in dread. "I won't sleep with you. I'm still gay."

Vinnie chuckles. "Is it that obvious I still want your smokin' hot, *yaoi*-prince self? Relax, studpuppy. I'm not going to try jumping your bones. I can appreciate your perfection without fucking you."

I have to say, I really like the sound of that. I'm wondering if we could get together and hang out sometime. Then I remember that I have vengeance to wreak.

"Great to see you," I say. "But I really gotta fly."

"Got a hottie waiting for you?"

"Something like that."

"Far be it from me to cockblock, but could I have just two more teensy minutes?"

"Sure, what's up?"

"So if you're going to go sincere with this cosplay, I'm wondering if you already have someone to run errands for you and whatnot... during the daytime, I mean."

I hadn't thought about that. All of the stories I've ever devoured about vampires agree that they sleep during the day and go out at night. So, I'll need a place to hole up, with someone to make sure I'm not bothered. I make one of my patented snap decisions.

"Okay, you might as well know. I'm a real vampire, and no, I don't have anyone to help out. Do you know someone who would—?"

"Me!" she interrupts. "Me, me, me. I know everything there is to know about vampires. You can stay at my place until you get yours fixed up right. Gimme your phone and I'll put my number in. Just call me whenever, and you'll have a safe place to crash."

"Cool." I hand her my phone. "By the way, what do I look like?"

"You look like sweet, romance-*yaoi* perfection. Your hair is thick and jet-black and spiky. Your skin is like fucking marble and your eyes are pools of midnight. You totally rock the frock coat and boots thing. Plus you're exquisitely slender and supple, if you must know." She gives me another long look. "If *Matrix* Keanu Reeves fucked *Sleepy Hollow* Johnny Depp and they had a baby, it would grow up to be you. If that was possible, I mean."

Ironic, isn't it? I finally perfect my "look" and I can't see myself.

But anyway, that's how I come to be sleeping in a cabinet under the stairs in Vinnie's loft apartment. I don't know how she can afford this place. It's enormous—the entire top floor of an old cigar factory. The wood floors still smell like aged tobacco. At least to me they do. Vinnie says she can't smell it, but then again, she doesn't have a vampire's heightened senses. Did that sound stuck-up? Am I developing the cool superiority of a top-of-the-food-chain predator? Or am I just being a dick? Help me out here. This is all new to me. And I don't mean to diss Vinnie. I'm grateful she's letting me stay here. Damn, I *did* sound like a dick.

So this loft is pure awesome sauce. There's just something about a big, open space partitioned off with textured rice-paper screens. I like that all the furnishings are made of natural materials in colors that remind you of the beach: sand, cool blues, and cream. It's the sort of simple design that costs buckets of money to achieve. And it's exactly the sort of décor I *wouldn't* expect from Vinnie Testardo.

I'm not making any taste judgments, just saying that I would've expected something more in keeping with her cosplay-loving spirit. Something more like the contents of a Broadway musical actress's trunk dumped over Barbie's dream house. Not that there's anything wrong with that. It's just more what I expected. Not these clean lines and groupings of unvarnished wooden furniture like pieces of modern art. It's the definition of unfussy.

The place where I sleep is an enclosed triangular space under a freestanding flight of stairs on wheels. I can't imagine the mind that invented the rolling staircase with storage, but it works. It's totally lightproof, and after Vinnie lines it with cushions and a velvet cape, it's pretty comfortable. And once I close my eyes, it wouldn't matter if I was lying on broken glass. I sleep the sleep of the dead: deep, dark, and dreamless, like drowning for hours.

When I surface at sundown—I check, it's officially sundown—I find a note from Vinnie that informs me she won't be back until seven-ish and to make myself at home. P.S. Please don't suck my cat.

*Cat?*

Wow, I'm really hungry. The stuff in the fridge verifies that normal food is not what I crave. I need blood. I guess that shouldn't surprise me. Now, where is that cat?

The cat is either in another dimension—which I believe to be highly possible—or is just very, very good at hide-and-seek. Looks like I miss out on the chance to see if I'd actually suck cat blood. It's six thirty now, so I'm going to sit down in this chair the color of a shore bird's egg to wait for my... what's the word for someone in Vinnie's position? In relation to me, I mean. Besides friend, what's the word for a vampire's personal assistant? You'd think someone with a measured IQ of 158 could come up with the right word, but no.

I can't come up with a plan to find the jerk that Turned me either. I don't have a name other than Troy—like there aren't 27 million Troys in the South—if that was even his real name. I don't know a single thing about Troy except what he looks like, which I've already lovingly described for you. But I will say again that he's smokin' hot. Way beyond soap-opera-actor handsome and far into Prada-runway-model territory. He had no trouble convincing me to leave the club for somewhere more private. Yeah, I guess I'm kind of a slut, but I'm twenty-one and male, so I'll ask you again to cut me a little slack, *s'il vous plaît*.

Hold the power brooding—I sense Vinnie. How weird is that? I can actually feel what she's doing like I'm the one doing it. I guess my vamp powers are starting to kick in. Vinnie's getting on the funky freight elevator that doesn't have doors. I can smell her scent now: the last fumes of Uninhibited perfume mixed with lady sweat—in Florida, everyone sweats. But beyond that even, I can feel her excitement through the weariness of a full day of work. I can feel the beating of her heart, the blood flowing in her veins. The *blood*. My brilliant mind makes a connection, and I run to the elevator with the same enthusiasm I used to show for the arrival of the pizza-delivery guy.

*Whoa*. Back it up, Bubba Vamp. Vinnie's a friend. She's sheltering me. She thinks I'm the hottest thing on two legs—with the possible exception of Count Greyce, the beautiful, tortured, vampire hero of her favorite anime series... but he isn't real, so I win.

I hear the chunky clunk of the elevator stopping and Vinnie's footsteps on the cypress plank floor of the foyer area. And yes, I know how gay I sound when I say things like "foy-ay," but that's what it's called, and as I might have mentioned, my gayness has been confirmed beyond a doubt and many times. But who cares? It's dinnertime.

I'm having a really hard time fighting the urge to run to the warm pink and suck until I'm full. *Shit*. My mom's dogs have more self-control.

"Vlad?" Vinnie calls out. It's so cool of her to call me that.

"I'm right here," I say as I appear beside her. I don't literally disappear and reappear, but I move so fast that she can't see me.

"Wow!" Vinnie blinks eyelids shadowed in satiny taupe. She's wearing full-on Snow White drag: puffy little sleeves, hair ribbon, enamel-red lips, and all. The black wig makes her look like a completely different person... a completely different person with identical 48 double Dees. I swear I'm afraid I'll fall into her cleavage and like it so much that I'll curl up and never move again. It's *not* a sex thing. Sheesh, gutter-brain.

"Where you been?"

"Who's your best friend?" Vinnie counters archly.

"Not a good time for a pop quiz," I say.

"Oh, poor baby, you're really hungry, aren't you?"

"Well, I had instructions not to suck the cat, and I couldn't go out. My only shirt looks like a crime scene."

"Right, so… who's your best friend?" she coos again.

"I'm guessing you are. Tell me why."

"Ooh, I love a pouty *bishie*." Vinnie checks her makeup in the agate-framed mirror hanging from fishing line in front of one of the rice-paper screens. "I have dinner—or is it breakfast?—all lined up for you."

"I like what I'm hearing. Tell me more."

"Give me two shakes to change, and I'll take you there."

I go to the wall of floor-to-ceiling windows and practice looking out over the city in a sinister manner. Vinnie is back way before I expect her. She's the queen of quick change.

Her Snow White wig is still in place, but the red hair ribbon is gone, as are the yellow skirt and the red and blue puffy-sleeved top. Now she's wearing Japanese schoolgirl Goth with a pair of full-bore, ass-kicking Doc Martens boots. In her hand is a poet shirt, all billowy, with a hundred tiny laces. Unfortunately, it's black. I don't do all black. That's for posers. Unless you're a genuine ninja, of course.

"I don't do all black," I say.

"Understood." She eyes me. "How do you feel about bare chest?"

"It's kind of show-offy, you know?" Truthfully, I'm not in that great of shape. I'm slim, and I have fairly broad shoulders and long legs, but I'm not exactly Harry Hardbody, you know? I don't go around shirtless, but I have to take this one off eventually.

Holy shiz! Imagine my surprise! Apparently vampirism has gifted me with a set of nicely defined muscles. I'm not Bruce Lee, but I look damned good. I guess that sounds a little conceited, but I don't feel like it's my body I'm complimenting, you know?

"Wow, this is the body I've always wanted."

"No kidding," Vinnie says. "I say flaunt it. Otherwise, the only other thing I have that you could wear would be the T-shirt I sleep in when my baby sister stays over."

"I forgot about her. What was her name again?"

"You're bad. Her name's Petronia, and you know she's always had a mad crush on you."

"Do all the women in your family have such fabulous taste?"

"Pretty much. Come on—let's get you fed." Vinnie grabs a transparent vinyl umbrella on the way to the elevator. "Just in case," she says, and her eyes twinkle. I'm not making it up; they actually twinkle like a shower of blue glitter.

I toss my crusty shirt over the driftwood hat rack and button my knee-length frock coat as I get into the freight lift with Vinnie. She removes her black lace choker and fastens it around my neck. I wish I could see what it looks like. So far Undeath is nothing like I thought it would be. For some reason, the basic conflict between my love of dressing-room mirrors and the fact that vampires have no reflections never occurred to me when I was mortal.

"Isn't this the coolest?" Vinnie chirps. "I'm procuring victims for my vampire lord."

When she puts it that way, it does sound kind of cool. "Where are we going?"

"Don't laugh, but it's a coffee house where role-players hang."

"RP Gamers? Really?"

"Their hardware is the shit." She shrugs.

"Geeks," I say, and I ought to know. I used to be their king… and then I got a job.

"Well, if you're picky?" Vinnie looks at me likes she expects an answer.

"How come you're going all Mama Hen on me?"

"I'd like a baby, but I'm not ready to be pregnant yet, so I'm gonna practice on you. Now, do you really want me to waste time describing your dinner to you?"

"No. I'm sure if you picked him out, he's all that."

"Damn right he is. I met him at a manga con during Guavaween. He was dressed in this retro Sonic getup with his hair in royal blue spikes that totally matched the collar of my Sailor Moon dress. *And* we were both wearing red knee-high socks over our high-tops to simulate superhero boots."

"Destiny," I say.

"You'd think, but he loves the cock." Vinnie sighs. "I'm beginning to think it's true that all the really hot men are gay." She pauses. "Shit, I forgot about the cat."

"Are you sure you have one?"

"It's really my sister Frankie's cat, but her husband is allergic. I don't think it likes me."

"Maybe if you didn't refer to the cat as 'it'?"

"Fine. *He* doesn't like me. Probably because I had him fixed. He was spraying everything in sight, including my shoes."

"I can understand why he'd hold a grudge, but you did what you had to do."

"Well, yeah. Anyway, I left food out and he has a litter box, so I reckon he'll be okay."

"Does he have a name?"

"D'Artagnan. I call him Dart. It seems to fit," Vinnie says as she leads the way into the parking garage.

Vinnie doesn't have a car. What she has is a motorcycle that she keeps chained up in the two-story parking structure. Before you get visions of a badass chopper, let me describe the fail that is the Honda Gold Wing. This abomination has such bourgeois accoutrements as an airbag and seats that are not only miniature easy chairs, but they're heated. And that's not all—the *handgrips* are heated. I can almost understand the need for a radio—music *rules*—and a GPS, but really, Butch, *heated handgrips*? Just doesn't square somehow with the primal struggle of man against the elements that a motorcycle should symbolize.

I said all these things to Vinnie during the ride to her place last night—the helmets have intercoms, I shit you not. She said her uncle left it to her in his will and it was good on gas. Her tone said "don't diss my ride."

So I don't bitch as I climb on behind her, leaving the helmet where it is. It crushes my hair, and since I'm immortal now, I figure I don't really need a helmet anymore.

Vinnie drives us to a place near the waterfront that's sandwiched between a seafood restaurant and a closed tattoo parlor. Predictably, it's called Starbase.

Inside, the place is half geek boutique and half coffee shop with free Wi-Fi. Young men and women in utilitarian clothing sit in circles facing one another, eyes on their laptop screens, buds in their ears, soy lattes or Red Bulls close at hand, swinging swords and casting spells in dark castles and magical forests, absorbed in the roles they're playing in a world built of collective imagination. *Ah, the memories.* I feel tired just looking at them.

"This way." Vinnie takes my arm, proud to be seen with me.

I like how that feels, and I do my best to look haughty as we walk past the baristas at the counter. They actually pause in their sacred ritual of preparing the divine bean nectar to watch me go by. I like how that feels even more. I swagger a little.

"His name is Logon." Vinnie's voice breaks my spell of self-satisfaction.

"Logan?" The only Logan I know is Wolverine, and hairy men are not my kink. I'm more partial to honey than bears.

"It's pronounced Logan, but it's spelled ell, oh, gee, *oh*, en. Log *on*," says a guy with a scratchy tenor voice.

"Clever," I say, because I know which side of a nerd the butter goes on.

From the shadows of a booth between the counter and the wall of the restrooms rises a towering figure cloaked in…. I wish. Logon stands up and is revealed as a *gipster*, which is a name I made up for the geek/hipster hybrid—*heek* sounds too ridiculous even for me.

Logon's hair is very blond and very long and is, of course, parted in the middle and pulled away from his face into a ponytail, thereby negating the entire process of growing long, flowing tresses. His bittersweet-chocolate eyes are framed by plain black glasses. His pants are black and narrow, and his putty-colored T-shirt is emblazoned with flowing letters that look like Tolkien's Elvish. I take the time to decipher the message, which is actually in English. *If you can read this, I found your ring.* Clever, and of course, it's an in-joke.

"Well, I have to hand it to you, Vinnie, he sure *looks* like a vampire." Logon's husky, whispery voice isn't too hard on the ears, but he just rubbed me the wrong way.

"I don't like it when people talk about me like I'm not here," I say sinisterly—wow, talk about awkward adverbs; just try saying sinisterly a couple of times.

"Logon, meet Vlad," Vinnie says.

I'm so not sure about this, but I do what Troy should have done for me. I woo the gipster. I really need a drink.

"Nice to meet you, Logon," I say. "Love your Ringer shirt."

"I got it at Dragon*Con," he answers to establish his credentials as a serious *otaku.*

"Atlanta's a zoo, sensory overload," I say to let him know that I *get it.* Having a frame of reference is so important.

Vinnie's rummaging in her Hello Kitty backpack. "Hang on," she says. "I know I have a tape measure in here somewhere. As soon as I find it, you two whip out your fanboy dicks."

My eyes meet Logon's in a mutual roll. So, rapport established. Vinnie's right; this could be fun, even if it isn't the embodiment of my dark fantasies.

"So Vinnie claimed she knew a real vampire," Logon says. "You sure look like the real deal. Excellent fangs, by the way, but they could be implants."

*I have fangs?* I shoot Vinnie a reproachful look for not telling me as I feel the tips of my pointed canines with my tongue. I have *fangs!* This is beyond awesome. I have to try them out.

"I need your blood," I tell Logon.

"That's... pretty convincing," Logon says.

"Look, I don't want to get all date-rapey, but I need your blood now."

Logon does that little looking to the left and right thing like he's about to tell a non-PC joke. "Yeah, okay. Should we go somewhere more private or something?"

It hits me that I probably don't want my maiden suck to be in front of an audience, but the vague, nonlocalized, grinding hunger pain is now a terrible, freezing emptiness. Even my bones hurt.

I slide into the booth and sit next to Logon. Referencing my favorite vampire movies, I reach out to pull him closer. I'm thrilled when he flinches. I give him a little shake of my head and the infinitely sad look of the misunderstood outcast. He stays put when I take the elastic band off his ponytail and let his hair fall around his face. It's a rather nice face if you're into the whole pale and delicate, Nordic-Anglo thing, and so what if he was a Ringer? I may not worship Professor Tolkien and his epic piece of literature that legitimized an entire subculture, but I'd do that Elf from the movies in a heartbeat. In fact, Logon kind of reminds me of the golden-haired, lithe-limbed badass out of Mirkwood. It's kind of a turn-on.

I lean toward Logon, and he tilts his head, baring his jugular, making it easy for me. I sense Vinnie is about to open her umbrella like she's expecting a large amount of spray as she moves to block the view from the rest of the place. My lips touch the soft skin of Logon's neck, and he shivers. Like the tines of a dessert fork into cheesecake, my fangs sink into his flesh. I don't think about it; it just happens. Blood wells up, and I wipe it away with my tongue. I swallow and oh my goolies! This taste, it's... it's.... I have to have more. *Now!*

# CHAPTER TWO

HEY again. I'm sure you're wondering what happened after I bit Logon. By the way, I know it's awkward and kind of lame to cut to black and catch you up later, not to mention narrating my own story, but it has a distinguished tradition—Dickens, Melville, et cetera—so no snark, please, about how *some* people are *so* self-involved.

BTW: *Moby "Dick"*? Is it just me, or does that title make you smirk like a seventh grader? Random, I know, but let's remember that you're privileged to listen in on the innermost thoughts of a prince of darkness, so again, *no snark, please.*

And yeah, I'm still lazing around in what passes for my coffin. I'm waking up slowly tonight, the better to snuggle with my new squeeze. It feels good to have Logon tucked in at my side with my arm around him, all protective-like. I like the way his long, blond hair drapes over my chest, and I especially like the way his left leg is draped over my thigh. He's totally mine. Turns out he's a complete and total *uke*—submissive and loving it—*and* his blood trips me out big time. *Sweetness.*

The first taste of his blood electrified me. As soon as it touched my tongue, I was all jazzed, and buzzing, and full of energy that wanted out. I felt powerful, and also like I'd just had the best orgasm ever, and the afterglow just went on and on. Vinnie finally had to pull me off Logon to keep me from sucking him dry—her reaction time was delayed because she was *so* getting turned on by the action.

Logon's eyes were all soft and faraway, but I could tell I hadn't hurt him. Then he focused on me and gave me a mega-hot kiss and asked if we could do it again. *Soon.* Pretty cool.

It's always been kind of a dream of mine to lead a group of badasses with supernatural powers. Who hasn't imagined himself as a Dark Lord from time to time? Not you? Really? Never? That's weird. Anyway, it's awesome that I have peeps like Vinnie and Logon. Not only do they accept me for who I am, they think I'm *awesome*.

Did I mention what a rush it was, drinking Logon's blood? Sorry if I'm repeating myself, but damn! It was *that* good. I can still kind of feel it even... but I'll need more soon.

Yeah, it's like that. Crimson crack. Now that I've had a taste, I crave it like I've never craved anything before. But no worries, my next fix is lying warm and soft against my side. I guess that sounds a little cold, but it's just a fact, and as it happens, I care deeply about Logon. I want him near me always. I'll never let him go, and I'll destroy anyone that tries to hurt him.

Dracula had his brides of darkness, and I have Logon, my blood-boo. Logon of the long, silky hair. Logon of the shy smile. Logon of the three nipples. Yeah, it's like that. He makes me as gooey as a toasted marshmallow. And don't think I can't sense you going, "Hey, wait a sec... *three nipples*?" Simmer down; it's not that uncommon. Marky Mark has an extra one. Hey, you know why men have nipples? Give up? Men have nipples because women do. It's not a joke. Everyone starts out female. It's grade-school biology. Moving along.

Vinnie and I made an addition to our budding family when Logon asked if he could come home with us. Vinnie's delighted. She finally has live gay porn in her apartment. Because Logon can't get enough of me. The ultra-amplified vampire orgasm is no myth; at least it isn't for us. I can make him hard just by breathing near him. When I suck his blood, he gets so aroused that he comes as soon as I touch his dick. And to judge by the noises he makes, his world is well and truly rocked. Logon comes so fast and so hard, and he's not shy about telling me how good it feels as I move in and out of him until I come. Just another thing to add to the list of wrongs for which Troy owes me. My first time with a vampire could have been like that, but no. Sucked dry and tossed at the dumpster like an empty juice pouch.

This will sound like bragging, but I lost count of how many times me and Logon did it before the sun came up. I dragged my shag-weary ass into the velvet-lined cubby and pulled Logon in with me. In the haze of my infatuation, I lost sight of Vinnie, but I trusted her to lock up. And I know she got an eyeful of me and Logon making volcanic love on various surfaces covered in 100-percent natural fibers, so she has to be happy.

Hmmmmm, so this is what smug feels like.

When Logon wakes up, I'm going to have breakfast while I fuck him so slowly that he'll beg me to go faster. When I finally let him come, he'll be delirious with pleasure. *Smug.*

Then we'll bathe and get dressed and take Vinnie out on the town. Everyone that sees us will want us. *I am the Sultan of Smug.*

And Logon's waking up. Excuse me.

Um, why aren't you gone? Really? You're sticking around? Suit yourself, but I'm gettin' busy.

Logon's skin is smooth and his muscles are firm. His body is slim and limber and rises like the tide to the stroking of my hands. Indulge me here, because I love every inch of him. I love running my tongue into his belly button, up between his pecs, around his nipples—all of them—and up his neck. I love sucking at the soft skin of his throat, his balls, and his inner thighs. I love the taste of his sweat, his cum, his ass. I love the moans and whimpers he makes when I'm going down on him. His cock is my salty candy, and I'm a greedy boy. I love the way he looks at me and touches me like I'm the most desirable dude on the planet. I love the way his eyes widen when I finger him. Without his glasses on, his eyes are softer than brown velvet, and right now they're melting in the heat of our righteous roll in the hay.

Logon pulls me down by the back of my neck and presses my face to his neck. He holds me close with an arm around my back and both legs around my hips. It's hard to get a hand between us to get hold of my dick. Logon groans deep in his chest when he feels my pink ninja rubbing against his crack. He pulls his knees up and opens to me.

I can't hold back anymore. My fangs sink into his throat and the warm, salty-sweetness flows into my mouth and over my tongue. The head of my cock pushes into Logon and nudges his man-gland. His hard dick is leaking onto my knuckles as a couple of tears leak from the corners of his eyes. And it happens again.

We're connected on every level: physical, mental, emotional, spiritual, and whatever else you got. We are one, and we are bliss. I sink into him, and he absorbs me. We rock together in a warm, red sea, our bodies, our feelings, our souls meshed in a perfect synergy. Logon meets each thrust with a lift of his ass. His fingertips knead the muscles of my shoulders, my back, and my butt, encouraging me to thrust deeper. I withdraw my fangs, bite him a little lower, and he comes like a volcano erupting. Cliché, I know, but I'm in the middle of fucking here. I'm one with the universe. Don't ask me to think up clever metaphors.

"Vlad! God, yes! Yes! Don't stop! I want to feel you moving in me."

That's Logon's voice in urgent mode. Damn. It happened again. I was gone into the warm, fuzzy, mystical thingie that happens when we do it.

"Fuck me," Logon groans.

Gladly. Time to pull out the aces and give my boo the bang he deserves. Logon loves being fucked after he comes, and I have no reservations about that. By the way, this is where I'd thank my mom for making me take dance lessons if she'd done that, but she didn't. Vinnie's the one who taught me how to shimmy and do a bump and grind. I'll never be as smooth as she is, but I ain't too shabby. In fact, this is one thing I'm pretty good at, as Logon will testify.

"Oh, fuck yeah! Come on, Vlad. Give it to me. Give it to me like that. Just like that. Yeah. Oh yeah! That feels so fucking good! So fucking good."

See what I mean? What? Smug? Me? No way. It ain't braggin' if it's true. Ask my Aunt Bootsy.

Logon writhes under me, legs pumping as he thrusts upward, one hand wrapped around his dick, the other curled around the back of my neck. His skin is slippery with sweat and the air is heavy with the dark-brown musk of full-bore sex. It's like I'm breathing him in, and I know I need him as much as I used to need oxygen. I've known him for slightly less than twenty-four hours, and he's the center of my new universe. I don't understand it, but I don't understand a lot of things, like daylight savings time or how bumblebees stay in the air. I just accept them on faith, but this thing with Logon is another few orders of magnitude higher on the scale of the ineffable.

He says my name in a strained little whisper. His delicate, WASP features tense up and then relax like he just came again. I run my tongue over a patch of bloodstained sweat on his left collarbone, and he rises languidly against me, murmuring my new name over and over. His taste fills my mouth, and I come like I've never come before. I don't have an analogy for it. I'm wrung out and breathless. All I can do is lie on top of Logon as the warm, liquid, tingling rush of energy reverberates in every part of me, fading just a little with each echo. Wait, I've got an analogy. It's like when you're surfing and you lose it on a really big wave and you get swept under, being tumbled around until it spits you out on the beach. Except instead of feeling pummeled at the end, you feel this really good, tired feeling. You know what I mean? Hope so, 'cause I'm done 'splainin', Lucy. Piss off for a while, perverts. Logon needs some cuddle time.

HEY, you're back. Let me catch you up—yes, I'm being ironic.

So I totally forgot about Troy while I was wallowing in carnal bliss, and yes, the sex is ultra for me too. My cum is pink, but that's a small price to pay for a climax that lasts for hours. We never got around to going out last night, just hung out at Vinnie's. I was all about sexing Logon and sipping from him whenever I felt the high wearing off. Logon didn't complain and neither did Vinnie. In fact, Vinnie fixed snacks for Logon whenever he'd start to fade. Okay, I admit it; I was a total animal going on pure instinct, but you should spend an entire day naked making love, if you haven't already. It's incredibly liberating. I didn't even care when Vinnie set up the video camera. We watched some of it before the sun came up. Weird, but sexy footage of a pretty blond guy seemingly being fucked by the Invisible Man. And going down on the Invisible Man. And so on. Vinnie and Logon threw popcorn at each other until I pounced on his delicious body and wrung another orgasm out of him. By that time, we were all exhausted.

Now the dark lust to seek out Troy has risen in me again… to use vampire-speak. Now that I'm awake, I should I ask Vinnie if she has any ideas.

"What a jerk," she says when I tell her the whole sordid story of my Turning.

Logon looks sympathetic too. "You should definitely kick his ass," he says.

"I have to find him first."

"Don't you have some kind of vamp sense that… senses other vamps?" Vinnie asks.

"Not so far."

"Maybe we should look in Samarkand," Logon says.

I rack my brain. "That's in Russia, right?"

"No, it's a bar on Adamo Drive," Logon says.

"And we're not going there," Vinnie adds.

"But that's where the vampires hang," Logon says.

"Not real vampires," Vinnie says quickly. "Just a bunch of skank posers that can give you diseases at twenty paces. There's no point in checking there."

"Why not?" I'm really pissed she didn't tell me about this place and even more pissed that I didn't know about it already. "How come I don't know about it?"

"I don't know," Vinnie says. "But it's phony, seriously."

"They don't advertise," Logon says. "And they don't like people talking about them."

"But the two of you somehow know about it."

"I just know a chick that worked there." Vinnie pretends to inspect her manicure.

"A guy invited me once," Logon says. "I could call him."

"No," Vinnie and I say at the same time. We look at each other, and I clear my throat. "If we're gonna do this, we're gonna do it on our own. No former boyfriends. Cool?"

"He wasn't my boyfriend." Logon looks at me from under lashes that no blond should rightfully possess. "And, you don't need to be jealous. I don't want anyone but you."

Vinnie makes a gagging noise, which I ignore as I sweep my sweet baby into my arms and nuzzle him severely. Logon squirms like a Labrador puppy in my dark embrace, clearly communicating his delight at being manhandled.

"Please," Vinnie says. "You met like forty-eight hours ago. Remember? I was the one who introduced you. It's not like you've been soul mates through the ages."

I suppress the urge to ask, "Jealous much?" I take pity on her. "You don't have to go to Samarkand if you don't want to."

"You don't think for a minute I'd let you go in there with no one but Scrappy Doo for backup."

"Oh no, you didn't." Logon glares at Vinnie. "I'm not a Cousin Oliver. Vlad likes me."

I see the future, and it is a buzzkill. My new bf and bff are flinging retro pop-culture mud, gearing up for a round of *mom likes you best*, and I'm having trouble controlling the urge to smack both of them. What happened to the big happy family of last night?

"We're *all* going," I say in a total *the dark lord has spoken* voice.

Vinnie pauses for a beat before she speaks again. "I gotta change," she says. "You look fine, Vlad, but Logon won't make it through the door dressed like that."

"Where's that black poet shirt?"

"I'll get it. I might have a pair of leather pants too."

Logon grimaces.

"You a vegan or something?" I ask.

"No, but leather makes my butt crack sweat and then it itches, and I can't scratch it in public."

"Baby powder helps."

"I'm just not that into clothes that I'd sacrifice my comfort to style."

A crack in my seamless fascination with Logon. Maybe it can be fixed. "I thought you liked cosplay."

"Well yeah, it's fun dressing up as a character."

"Right. So just think of your clothes as a costume."

"I'll wear whatever you want me to," Logon says. *Bliss restored.*

Vinnie comes out of her room and tosses a silky black shirt at Logon. "And I found these," she says, holding up a pair of black leggings and flat-heeled boots. Luckily, Logon has small feet.

"We're not going to a Renaissance Fair," Logon says.

"Put 'em on, okay?" I say. I have the sudden intense desire to see him in the skintight leggings and knee boots. I wonder briefly if he's into archery at all. Is my RP geekness showing? Deal with it. My fetishes are pretty vanilla as these things go.

"They should fit," Vinnie tells Logon. "They're Petie's, and you look like you're about the same size as her."

"And leave your hair down," I say. His ass looks great in the black leggings, but it's a good thing the shirt comes down to mid-thigh, or he'd be arrested on the street for indecency. He isn't wearing underwear, and his junk sort of hangs in the crotch of the leggings like a sloth in a hammock—a very handsome, seven-inch sloth when aroused.

Vinnie's still wearing the Snow White wig and Doc Martens, but she's changed the plaid skirt and white blouse for a red brocade *cheongsam* and elbow-length gloves of black leather.

"We look like an Emo Three Musketeers," I say.

"We'll fit right in," Vinnie says. She cocks her head at Logon. "You don't look like a gamer-boy anymore," she says. "Now you look like the cousin the Malfoys lock in the attic when company comes over."

"I don't disagree," I say. "But do you have to point it out? Can we have a civil evening?"

"You want to bring out the brass tacks? Let's get down to it then, because I have one or two safety concerns." She points at Logon.

"Have you bothered to ask your playmate if he has a job, or friends and family that might miss him?"

I refrain from pointing out that it was Vinnie who introduced us as I look a question at my lover.

"Not really." Logon does one of those shrugs that say, "I'm very uneasy with this subject and not adept at thinking up lies."

"If you have a job, you'd better tell me, technopup," Vinnie says. "I can't support all of us." She pauses. "Well, actually, I can... but it isn't fair."

Ah, those three little words. It. Isn't. Fair. The cry of four-year-olds everywhere. Vinnie's been so together up until now that I'm surprised she uttered those supremely bratty words. I say the first thing I can think of to divert unpleasantness.

"Where do you work?"

Vinnie lifts her chin. "I'm a mobile dominatrix specializing in fantasy characters."

"So... you make house calls?"

"That's right. I took the job to pay for nursing school, and it pays so good I decided to put school on hold for a while. Besides, it's fun."

"Do people really want to be Dommed by Snow White?"

Vinnie smiles. "You have no idea how weird it is out there."

"Then let's find out." I think this is a great exit line, and I go to the elevator. Logon is right beside me and Vinnie kind of trudges behind us. Again, this is not like her. Granted, I haven't seen her for almost five years, but this is a girl with the soul of Julie Andrews in *The Sound of Music* crossed with that chick from *Cabaret* and every drag queen I've ever seen. It would take a concentration camp to dim her optimism. Even that might not do it. Forced repeated viewings of television reality shows might be required. It's not very vamplike of me, but I don't want Vinnie to be depressed. I'm thinking about that when another thought strikes me.

"We won't all fit on the Gold Wing," I say.

"Then I guess *I'd* better arrange for alternate transportation." Vinnie's voice isn't suited to sarcasm, but I don't laugh, even though she sounds kind of like a snotty Betty Boop. "Would Master prefer a stretch limo or one of the cute short ones?"

"Bitchy much?" Logon mutters.

"It's only a few blocks to Adamo," I say. "We can walk."

"Like this?" Logon indicates his Elizabethan Emo ensemble.

"Hell yeah," Vinnie says. "Let's parade!"

*Much better.* I link arms with Vinnie and Logon, and we saunter down the sidewalk, gaining more swagger with each step. I'm thinking that I could kick the ass of any jerk that looks at me sideways, and Vinnie and Logon are thinking that they're with someone who could kick the ass of any jerk that looks at us sideways. I know that kind of makes *me* sound like a jerk, but when you grow up weird, you tend to get bullied a lot, which makes you wish for the power of ass-kicking a lot. Anyway, by the time we get to the corner, we're doing a synchronized sashay. By the time we reach Adamo, it's a full-on strut. But very cool and understated, you know? We're creatures of the night, not showgirls.

Vinnie takes us down an alley lined with Harley Sportsters—all basic models, black and chrome, but tricked out with skulls, bats, eyes of Horus, all the usual Gothy regalia. I can't believe I didn't know about this place. Not that I'm a Goth. I should have clarified this already. My "look" has Goth elements, but that's the fault of the artists who create the characters for the mangas that inspired me. *Black Butler* would be near the top of the list, *Descendants of Darkness*, and the demons in *Death Note* were very cool. So yeah, a little Goth, a little Victorian, a pinch of J-rock star and a dash of demon ninja. Of course, that's a very simplified capsule summation of my vibe. It's too complicated to go into now.

At the door—which is one of those metal roll-up affairs with a chain on a reel, just like a castle gate in a cheesy kind of way—the multipierced hulks on guard take one look at us and stand aside. This is how I've always wanted to enter a nightclub, as a commanding presence reeking of mystery with a hottie on each arm. Everyone in the place looks at us. Luscious, as my Aunt Bootsy would say.

"Everyone's totally checking us out," Logon whispers.

"As well they might," I say, which is also something Aunt Bootsy says. Thinking about her brings on one of those *what the hell* moments. I stand up really straight, trying to be as tall as possible, and do my best to channel aristocratic disdain. "Who rules here?" I say loudly.

My voice cuts through the jangly, *I need an opium fix* music, and I sense stirrings around the room, which is decorated in just the sort of industrial grunge mated with high tech that you'd expect. It's like William Gibson's attic up in here.

"Come with me, my lord," says a skinny guy wearing a black leather vest and chaps over a red lace bodysuit. What a shame he's a member of the Noassatall tribe.

We follow his inadequate booty behind the bar and down a short hall with three doors. He scratches on the door at the end of the hall with one of his long, silver-painted fingernails and gets permission to enter. We walk into the brothel of blood.

I've seen tacky, okay? My mom is the queen of kitsch and infected me in utero, so I know what I'm talking about when I say that the lair of South Florida's mistress of the dark is a towering tub of tack. Flocked wallpaper in a scarlet-and-black damask pattern. Beaded lampshades with arterial-red fringe. Velvet-upholstered love seats. Need I go on? Didn't think so.

"Mistress," Buttless says. "These unworthy ones crave an audience." He might be assless, but his RP is sincere, and I have to admire that a little.

"Who disturbs me in my inner sanctum?"

I turn toward the sound of a woman's voice speaking in a sixth grader's idea of an East European accent. Wow, she matches the curtains. Five feet of hell in an Elvira beehive that adds another ten inches to her height. She's wearing something that looks almost like a pair of black rubber suspenders attached to a black rubber tool belt. More black rubber in the form of stocking-boots is attached to the belt by little chromed chains. None of this rubber in any way obscures the view of her lady bits. I probably don't need to mention that her pubes are shaved into a bat-shape, but I will.

"Do you know who I am?" I say. I immediately realize how stupid this sounds, since the faux-vamp queen just asked me who I was.

"Do you know who *I* am?" she counters, and I relax, recognizing I'm not dealing with a rocket scientist.

"Your...." Damn, what's the word for a servant of the dark nobility? "Your servant didn't tell us your name."

"I am Sybaris." She goes all Sphinx-faced when she says her name; at least I think that's what she's going for. I'm thinking that her only credentials as vampire royalty are an admittedly smokin'-hot bod and a complete lack of self-consciousness about said bod. She looks the part, but she's as human as an episode of Jerry Springer.

"My master is known as Vlad the Paler," Vinnie speaks up. *Nice. I like bad puns.*

Sybaris does the regal nod thing and succeeds in looking like a smack-head nodding off. "Why do you seek me?" She poses in a full-Vallejo against a nest of red velvet pillows and gestures for us to be seated.

"I'm looking for one of my brethren." I can match that pseudo-olden days talk.

"There are no strangers of our kind in the city," she says.

I want to call her a poser, but she's so into her role that I'd feel like a total buzzkill. Why harsh her gig if it isn't necessary? "Are you certain? I saw him at the Inferno two nights ago."

"Impossible."

"He said his name was Troy."

"Troy?" Sybaris's red contacts look like panic buttons as her eyes widen. "Nevah hoid of 'im." Suddenly, she sounds like she just got off the bus from Brooklyn... 1920s Brooklyn. And she's lying. I can smell it as clearly as her overpowering perfume.

"If you know where he is, you better tell me," I say like a hard-boiled dick. Yeah, gross, right? How'd you like a side of hard-boiled dick with that? But it's a film noir thing. There's always a femme fatale and a hard-boiled dick. Check if you don't believe me.

Sybaris commands her minion to leave.

Yes! *Minion.* That's the word for a vampire's servant.

"You're real, aren't you?" she says.

"If you mean do I suck blood and cause megaton orgasms, then the answer is yes."

"Thought so." Sybaris sighs. "Thanks for not being a snot, by the way. Most real vampires are total snotbags, Troy included."

"Just tell me where he is."

"He laughed when I asked him to Turn me. He said the last thing the world needs is a bimbo vampire."

"Harsh," Vinnie murmured.

I raise an eyebrow at her.

"Just sayin'. Even if it's true, it's harsh."

"I'm not a bimbo," Sybaris says. "I used to work for NASA before the budget cuts. Damned Republicans."

I hide my reaction to the possibility that she might actually be a rocket scientist. "Mistress Sybaris, if you know this fiend's hiding place, I will avenge your honor." I'm understandably proud of this ad lib.

"There's this rich guy that lets him sleep in the basement of his mansion whenever Troy feels like it. His name's Robert Massey."

"Fuck me sideways!" Vinnie exclaims.

"You know this guy." I make an informed guess.

"Yeah, and so do you. Big Bob Massey from the late-night commercials. I rent space from him sometimes. He owns the biggest dungeon-for-hire business in the Southeast."

"Oh, *that* Bob Massey," I say.

"Don't sneer."

"Rent-a-dungeon?" I give her the eyebrow again.

"Like I can afford to build my own?" Vinnie glances at Sybaris, seeking solidarity. "Sometimes customers want a certain atmosphere, and Massey provides that for a fair price."

"Are the walls made of stone?" I ask.

"Yes."

"*Real* stone?"

"Well... no."

"Maybe I should see for myself." I bow magnanimously to Sybaris. "Farewell," I say as I make a sweeping turn. I'm very relieved when my minions turn with me. You know what? That word's not working for me. It's kind of demeaning. I'll have to come up with something else.

VINNIE gives the taxi driver directions and sits back. With Logon, me, and her in the backseat, it's pretty tight, but neither of them would agree to sit up front, and it wouldn't look right for me to sit next to the driver. Besides, I'm afraid to leave Vinnie and Logon alone. They're on each other's last nerve, and my eyes are tired from so much rolling.

"Why are we going to the dungeon if Troy stays at this millionaire guy's mansion?" Logon asks.

"So I can ask my friend Tibbie if Bob's there before we go bustin' in," Vinnie says.

"Why don't you use your phone?"

My superior senses can hear Vinnie's teeth grinding together.

"Because I also need to leave a check," she says.

"Oh good," Logon says. "So even if we don't find Troy, the cab ride won't be a *complete* waste of time."

I pinch my blood-boo's inner thigh in a reflex reaction to the bitch-tone in his voice.

"She started it," Logon yelps.

I give him my best incredulous look, and he has the grace to look embarrassed. He's so cute that I have to kiss him. The need to taste his sweet blood is strong, but I can feel the cabbie's attention on us like a persistent fly. I look up and meet the driver's eyes in the rearview mirror. He looks away and keeps his eyes on the road until he pulls over at a building that looks big enough to house a blimp.

The purple and yellow neon sign spells out *Welcome to the Pleasure Dome*. Vinnie vouches for us at the front door, and we walk into a small lobby like you'd find at an economy motel. The three girls behind the long counter are wearing skirts and blazers, and I expect them to try to sell me some real estate any second. Which is pretty much their job, I guess, only they're renting by the hour.

"Hey, Lauren," Vinnie says, and one of the girls looks at us.

"Mistress Lavinia." The warmth in the greeting is genuine, and Lauren smiles as Vinnie walks over to her. "What can we do you for tonight?"

"First things first." Vinnie takes a check from her purse and slides it across the counter.

Lauren opens a drawer and slides the check into it. "What else?"

"I'm looking for Tibbie."

"She's here." Lauren looks past Vinnie's shoulder and smiles at me and Logon. "Who're your good-lookin' friends?"

"This is Vlad and Logon," Vinnie says.

"So cool you got a crew now." Lauren winks at Vinnie. "You want to go inside, or you want me to give Tibbie a call?"

"I don't want to bug her if she's busy."

"Hell no, girl. Would I do that? She's primpin' for a midnight special." Lauren's hand drops below the counter and a door opens to our left. "Go on in."

"Thanks a million," Vinnie says as she leads us down a long hall with numberless doors on each side. Near the end, she stops and knocks on a door.

The door swings open. "Who the fuck—? Hey, Vinnie! Get in here, girl, and gimme some sugar. I'm about a quart low." A slender black man in a purple thong grabs Vinnie and hugs her, pulling her into the room with him. I note the presence of racks of shiny clothing and tables with mirrors attached and cleverly deduce that we're in a dressing room.

"Vlad!" Vinnie says. "Meet Tibbie, the finest female impersonator in the business."

Tibbie's skin is as smooth and golden brown as caramelized sugar, and he has the bone structure of Nefertiti. "I don't doubt it," I say.

"Ain't you sweet?" Tibbie bats his eyelashes and I feel the breeze. "What's your name again?"

"Vlad," I say. "Short for Vladimir," I add when he looks puzzled.

"Don't feel bad, honey," he says. "Tibbie's short for Tiburon." He gives me a look of commiseration before sitting down at one of the tables. "Y'all don't mind if I get ready for work while we talk, do you?" He picks up a compact of bronze powder and begins brushing it over his eyelids.

"We're looking for a guy named Troy," Vinnie says. "He stays at Massey's mansion sometimes."

Tibbie's big dark eyes meet Vinnie's in the mirror. "Why you lookin' for him?"

"Vlad owes him something."

"He's bad news, child." Tibbie uses a cotton swab to dab a line of gold dots down the center of his lids.

"Can you tell me if he's at the mansion or not?"

Tibbie picks up a pencil and outlines his eyes in smoky black. "I wouldn't be doing you a favor."

"I appreciate your concern," Vinnie says. "But I've got my big girl panties on."

"What's all this got to do with you, Vladimir?" Tibbie asks as he uses the same pencil to define his eyebrows.

"I need to find Troy," I tell him.

"Vinnie must like you to do you a solid like this."

"You can stop fishing," Vinnie says. "Vlad's a vampire, and I'm his...."

Tibbie raises his perfectly arched eyebrows as Vinnie flails.

"We haven't settled on a suitable title." I step in and save my Girl Friday the 13th.

"A vampire, huh?" Tibbie doesn't seem terribly impressed. "What you want with Troy?"

"It's personal."

"Uh-huh." Tibbie stands up and wriggles into a pair of pantyhose. "Y'all stay here a minute while I run see if my dress is through bein' steamed. I'll see if Kaneesha saw anything when she was cleanin' up at

Mr. Massey's house this mornin'… if she ain't run off and got a job with the TSA by now."

"Thanks," Vinnie says as Tibbie stalks out of the room in pantyhose, crocodile platforms, and a wig that almost defies description. It's a mass of tawny frizz festooned with swags of Rasta braids. Seriously though, that doesn't begin to give you the picture. Somewhere between a dandelion and a chandelier made of hair.... Nope, I'm not even going to try. It's cool, though. Reminds me of some of the futuristic hair in the old-school *Star Trek*.

The door opens slowly, and a guy kind of hangs there like he thinks he's a gunfighter at a saloon or something. Actually, it's a pretty good entrance, but my envy won't let me acknowledge it. The stranger is tall, lanky, and wearing classic bluesman drag. By that, of course I mean a plain black suit and tie with a white shirt and a fedora. Isn't it kind of interesting that Amish men and musicians with names like Ramblin' Crawdad King dress alike? But this party crasher is no sharecropper's son of the sultry Mississippi delta. This is an obviously white guy with brindled gray and brown hair that looks like it was cut with a broken bottle. The brim of the hat and thick bangs put the stranger's eyes in shadow, but you can still see that they're a really bright blue, like lighted swimming pools.

"Can we help you?" Vinnie says in the tone that means *can't you see you're in the wrong place, you ignorant, crap-lousy oaf?*

"Well hello, cher." The stranger's voice is a thick drawl that I associate with movies located in New Orleans; he even says "cher" like it's spelled "shar." "Had me a devil of a time keepin' up wit' you fine folks."

"You've been following us?" Vinnie's all indignant, aiming her rack like a pair of M16s.

"Off and on. Been keepin' my eye on you for sure."

"Why?"

"You sure are feisty."

"And who are you?" I ask. I don't even mumble. I'm feisty too.

"Call me Bon Tom." The tall man takes off his hat and bows to me.

Slut that I am, my balls skip a beat when he looks up. He has one of those lean, hungry-wolf faces that makes me want to roll over and beg. And his eyes are just as blue as a Siberian husky's. He's not just attractive, he's got the kind of sexiness that bypasses the brain and goes directly to the pecker. Predictably, my instant, unwelcome lust for him makes me cranky.

"What do you want, Bon Tom?" I ask.

"Looky here," Bon Tom says. "I can see you the big dog on this porch, but you just a puppy, ain't ya? All Bon Tom askin' is the common courtesy what you'd give any stranger. Use the manners your mama taught you."

"If it's not too much to ask, why are you stalking me and my friends, Bon Tom?"

"Lookin' for Troy calls hisself Sanger." Bon Tom grins. "You sure spend a lotta your time humpin' Blondie."

"Jealous much?" I hope my sneer is icy.

Bon Tom shakes his head. "Bon Tom like the ladies," he says.

"No one's perfect," I assure him. "What do you want with Troy?"

"Troy a foolish man took somethin' what don't belong to him. I find him, I gonna take it back, along with him sticky little fingers."

"Ick," Vinnie says.

"Oh, it gonna be major league ick, cher," Bon Tom says.

"You know Troy's a vampire, right?" Vinnie turns a little to give him a better shot down her cleavage. It's a purely reflex move.

"If I don't, I figure it out pretty quick when he bite Mr. Boy Toy." Bon Tom nods at me.

*Boy Toy? Really?* "Hey, what about the courtesy thing? It's a two-way street. And just by the way, you saw him attack me, and you didn't do anything?"

"Not my business, cher."

"Just what is your business? Are you some kind of Blues Brother hit man?"

"I a priest mostly."

"Get out!" Logon exclaims.

"Bon Tom a *bokor*, same as a priest."

"Not exactly true, honey." Tibbie strides back into the room in a drapey, swingy red dress. "A *houngan* is a priest. A *bokor* is a sorcerer."

"Hello, cher!" Bon Tom gets an eyeful of Tibbie and likes what he sees. "How come you know so much 'bout Vodou?"

"I don't trifle with your type. Go on and get out of my dressing room now."

"Cher, don't be like that."

Tibbie whips a knife from somewhere and sticks it in Bon Tom's face. "You like this better?" Tibbie doesn't realize that Bon Tom has a knife too until Bon Tom taps Tibbie's belly with it. Tibbie slowly lowers his weapon and Bon Tom steps back... after ostentatiously sniffing Tibbie's perfume, which is a very cool and sinister move, but clearly shows that Bon Tom hasn't caught on yet that Tibbie's a dude. *Lusciousness.*

"So that's what? A holy knife or something?" Logon says.

"Enough jabber," Bon Tom says. "Where's Troy?"

"If we knew, would we be standing here wasting our time with you?" I say.

"Why not? I been told I got my charms."

Logon snorts. "I've been told piss is lemonade, but I'm not going to drink any."

I glance at him.

Logon shrugs. "My mom. She calls taking a dump making Tootsie Rolls."

"Weird," Vinnie says under her breath.

Bon Tom clears his throat. "Gettin' back to Troy. I figure you gonna find him like a blind pup finds a tit, but I'm tired of trailin' you. Thought we could join up."

Tibbie picks up his phone. "I'm callin' the front desk right now. In about three hot seconds, some very large, very pissed-off mens gonna be comin' through that door."

"We can help each other if we work together," Bon Tom says.

Tibbie meets his eyes. "One."

"Come on, cher, be sweet."

"Two."

Bon Tom turns and saunters out the door like he has better places to be.

"*Bokor*, my ass," Tibbie says. "I ain't never heard of no white *bokor*."

"I have," Logon says. "But only in that game *Zombie Bayou*. The Papa Sugar character is badass. The game isn't very challenging though, and the graphics are…." Logon's words trail off as he realizes no one cares about the quality of the graphics.

"Well that was useful," Vinnie says as she turns to Tibbie. "So did Kaneesha know anything about this Troy guy?"

"He's at the mansion."

"Let's go," I say.

"Hold up, Mr. Last Samurai. Maybe you should think about this first. I don't know what y'all want with Troy, but don't forget that he's got a lot more experience than any of you."

"You don't know me," Logon says. "I could be a powerful sorcerer."

"No, you couldn't." Tibbie disses my squeeze.

"You can't judge a book by its cover," I say.

"These days you can," Vinnie chimes in. "Have you seen some of those romance novel covers? Hot stuff!"

I scowl at her for contradicting her master and get back to the point. "So tell me, Tibbie. Do you only have insults and dire warnings, or do you have some useful advice too?"

"That was pretty good," Tibbie says. "Keep practicing and you'll sound like a trifling movie vampire yet."

Now she's dissing *me*. And I'm referring to him as her. Though I guess I probably should if I want to be politically correct about it. Yeah. Right.

"You're sassy," I say, once again channeling my Aunt Bootsy. "And clearly you're no ordinary mortal." I can see I have Tibbie's interest now. "If you have time, could you let me in on a few of your secrets?"

Tibbie gives a big, dramatic sigh. "Okay, but only because I have a strong feeling that you intend to open a large can of whup-ass on Troy. That boy's got it comin' to him."

"You mad at him too?" Vinnie says. "Mistress Sybaris has a real hard-on for him."

Tibbie sniffs. "So-called Mistress ain't nothin' but a titty dancer wannabe. And Troy a fool messin' where he shouldn't be messin'." He looks at the clock. "Two hours. I can just make it."

"Does that mean you'll come with us?" Vinnie practically squeals.

"The spirits of my ancestors would give me nightmares if I let you lambs walk into a slaughter."

"Were your ancestors vampire hunters?" Logon asks.

"Baptist preachers," Tibbie answers.

# CHAPTER THREE

SO THE mansion…. Let me try to cast it in words for you. The home of Robert Milton Massey is one of those horrendous piles of pink faux adobe that's supposed to look like a Spanish castle. Maybe he fancies himself a conquistador; I don't know. What I do know is that the last thing Florida needs is another Pepto-Bismol Castillo.

"Could you just expire from tackiness?" Vinnie says as we get out of the taxi and stare through the wrought-iron gates.

Naturally, the gates are wrought iron with a big, swirling capital letter M in the center of each. I've been seeing Bob Massey's commercials on local broadcasting since I was in fifth grade, and if there's one thing I'm sure of, this is a man who likes to claim things as his. I'll bet he was a real treat for the other kids in day care. If this was a movie, I'd totally put a flashback right here. A few adorable toddlers in a playpen in a shaft of golden light as nostalgic music plays in the background. One of them grabs a toy from another and—*wham*—hits him upside the head with it. Fade out on gleeful face of toddler Bob clutching toy as the music changes to a spawn-of-Satan theme.

"So do we just knock?" Logon asks. I'm discovering that he has a real knack for recognizing the key element of any situation, which can be a useful talent. But then he has to point it out in this dry, condescending way, like an I.T. shoving you aside and sitting down in front of your computer. I love him and all, but if he ever utters the words *have you tried rebooting*, we're finished. I'm serious. At work, those guys are my archenemies.

*Work! Yikes!*

I've been so busy since I Turned that I haven't once thought about my job. Technically, I'm on vacation, but I should at least check my messages because I told the boss he could call me in if he needed to. It wasn't like I was planning on going out of town, and I can always use the money. My vacation "plans" involved nothing more ambitious than hitting the clubs every night, getting hammered, and trying to pick up a hottie for the purpose of pure pleasure. I actually prefer going to work with a hangover; it's less real that way.

Most of the people on my shift are okay, but Metro Media, or M&M—or M Squared as I like to call it—is like the Walmart of electronics. It's huge, brightly lit, and stacked to the ceiling with all manner of electronic thingies and their accessories, all at a reasonable price. And they make us wear pseudo-uniforms. Someone's mistress in corporate must have thought all M Squared employees would look cute in vests, so we have to don these polyester one-size-fits-most abominations in the store colors, which are screaming blue and melt-your-eyes yellow. Plus, twice a year they make their employees attend half-day seminars on customer relations. Why don't they just nail me to the floor and walk on my goolies in stiletto heels?

I do understand that customers are M Squared's reason for existing, but I'm not too clear on why *M Squared* needs to exist. Sure, they provide apathetically crafted technology for a price that won't break most people, but here's where it all fails for me: Metro Media only stocks the most popular brands of whatever. So if you like to watch movies that are a little more obscure or listen to bands that aren't mainstream, you're SOL at M&M. You can find a jillion copies of whatever the major studios are barfing up this week, but if your taste is more, shall we say, independent, once again, you're shit out of luck.

I used to dream about opening a little video store called The One Hundred. It would only stock one hundred titles: movies handpicked for excellence, films that would make you a better person merely for having watched them. But after making about a zillion lists, I realized

I'd never settle on the perfect hundred. And then I realized that if I opened such a store, I'd be one of those boring jerks who're certain they're vastly cooler than everyone else. You know the type. They know they're superior to you, but they're willing to help you if you're ready to learn. My first serious boyfriend was one of them. What a pompous, pretentious, passive-aggressive ass. I'd like to run into him again now that I'm a vamp. Have I always been this vengeful?

*Oh yeah, right, revenge.* Vamp business. We need to get onto the grounds of Massey's place.

I grab hold of the gates and wrench them open like they're made out of bendy straws. I sense the awe of my companions at my back as I step onto the driveway of the dark mansion. My shadow stretches across the billiard-table lawn like an accusing finger. Can you feel the drama?

"Hope you don't have to pay for that," Tibbie says as he walks past me.

"As if," Logon says. He might be kind of a know-it-all, but he's always got my back.

"Yeah," Vinnie says. "Send the bill to Castle Dracul, Transylvania, care of Mr. Harker."

They're a good crew. I put my arms around their shoulders as we follow Tibbie.

Tibbie rings the bell, and after a moment, the door swings inward. The foyer light is blocked by a dark, bulky figure.

"Welcome, please come in."

I recognize the booming voice and transplanted Michigander accent from late-night TV commercials. There I'd be on a typical teenage Friday night, several beers and tokes into the evening, sprawled in comfort on a couch molded to the shape of my ass, watching a campy old horror film presented by Elvira and her twin creamy-skinned co-hosts. Just as I'd be getting into the craptastic film, it would be interrupted by a bellowing man with a white-guy Chia Pet 'fro and a big gold chain tangled in his chest hairs. For what seemed like an eternity, he yelled at me while pictures of the wares he was hawking were projected behind him. How was it possible that he approved these commercials? Had he not seen them before they were aired? Did he not realize how inherently ridiculous a man appears when he seems to be floating like a middle-aged fairy of soft-core porn in front of a gigantic display case featuring such "adult" items as chocolate boobs, edible panties, and dick-shaped bottles of self-warming massage lotion? Now's my chance to ask the questions that had plagued my beer- and bong-addled brain. But I don't really care anymore.

"Hey, Bob," Tibbie says. "Sorry to drop by so late, but I figured you'd want to meet my friends."

"You know what I always like to say: It's never too late." Massey stands aside to let us enter. "I like your playmates," he says. "Can't wait to see you in action with them."

"I'm just dropping them off," Tibbie says. "Got an appointment at midnight."

"A shame," Massey says. "You'll be missed. Great outfit, by the way."

"Let me introduce Vlad." Tibbie waves a hand at me and my entourage. "I'm sure you can see that he's no ordinary dude."

"No indeed." Massey's dark little eyes gleam like those of a flesh-eating pig. "Let me welcome you again, my lord," he says to me.

Well, well, so good ol' Bob Massey is a vamp-hag. I probably should have guessed, since he was letting Troy sleep over, but seriously, he's like almost the last person I'd expect to be into Goth culture. He's so... insincere. The dark princes of pain and duchesses of despair care very deeply; it's why they're so wounded and alienated, longing for the powers of the undead. They fantasize about "chucking a Carrie." I'm talking about the young ones of course, the Gothlings, which Massey is definitely not.

Looking at him now, I'm thinking *he's* thinking that he's the Hugh Hefner of the Bay area. First off, there's the martini glass in his left hand; you just know he keeps the right hand free in case he has to shake with someone. Salesmen and politicians... I see no difference. Then there's the smoking jacket, an item of apparel I considered somewhat cool until a few seconds ago. So while I give him points for not totally copying Hef's robe and pajamas look, I have to take points away for the belly that parts the skirts of the smoking jacket like curtains pulling back to display his crotch.

"I knew you'd like Vlad," Tibbie says to Massey.

"He's superb," Massey says. *Superb*. That has a really nice ring to it.

"Thank you," I murmur, going all humble and polite. "I'd like to ask you a question."

"Ask me anything you want, but let's not stand around in the front hall." Massey turns and moves away with the Belushi-style light-footedness that some heavy people have. He leads us into a genuine lounge with a small bar and several groupings of comfy chairs around bottle-cap tables. We all perch on bar stools as Massey claims the space by walking around to the back of the bar. "Shoot," he says to me as he leans his elbows on the polished wood.

I decide to approach the subject in a roundabout way. "You know what I am," I say.

Massey nods. "A nearly perfect being."

This isn't one of the answers I'm expecting. It's flattering, but it's odd. "Um, yeah. So I guess you know other vampires."

"I've been lucky enough to meet a few." Massey looks at me intently. "You look like you could use a drink, am I right?"

He's right. It's been almost four hours since I've had any blood, and I'm feeling it. It's not bad yet, just a little tickle, like the one that warns you you're going to have a sore throat or maybe even several days of misery wallowing in your secretions while the flu has its way with you. Yeah, I could use a drink.

I smile at Massey, just giving him a flash of fangs like the tease I am. He nods and opens a little fridge under the bar, staying bent over as he pours and replaces a container. Putting the brandy snifter in the microwave, he zaps it for a minute. With a little flourish, he sets the glass of warm, red liquid in front of me and takes drink orders from my friends. I can smell the blood, and I wonder where Massey gets it as I raise the glass to my lips.

"It's mine," Massey says as I swallow. "I siphon off a pint every other month, just to have it on hand."

I might have to revise my opinion of Massey; he might be more Howard Hughes than Hugh Hefner. And his blood.... Well, it isn't vile, but it does lack a certain something. I can feel it making me stronger, but I'm not transported the way I am when I drink Logon's blood. The earth doesn't budge an inch. It occurs to me that I've never bitten anyone *but* Logon. What if it's just him that has that fantastic effect? Hm. Or maybe it's because I'm not drinking Massey's blood straight from the source. Excuse me while I swallow a little vomit back down.

I have so much to learn about being a vampire that it depresses me almost as much as talking about politics. I really need to just take a day and find out what powers I have. I really should do that before I find Troy. Yep, that would be the smart thing to do. But that's not how I roll.

"I'd like to meet some other vampires," I say.

"Then you should come to one of my parties," Massey says.

"I was thinking more like *now*."

Symmetrical bald patches catch the light as Massey lowers his head and leans toward me in the demeanor of a salesman about to offer a juicy deal that will get him fired if the boss finds out about it. "It's possible I could accommodate you," he says.

"Look, Monty, I'm not here to play *Let's Make a Deal*."

"All I want is a few drops of your blood."

"In return for?"

"I'll introduce you to one of my special friends."

"What are you going to do with my blood?" I ask. Shrewd, right?

"I'm going to mix it in a glass of wine and trip my balls off." Massey grins. "Just kidding. I like to drink it before I entertain a lady friend. It enhances the experience."

"Seriously?"

"For real."

I suspect Massey is mocking me, but it's just a feeling. "Fine. Give me something to put it in."

Massey whips an eyedropper from under the counter and looks at me like a dog whose dinnertime has long since passed. I pretend I know what I'm doing and raise my thumb to my mouth. I press the pad of my thumb to a fang and hold it out to Massey. A bead of red wells from the puncture and is sucked into the tip of the dropper. Massey collects three before the tiny wound heals. *Heals*. Before my eyes. This is *so* cool. I really need to find someone who knows about this shit for real.

All of a sudden, I understand Rice's dreary doormat Louis a lot better. I've always identified more with Lestat, and I totally agree with movie Lestat's opinion that Louis is a whiner. But now I empathize with Louis's need to find someone to explain things. For all I know, I can turn into a bat. How cool would that be? Yeah, way cool.

Massey puts the dropper of blood away in the fridge with the care of a master jeweler handling the Hope Diamond. He looks up at me with the smile of a man just waiting for the ink to dry on the contract. And no, I *can't* talk without using analogies. Get used to it.

"Well, I think it's time for a trip to the basement," Massey says, and we all follow him.

It's a fiasco. I knew things had been going too well for too long. It was time for another setback. This one comes in the form of an empty coffin. Said coffin is lined in black satin and sits on a genuine marble catafalque. The catafalque occupies a room designed to look remarkably like a chamber in Hollywood's idea of a medieval castle. Wine racks line one wall, attesting to the room's original purpose.

"He was here when I came up to answer the door," Massey says, fake-apologetic. "I don't know where he could've gone."

"We ain't got time for foolin' around," Tibbie says. "What about the other rooms?"

"Well...." Massey does the worst *I just remembered something* act I've ever seen. He actually bugs his eyes, his mouth actually drops open, and he actually says, "Hey, wait a minute. I just remembered something." *Lame*. I can't wait to get out of here.

"Are you gonna let us in on it?" Vinnie asks. So sassy.

"There *is* a place Troy goes sometimes." Finally, the elephant in the room has a name. "It's a little ways away though."

Confusion in the ranks as Vinnie, Logon, and I exchange the panicked looks of losers without cars.

"How far?" Vinnie asks.

"Up 19 to Indian Rocks."

"Indian Rocks!" I can't help my incredulity. What would a vampire be doing in Indian Rocks? It's an "Old Florida" tourist town on a strip of sand separated from the mainland, pretty evenly divided between beehive resort hotels and crappy little motor courts. You can get great seafood, but a vampire wouldn't care about that.

"He's mentioned wanting to go there several times on this visit," Massey says. "I was planning on driving him up tomorrow night, but I guess he couldn't wait."

"So you have directions?" Vinnie asks.

"Sure, no problem.

"Uh, hey," I say. "That's gonna be a hell of a long cab ride."

"You don't have a car?" Massey says as though I'd just mentioned that I only have one ball. Not true, of course. That was just for the purposes of illustration. I assure you that I have twin balls, both high-functioning.

"Never needed one," I say suavely with the confidence of a man who has all the equipment he needs—and very attractive it is too, thank you for asking.

"A man's gotta have a car," Massey says. "Are you some kind of socialist or something?"

"I don't discuss politics with my friends, much less strangers." I love it when my brain manages to provide a retort other than *I know you are, but what am I?*

Massey's chuckle sounds indulgent, which annoys me intensely. I may look like a kid, but I'm a junior college graduate, damn it.

"I'll loan you a car," Massey says. "The least I can do."

"No thanks," I say as Vinnie and Logon gape at me.

"I insist," Massey says. "I owe you one, and I don't like owing."

"Take the car, white boy," Tibbie says. "That way, you can drop me off at sin city in style."

MASSEY has a six-car garage, and it's at capacity. In this one area, he has a smidge of style; I'll give him that. Instead of the usual stable of Porsches, Ferraris, and BMWs, the discount-dungeon king has a collection of slightly less popular, but infinitely cooler models: a red Mazda Miata from the first year they were made, an ivory Studebaker Avanti, a black 1963 Ford Lincoln with suicide doors, a cream-cheese blue American Motors Javelin, a front wheel drive Oldsmobile Toronado, and a 1961 Willys Wagoneer Woodie. I'm truly surprised.

"I recommend the Wagoneer," Massey says. "I had black-out shades rigged in the cargo area. A vampire who got caught out in the daylight could sleep back there until sundown."

"It's certainly roomy," Vinnie says.

Massey's already taking the keys off a pegboard in the hall we just walked down. When he holds them up, Vinnie's hand shoots out. Massey glances at me before handing the keys over to Vinnie. Then he caps the visit for me by uttering the following.

"Guess you won't need the air bag, sweetheart, since you already got two of your own."

My fangs itch. Something is blooming at my core and spreading outward—kind of like an orgasm, only this is a climax of rage. I feel taller, and I'm pretty sure my eyes are blazing.

"Vinnie, would you like an apology for that piggish remark?" I ask.

Vinnie's smirk is an evil thing, but then she shrugs. "I've heard worse," she says. "Not much worse, but a little. Honestly, it was too stupid to really be offensive."

"Okay, but I'll make him cry like a little girl if you want."

"Doubt that," Tibbie says. "Whatever you can threaten him with vamp-wise would just turn him on, and that's gospel."

She's... *he's* probably right. Oh what the hell, *she's* probably right.

"Let's just go," I say.

Vinnie gets in and fires up the behemoth. Tibbie climbs into the front passenger seat and settles herself.

"Just a sec," Massey says to me. "I know you're in a hurry, but just one question. When you get back with the car, you think there's any chance I could watch you feed?"

"None whatsoever." I pull Logon into the cavernous backseat of the Wagoneer. "Let's go, Vinnie."

Vinnie hits the garage door opener that's clipped to the sunshade and rolls out of the garage. On a covered concrete pad sits a pearly Cadillac Escalade, which I assume is what Massey drives to work. What a dildo. He has all those excellent cars and drives the ludicrous contradiction in terms that is the Cadillac luxury sport utility vehicle, possibly one of the most absurd status symbols in American history, and that's saying something. It's also one of the clearer signs of the Apocalypse, along with test audiences for movies and vote counting in the Florida 2000 Presidential election.

"You're sure you can find this place?" I ask again.

"I told you, I know exactly where it is. My folks made me go to Indian Rocks Beach with them every summer until I was thirteen. After that year, they let me go to camp like I wanted."

I know this story. Vinnie, an early bloomer, had caught the eye of a local lifeguard named Kip, or in the words of Vinnie's father, *that scumbag preppie pervert.* He wanted the country-club Casanova charged and sent to prison, where it was to be hoped he'd be subjected nightly to poetic justice at the hands of large, sex-starved convicts. Vinnie's mom begged him not to humiliate the family and make Vinnie relieve the horror of being molested. In fact, Vinnie had enjoyed fooling around with the eighteen-year-old local golden boy, but he should have known she was a child no matter what her bra size was. Anyway, her folks decided that a supervised summer camp was the best solution, and as Vinnie puts it, facilitated her early expeditions into

Lezland. Have I mentioned that she has dual citizenship? Bats for both teams? Goes both ways? Get my point? Can I stop now?

Something bounds into the road from behind a tall hedge.

"Look out!" I yell at the same time that Tibbie hollers, "Punch it, girl!"

Vinnie swerves and hits the brakes. She seems a little rattled. Nearly hitting someone with a car will do that to you.

"What in hell is he doing here?" I say.

Tibbie rolls her eyes. "Oh, sweet Jesus on a Rose Bowl float! Come on. You had to know his ass was gonna follow us."

I roll down my window when Bon Tom taps on it.

"Goin' my way, cher?" he asks.

"Do you have a death wish?" I reply.

Bon Tom grins. "If you knew what you sayin', you be funny. Come on now. Scootch over a skoshie and give Bon Tom a ride."

"We're taking Tibbie to work," Vinnie says.

"And then you goin' to wherever Troy is."

"What makes you think that?"

"Don't think it. Smell it."

"Pull your lacy socks up and get back on the road," Tibbie tells Vinnie. "You don't want me to be late for my date."

So we drive Tibbie to the Pleasure Dome with Bon Tom making less-than-subtle overtures to the female impersonator the entire way. Tibbie shuts him down each time, but he's not daunted. He blows her a kiss as she gets out of the car. Tibbie swats the kiss to the ground and crushes it under her high heel.

"Hot," Bon Tom murmurs.

Logon and I giggle a little.

"What?" Bon Tom gives us the evil eye.

"Why don't you move up front?" I say. "Give me and Logon a little room."

Bon Tom moves up to sit with Vinnie and we get going again. When we merge with Highway 19, Bon Tom sits up a little straighter and asks where we're going.

"Some place in Indian Rocks," Vinnie says.

"Do tell." Bon Tom slides down in his seat again. "Wonder why he send you there."

"You know where we're going?" I say.

"Pretty sure."

"So what's it like?"

"Bon Tom not the sort to spoil surprises."

Screw him. It's only about a half hour to Indian Rocks, depending on what time of day you decide to get on the road. But Vinnie isn't used to a vehicle as large as the Wagoneer and steers it like a ski boat in quicksand, staying several miles below the speed limit. Logon is stroking my inner thigh and that lovely warm tide is rising in me. The microwaved glass of Massey's blood quieted my hunger pangs but did nothing for my pleasure centers. I need a hit, and Logon is not so subtly hinting that the neck bar is open and it's happy hour. Vinnie and Bon Tom surely wouldn't begrudge me a nip.

I pull Logon onto my lap, and he leans his head against the window behind him. The moonlight pours over his fair hair, his pointed profile, and the curve of his throat. I feel a fierce ache in my goolies, and I know I'm a goner. Logon might call me master, but really, I'm his slave. He must never find out about this, but I want him as much as he wants me, more even.

His skin is so warm and soft against my lips. It's like a baby's butt or a horse's nose. I know those aren't very romantic images, but they *are* extremely warm and soft... velvety too. His breathing goes shallow, and I can feel how fast his heart's beating. He turns his head slightly, offering easier access, surrendering completely. All mine.

I have to wonder if it would have been like this with whoever I bit first. I mean, it was just random that Vinnie knew someone that wanted to be bitten. Well, actually, she probably knew quite a few, but she chose the cutest unattached gay male out of the bunch, and that was

Logon, my buttery, blond bunny-boy. You see how bad it is? Yeah? Then eat your heart out with envy.

My fangs slide easily into his skin and blood flows over my tongue, so hot and sweet and tart and salty and a dozen other things I don't have the words for. It fills me with the best feeling in the world. Like slipping into cool water after a long hot day. Like seeing something familiar when you think you're lost. Like the moment that climax becomes afterglow. I could talk about it for the rest of my life, and I doubt I'd ever come close to describing it. It's one of those things that has to be experienced, and even then, it's what you'd call highly subjective. Does the phrase "frame of reference" mean anything to you?

Logon moans a little, and I shift to my back on the bench seat with my thigh pressed against the bulge in his leggings. I suck softly as he rides my thigh. He bites his lip to keep from making any noise. Somehow, he gets his hand on my junk—I can't imagine the position his elbow must be in—and he squeezes it. I feel about fourteen, getting my first hand job in the band room coat closet. And it's like this each time I bite him. Like the first time: overwhelmed by excitement and powerful new feelings, stimulated to a degree that interferes with coherent thought. Standing on the threshold of something wondrous.

"Are you finished, cher?" Bon Tom asks.

*Shit!* Logon's shuddering against me in the throes of mega-orgasmic bliss, and I'm so close I can taste it, but our uninvited guest has ruined the moment for me. I'm a powerful vampire living outside the laws of society and all that, but now that I've been reminded that Logon and I aren't alone, I can't stay hard. I was really hoping that I'd left all those stupid hang-ups behind when I died. *Heavy sigh.*

I sit up, and Logon pulls his shirt back down. I don't envy him the mess in the crotch of his leggings, but the smile on his face convinces me it's worth it to him. The wounds in his neck are already closing. I time it, and it takes 36 seconds for the punctures to heal. How cool is that?

"Did you need me for something?" I ask Bon Tom.

"We almost there. Thought y'all might want to button up."

"Your timing is prodigiously bad."

"You know some mighty big words, cher. Do people call you a know-it-all?"

"Where the hell are you from? Your accent sounds totally phony."

"Easy, cher. I sure am sorry I give you the blue balls. Go on and bitch about it if it make you feel better." Bon Tom doesn't show any visible remorse as he faces front again. "Turn here," he says to Vinnie.

We start down a long, dark driveway lined with overgrown hedges that scratch the sides and roof of the car like fingernails on a chalkboard. At the end of the torture tunnel is a typical cracker shotgun house, a long narrow building of five rooms in a row with a clear line of sight between the front and back doors. Someone told me once that the design has something to do with hurricanes, but damned if I remember what.

"Who lives here?" I ask Bon Tom, since he clearly knows where we are.

Bon Tom chuckles. "Y'all come with me." He opens the front door and steps inside.

The light is dim, of course, and the air is layered with smoke.

"Watch your step," Bon Tom says, glancing down.

Except for a narrow pathway, the floor is covered with wide, shallow dishes. The dishes are filled with water and floating flowers. I wonder who's responsible for replacing all the burnt incense and wilted flowers, not to mention changing the water in the dishes. That would be a job and a half. I had an aquarium once, and cleaning it got really tedious. Things grow in the water here in Florida, and most of them are nasty, like mustard algae, brain-eating amoebae, and cottonmouth snakes.

Bon Tom leads us straight through and out the back to a patio. There's a fire in a big brick barbecue pit and it's the only light out here except for a few candles. No Tiki torches. No porch light. Not even a bug zapper. Just the fire and the candles sitting among bottles of rum and plates of flowers, candy, and cigars.

"Who you brung me, Bon Tom?" A voice comes out of the shadows, and I have to admit that it makes me curious because I can't tell if it belongs to a man or a woman. It could be a guy with a high tenor voice, or a girl with a low alto. It's a light voice, what writers call "reedy," and it has a kind of scratchiness to it like you're hearing it on a car radio out in the middle of nowhere. Kind of like Logon's voice, but his is a little deeper.

"*They* brung me," Bon Tom says. "They lookin' for *you*, Orisha."

"Now they found me." Orisha steps away from the side of the brick hearth and into the light.

Bon Tom kind of straightens up, like a soldier called to attention. "Everybody say hey to Orisha now," he says.

"That ain't my real name," Orisha says. "But it'll do for you all."

I notice several things right away. Orisha reminds me of the evil pharaoh guy from *Stargate*—the movie, not the TV show. Big cloud of dark hair. Smooth Bahaman-brown skin. Bedroom eyes and sensuous lips. You've probably noticed that I'm avoiding pronouns, but I seriously can't tell if Orisha is a dude or a dudette. This is despite the fact that Orisha's black velvet bathrobe is hanging open, which is another thing I can't help noticing. And you'll love this: Orisha is wrapped neck to ankles in what must be miles of rope arranged in artistic patterns with intricate knotwork. You'd think the bare breasts pouting from between the lines of rope would be a clue, but when I look down—like *you* wouldn't—I see what is clearly, though small, a penis.

I almost said a *male* penis. You know, like a *man's* dick, which is something I've actually seen in the porn I occasionally read, e.g., "Wade pounded Troy's ass, letting him know he had a man's dick inside him now." I actually read that; I'm not making it up. Okay, so I put Troy's name in there. It made me smile.

"I'm Vinnie," Vinnie says. "Pleased to meet you. This is my master, Vlad, and his companion, Logon. We're looking for someone." *My master, Vlad, and his companion, Logon.* Do I need to tell you I like the sound of this? Didn't think so.

"Welcome, Lavinia," Orisha says. "Welcome, Cyrus. Welcome, Logan." Orisha laughs, presumably at the looks on our faces when we hear our real names. *Spooky.* "What can us do for you all?"

I never thought I'd get tired of weird, but I've had just about enough for tonight, and I'm nowhere nearer Troy than I was when I started out. Plus, my coitus was interrupted, which never puts me in a good mood. You like the way I'm apologizing before I even get to the rude?

"Personally, I'm looking for the vampire that Turned me, but I'm utterly flabbergasted by this whole scene. What do you have going on here?"

"What you most curious 'bout?"

"You appear to have breasts *and* a penis. Is that some kind of add-on, or did you come this way?"

"I come anyway I can, Shoog, but in regards to my equipment, like the first people, I am not male or female, but both."

"No way! Awesome!" Logon exclaims.

I glance at him.

"I've always wanted to meet a hermaphrodite since I first found out they existed," Logon says. "I'm not some kind of freak. I'm just, you know, fascinated by the concept."

"I got nothin' to hide," Orisha says. "And ain't you cute. I got more class than to flirt with you to your master's face, but you sure are a punkin."

Logon actually looks bashful, and that annoys me. I want him to save that look for me, not hand it out like penny candy at Halloween to every intersexual that knocks on the door. That's right, I know the PC term and, to be honest, I'm as fascinated as my boo—who is currently attempting the trick of simultaneous cock- and clit-teasing.

Before I can speak, Orisha says something to me. "You're new, which tells me Mr. Troy done fell back into his old bad ways. Makin' babies and not doin' right by 'em."

"Uh, yeah," I say. "Do you know where I can find him?"

Orisha laughs, a deep, throaty laugh that doesn't go with the prepubescent voice. "Oh, Shoog, don't I wish. Troy Sanger stole something from me two-three days ago, and I want it back. So far, Mr. Bird Dog over there cain't seem to put his hand to it."

"Bon Tom almost have him outside that bar," Bon Tom says. "But he feed on this one and use the energy to fade. Bon Tom cain't follow him after that."

"That's right. You were in the alley when he bit me." I sound as outraged as I feel, though this "fade" thing sounds *très* intriguing.

Bon Tom nods.

"You saw him leave me behind the dumpster."

Bon Tom nods again.

"Would it have killed you to at least drag me out of the puddle?"

"I done tol' you, cher, I was busy."

Bon Tom just became name number two on my Rainman-style hit list. I mentally add a note: *Left me in dumpster water to die.*

"Bon Tom was about my business," Orisha says. "If you got a bone to pick with him, you can talk to me."

"I guess things turned out all right," I say. I know how to pick my battles. "Being a vampire rocks mostly."

"Don't it, though?" Orisha says. "You get to live forever and visit heaven with Mr. Blondie Sugar-Britches whenever you take a notion."

"You've taken a real shine to Logon, haven't you?" I say.

Orisha laughs that groin-tingling laugh again. "And why not? Ain't he somethin' special?"

I can't argue with that, but the way Orisha is eyeing my lover is not just setting off alarm bells—air-raid sirens are blaring and I'm hearing Emergency Broadcast System warnings. I think we've learned all we're going to learn here and should leave right away.

"Relax, blood drinker," Orisha says, reading my mind again. "I got me a boyfriend *and* a girlfriend. And I think you and me can help each other, sure enough."

"How did you know what I was thinking?"

"I know a little somethin' 'bout your kind. Crazy jealous." Orisha shakes his/her head. "Listen here. I cain't leave this spot just now, or I'd find Mr. Sneak-Thief myself and drag him back here by the shorties for an old-time barbecue."

"Why can't you leave, if it's any of my business?" I ask.

"I gettin' ready for a drum dance. Cain't go out among the impure, Shoog, or Legba might not come when I call."

"Legba?"

"The god that open the way."

"God?" Crap, I sound like a not-too-bright parrot.

Orisha laughs again. "Find Troy for me, and I tell you all 'bout Nawlins-style Vodou, pretty vampire boy."

"What makes you think I can find him if Bon Tom can't?"

"Troy Turned you, yeah? So you should be able to sense where he is."

"Nope."

"You all don't feel a hot spark out there in the big ol' dark?"

I concentrate, but I don't feel anything beyond Logon radiating fuck-me vibes at my side. "*Rien du tout.*"

"Nothing at all? That ain't right." Orisha stares hard at me. "Things been out of whack for a spell now. Cain't ignore it no more, I reckon. Best look into it."

"The drum dance," Bon Tom says.

"You think I forgot, hound?"

It's petty of me, but the way Bon Tom cringes from Orisha's glare makes me smile. "So." I break the tension. "Any clues where I should start looking for Troy?"

"He a high roller." Orisha turns off the laser beams, and Bon Tom shakes once like a dog with wet fur. "Cain't stay undercover for long. The night life be callin' him."

"I doubt he'll go back to the Inferno," I say, even though I have no idea if it's true or not.

"He won't," Bon Tom says. "Bon Tom Marked that place."

"Tell you what, Shoog," Orisha says. "You find the place where the most coolest meet up, and that's where Troy be."

Oh hell, I guess I'll have to force myself to wade through the hottest clubs in the greater Tampa-St. Pete-Clearwater area, and perhaps Orlando as well.

"You take Bon Tom with you now." Orisha looks into my eyes. "He make you wanna slap the fool outta him sometimes, but he got his uses."

"Like what?"

"Ain't got time to educate you. Got other business tonight." Orisha casts a dark look at a neighboring house.

"Them heifers in your business again?" Bon Tom asks.

"They talkin' now 'bout makin' a Homeowner's Association." Orisha spits on the ground. "Got they panties in a bunch over a little chicken blood. Like they don't eat Kentucky Fried every Sunday after churchin'. They think them chickens die in they sleep?"

"Maybe I oughta stay," Bon Tom says.

"I just give you a job. You good at guardin', so guard these babies," Orisha tells Bon Tom, then turns back to me. "Find me that thief, pretty boy, and I'll do somethin' real nice for you."

"I'm going to find him," I say. Let him/her make what s/he wants of that. I *am* intrigued by the offer of "something real nice," though. What exactly would that translate into? The ability to talk to animals? A Vodou orgy of Roman proportions? A homemade possum pot pie? I can't get a handle on Orisha. Real or fake? Priestess or poser? I swear I can't tell.

"Best be goin'," Orisha says. "Night don't last forever."

Fine with me. "One more thing," I say. "I have to ask—what's with the ropes?"

"Oh, that. Forgot I had 'em on." Orisha lets the robe drop and strikes a pose. "I like goin' 'round bare-ass, but my girlfriend like to practice *shibari* on me and since it turn my boyfriend on…."

"It's very striking," Vinnie says.

"Comfy too." Orisha pulls the black velvet back up onto his/her shoulders. "My girl's an artist and bondage ain't 'bout pain. It's 'bout trust."

"Right on, sister," Vinnie says, obviously having none of my gender confusion issues.

"Hey, vamp boy," Orisha calls after me. "You take care of Sugar-Britches, you hear?"

I put my arm possessively around Logon and hear Orisha's sexy laugh behind me.


"WHAT'S the plan, boss?" Vinnie asks as she cranks up the Wagoneer. "Do we take this beast back to Massey tonight or wait 'til tomorrow?"

"He didn't exactly place any kind of time limit on borrowing it," Logon says. "I sort of got the idea we could keep it until we find this Troy douche-nozzle."

"Let's go home," I say. "There isn't much left of the night, and I don't feel like going anywhere else."

"What about him?" Vinnie points a thumb at Bon Tom.

"Oh don't y'all worry your pretty heads 'bout Bon Tom," Bon Tom says. "Just go on 'bout your business."

"Seriously, I'll ask you one more time—where the hell are you from? That's the most effed-up accent I've ever heard attempted."

"Poke all the fun you want at Bon Tom. Don't mean a thang."

"*Where* are you from?"

"You said you was gonna ask *one* more time, cher. That makes twice."

I grit my teeth. Why can't I make this Tarantino scarecrow answer me? Am I not a fearsome prince of darkness with a heart as black as midnight and an unquenchable thirst for blood? WTF? Maybe I should try and read *his* mind.

Bon Tom turns to look at me over the back of the seat. "Bad idea, cher," he says.

Who the hell *is* this guy? Besides the ass hat who left me to die *and* cockblocked me. Why did I let him come with us?

"You scared of Orisha like everybody else," Bon Tom says.

*WTF squared!* "Well, you have to admit that's a pretty spooky act with all the Vodou trappings," I tell him. "Not to mention the shock value of the nudity."

"Shock value." Bon Tom repeats my words and chuckles. "Tell you what, cher. Why don't you climb in the back and climb on top of Blondie? That make you sweet again."

*Smug son of a bitch.* He's right, though.

# CHAPTER FOUR

I WALLOW in silken billows of red until Vinnie slams the behemoth into park under a bile-yellow streetlight. Jostled from the warm, downy embrace of bliss, I am understandably grumpy.

Vinnie and Bon Tom appear to have become better acquainted during the drive. I'm judging by the complicit looks they exchange whenever I voice a complaint. They look like mommy and daddy indulging a toddler who's up way past his bedtime. I'll make them pay for this disrespect, but not right now. Right now, I want to crawl into my staircase surrogate-coffin and curl up around Logon.

"Hold it," Vinnie says as I head for the cubby. "We need to plan a little before you go to bed."

"What are we talking about?" I ask.

"We're going out clubbing when you wake up, right?"

"Right, and?"

"And you need new clothes. Also, we should plot a course, map out the clubs, and figure the best route so we don't waste time."

"No prob. I can do the map thing in like fifteen minutes with a laptop," Logon says.

"And I trust you to handle the rest," I tell Vinnie. "I'm out." I pull Logon into the closet and indulge in a few more close encounters with him.

LOGON is tonguing my left nipple like a kitten with a saucer of milk. I picture him with ears and a tail. *Nice.*

"Hello, gorgeous," he says. "I'm starting to get a sense of when you're going to wake up."

"I like the way you say good morning."

Logon laughs his soft little laugh, and I feel it all the way to my core. My heart beats faster, or rather it would, if it was still beating, and a rush of *need* blasts through my veins. *Mine. Mine. Mine.* I roll and pin Logon under me, nip his neck just a little, just a sip.

"Damn, that's good," Logon murmurs.

He moves restlessly, his bare skin sliding against mine, and I'm on fire for him. What the hell, just a quick one. We have time, and we don't want to show up at the clubs too early anyway. Logon does everything physically possible to let me know he agrees, and we wind up head to foot in a classic sixty-nine. For the first time, I bite him somewhere other than his neck.

My head's on his thigh, and I can feel the femoral artery racing under his skin. I kiss the soft, soft flesh and, almost by accident, my fangs slip in. Logon moans so loud that he startles me. His pelvis rises, and his hard cock brushes against my bangs. He moans louder, and I grab his dick. I keep sucking lightly while I stroke him, thumbing pre-cum from the tip of his hard-on. Even though he's distracted, he's still going down on me, deep-throating my cock and playing with my balls. An electric thrill runs down my spine when he runs a wet finger over my taint. The finger nudges my asshole and then pushes in. He finds my prostate. I gasp and a little blood dribbles down the crease where Logon's thigh joins his torso. I lap at the blood as I ease a finger into Logon and thrust.

Whoa! Now that's an orgasm. I'm surprised cum isn't squirting out my nose and.... Oh fuck! Fuck! *Fuck!* Here it comes. Yes! Yes! *Hell yes!*

Damn, I think I blanked out again.

"Wow," Logon says. He's panting like he just ran up five flights of stairs, so I couldn't have been out for long. "Wow," he repeats in case I didn't catch it all the first time.

"Yeah," I say cleverly. I'm concentrating on getting turned around so I can kiss Logon.

"Hey, lovebirds." By the sound of Vinnie's voice, she's on the other side of the room. "You ready to favor the world with your fabulousness?"

"Yeah, be right out," I yell back and hear her walk away. I'm focused on Logon's sweet lips. I want to stay here with him forever.

But I have a jackhole to track down.


WHILE I was recharging, Vinnie had used her day off, her ingenuity, and Bon Tom's bemused help to create ensembles for all of us. She was like Molly Ringwald in *Pretty in Pink,* only in black and with boobage. From the bounty of thrift stores and Vinnie's sewing machine came elegant, edgy outfits that stop just short of being costumes.

My black suit has a long jacket that suggests a frock coat without actually being one, and the satin-striped pants are skintight. Vinnie found me a tuxedo shirt with an Edwardian-style collar that she pins a huge silver brooch on in place of a tie. I already have boots, and Vinnie provides a finishing touch in the shape of a pair of black kid gloves.

"No wolf's-head cane?" I ask as she plaits a tiny braid into Logon's hair just over his left ear. She's a lot nicer to him now, and I like the clothes she picked for him.

My blood boo's wearing a white, piratey-type tunic thing over black leather pants. Vinnie wraps four or five cloth belts with tassels around his hips. The tassels dangle very enticingly, if you ask me, brushing his crotch and ass when he moves. His hair flows loose, except for the braid, catching the light. *Damn, he's fine.* I'm amazed that I ever saw him as a mousy gipster. He's all of the *bi-shonen* manga beauties I lusted after as a teen rolled into one. Suddenly, I want a picture of him just like this because he's going to get old someday.

*Oh hell no.*

The central angst of all vampire love stories is falling on me like a truckload of brick-shaped turds. Logon's going to die and I'm not. My *yaoi* angel is going to grow old.

"What up, cher?" Bon Tom says. "Look like somebody done walked on your grave."

"Shut up," I retort wittily.

"Did you just realize the sweet thang ain't gonna be 'round forever?"

"What part of shut up don't you understand?"

"You oughta be nicer to Bon Tom, cher. I might know somebody can help with your particular problem."

"You're my particular problem."

"Can you two stop for five minutes?" Vinnie says. "Sheesh. You can cut the sexual tension with a machete."

"Bitch," Logon says. Not a good idea when someone has hold of a handful of your hair. "Ow!"

"Grow up," I say loudly, halting the incipient hissy fit. "Both of you."

"Y'all make me miss kindergarten," Bon Tom says.

"Ha!" Vinnie snorts as she finishes off Logon's Elf-braid with a cute skull and crossbones barrette. "As if you've ever seen the inside of a classroom."

"Don't make fun of my ignorance, queenie," Bon Tom says, but he doesn't sound serious.

*Queenie?* Just what the hell went on while I was sleeping the sleep of the undead?

Vinnie giggles. Now I'm really suspicious. Has this mongrel been putting the moves on my homegirl? So not cool. *Whoa.* Dial it back a notch. Vinnie has the right to get some too. She must be horny as hell after being around me and Logon for the last three nights.

I have to admit that she looks roughly as hot as the surface of Mercury with her curvalicious bod poured into a basic Morticia gown in cobwebby black. The neckline plunges to her belly button, displaying a sweet red satin bra. Her wig is long, straight, and dead black, and she's wearing a heavy silver chain around her neck that disappears into her cleavage. It looks like Cher's closet blew up on her, but she carries it off brilliantly, and I tell her so.

Bon Tom is wearing the same black suit and tie with white shirt and fedora hat that he's had on since I first saw him. Have I mentioned the black on black wingtip shoes? It's almost a look, but the clothes are worn and a little frayed, as if he's been wearing them for years.

"What about him?" I ask Vinnie, as if she's now in charge of Bon Tom.

"He can walk a few feet behind us," she says as she snatches Logon's glasses off his face. She polishes the lenses and puts them back before he can protest. "Where's my map, technopup?" she says.

Using Vinnie's laptop, accompanied by a constant stream of complaints about the machine's configuration, operating system, and general counterintuitive nature, Logon conducts a few million searches with about a dozen keywords, cross-indexes his information with a map program, and prints out driving directions.

"Pretty work," I say and kiss the top of his head.

Vinnie pulls the chain out of her rack and looks at the Baroque watch attached to it. "Almost nine," she says. "What do you say, boss? Should we get going?"

I really wish I could see myself in a mirror. I think I probably look pretty close to the vampire I've always imagined. I don't have the long coat with the fur collar, but this *is* Florida after all, and even though it's October, it's nowhere near cold enough for a coat like that. Yeah, I know what you're thinking; I'm dead, so I wouldn't get overheated and sweaty. True, but when you're wearing a hulking winter coat and it's seventy-five degrees Fahrenheit at midnight, it attracts the wrong kind of attention. We don't need any cops searching us for illegal drugs tonight.

"I hate to sound ungrateful, but I wish we had another ride," I say as I lead my crew into the elevator. "I'm not saying it has to be a hearse, but a black limo would be nice."

"Can I bring up another practical matter at this point?" Vinnie asks. "What are we using for money? These clubs are going to have a cover charge and valet parking. That's going to add up fast. I have a credit card, but it ain't platinum."

Bon Tom chuckles. "Don't you worry 'bout a thang, pretty mama. When you look like that, you don't need money."

"It doesn't work that way," Logon says.

"Sure it do, sweet thang. Look here, Vlad. You just walk up to the door and keep walkin' on in. Ain't nobody gonna stop you if you step like a boss, you hear?"

"I might have to practice."

Bon Tom shakes his head as we step out of the elevator on the ground floor. "No, you don't need no practice, cher. You a vampire. *Be* a vampire."

Well, I *have* seen plenty of movie vampires make entrances. Maybe I can fake it.

WE ROLL up on Tango's Two, and Vinnie finds a parking place at a dead strip mall around the corner. Half the parking lot has been turned into a car show by a bunch of gearheads with tricked-out muscle cars. Some things never change, as my Aunt Bootsy would say, but she'd be wrong in this case. Something did change.

In her day, muscle cars were genuine phallic symbols—long, brash, and generally red. Nowadays, street racers drive these squatty little imports in colors usually found on the fingernails of showgirls. Yeesh. I sound kind of like a grumpy old man talking about the good old days and ragging on the crazy kids. That's not like me. I wonder if being undead is changing me in ways other than living on blood and sleeping all day. Wait. Scratch that last one. Sleeping all day is something I already did when I was alive.

I wonder if the night crew at Metro Media misses me. Man, I really *am* gay. BTW, this is where I'd put in the smiley face if I was posting to a forum. Which I used to do when I was into RP big time. But I don't want to get off on a role-playing tangent.

*Or do I?*

Could it really be that easy?

Bon Tom said *be a vampire*. I've always fantasized about it, and now that I am one, I'm frittering the experience away, just floating through it like I did with my life, just going with the flow. But now it occurs to me that I could take this into my hands and mold it into whatever I want it to be. If I look and behave like a suave, sinister vampire, well then....

Okay, I just need to get into character. I'm definitely an old-school vampire, vintage clothes, elegant manners, but also definitely an ass-kicker. I'm thinking somewhere between those British Count Dracula movies and Vampire Hunter D. Half Euro-nobility and half samurai. Yeah, that works for me.

Now all I have to do is pull it off.

Well, first of all, I *am* an actual vampire. I suck blood, and I'm strong as shit. I'm lookin' fly, and I'm on the prowl with my posse. Bitches better recognize; know what I'm sayin', play-ah? Attitude is the key. Or in this case, baditude. I think I'm ready.

The bouncer and the line at the door of Tango's might as well be part of the architecture for all the notice I give them. I am a sultan of supernatural *savoir-faire*. Bon Tom maneuvers around to hold the door open for me. Logon and Vinnie are right behind me, not so close that they look desperate, but obviously members of my entourage. The hostess inside takes a long look and surrenders to our drama. With a sweep of her arm, she invites us in, no cover charge.

And what now? On cop shows, detectives go into nightclubs and someone—usually a bartender—tells them something they need to know to solve the case. Note to self: stop relying on pop culture for advice.

"He ain't here," Bon Tom says.

"Just like that you can tell?" Vinnie says.

Bon Tom nods.

"No point in hanging around here, I guess," I say.

"Fine, we'll go," Vinnie says. "But I'm finishing my drink at the next place. I've always wanted to go to the Penthouse."

We brazen our way into the exclusive lounge on top of one of the city's restored Art Deco buildings. The crowd here is on the leading edge of fashion, but it's that brittle edge populated by young members of Society with a capital S. The girls have all graduated from college into jobs as buyers for the juniors' department at Neiman-Marcus—yes, we have them in Florida—and they spend their nights at cocktail parties or bars like this one, hoping to rope a free-range junior partner in a big law firm or the fabled land-rich multimillionaire's son whose only job is working on his tan on the deck of his yacht.

I give Vinnie a look as we find a place at the bar. Sure the décor is to die for, and the clothes are beyond fabulous, but no one here is having a good time, despite the liberal application of alcohol. It's full of dead-eyed people drinking grimly, like they're paying penance for something. It's like a miniature Vegas but without the annoying slot machine noises.

"This is the most depressing place I've ever been."

"One drink," Vinnie says. "Enjoy the scenery."

"Gah, the desperation." I fake a dying gasp.

Bon Tom grins and succeeds in looking like a coyote eyeing a chubby Chihuahua.

"Is he here?" I ask.

Bon Tom shakes his head. "You the only bloodsucker in here tonight. Couple shape-shifters, but nothin' else."

"Shape-shifters?" I look around the room

"You know, cher... werewolves and the like."

"Where?"

"Where what?" Bon Tom replies.

"Werewolves," I clarify.

"Cut it out," Vinnie says. "Mel Brooks already did that joke in *Young Frankenstein*. Now, what do you want to drink while my boobs have the barkeep's attention?"

"Water," Bon Tom says.

I pass, but Logon asks Vinnie to order him whatever she's drinking.

"Well, look at us," Vinnie says as she lounges back against the bright turquoise faux alligator hide with a martini glass in her hand. "This is how it should be."

"It's *very*," I say without enthusiasm. "Can we get back to the werewolves?"

"These two aren't wolves," Bon Tom says. He inclines his head toward two fit, forty-ish women in high heels and spandex. "Couple of cougars."

Vinnie laughs and Logon joins in. Bon Tom looks confused for the first time since I met him. I realize now that he wasn't making a joke, probably doesn't even know that cougar is a slang word. *Now* it's funny.

"Are you all in a play?" asks the man sitting next to Vinnie at the bar.

"Only in the sense that all the world's a stage," Logon answers.

The intrusive guy rolls his eyes at his friends and does the thing that flips my psycho switch: the limp wrist. Where does this come from? I've never seen a gay person in real life that held their wrist like that. It's not just insulting, it's stupid. I ignore the fact that anyone stupid enough to use that gesture is too stupid to appreciate a lesson in tolerance. I just want to scare the crap out of him so he knows what it feels like to be bullied.

"Do it," Bon Tom says in my ear. Is my mind really that easy to read? Don't answer that.

I move to lean on the bar, facing the jerk, standing between him and his friends. He looks surprised to see me, because I moved at vampire warp speed. "You're not funny," I say.

"Whut?" is his brilliant riposte.

"You *think* you're funny because your friends laugh when you talk, but they're a bunch of fart-smoking, shit-munching hyenas with taste as bad as yours."

"You want to get in my face?"

"You insulted my friend."

"I wouldn't have talked to you freaks at all if I wasn't wondering what such a hot babe was doing hanging out with a bunch of fags."

"Eat your heart out," I say. "Or I could do it for you." I look deep into his eyes and do my best to project an *I'll rip out your heart with my bare hands and snack on it* vibe.

It works, to judge from the ass hat's change of expression. "Who the hell are you?" he says in this kind of hoarse whisper.

I'm so tempted to tell him I'm his worst nightmare, but that's been done to death. As badass clichés go, it's as overused as telling someone you'll see them in hell.

"I'm no one you want to know," I say instead. "But if you keep being a bigoted assjack, you're going to get to know me better, and I can promise you that you won't enjoy it." I can actually hear him swallow when I lean toward him. Threat delivered, I use my super-speed again to go back to where I was. Wow, that was a rush.

"Good job," Bon Tom says. "You sure 'nough put the fear into that natural fool."

I glance over and see the jerk darting a nervous look over his shoulder. I smile at him, letting him see my fangs. He pays his bill and leaves. *Quickly.* Okay, so I know that this makes me as big a bully as he is, but I promise not to use my powers for evil ever again. Let's move on.

"Where to next?" I ask.

"The Tidepool," Logon says.

"The seafood place near the docks?" Vinnie frowns. "That's a pretty gritty neighborhood. How'd it get on the list?"

"The entertainment gossip blogs tagged it with three or more keywords."

"All right, Data," Vinnie says. She tosses back the last of her martini. "Let's go." She slides gracefully off the bar stool. "By the way, thanks for taking care of my light work. That shithead took off like his ass was on fire."

"You are *so* cool," Logon tells me as we leave the Penthouse. He takes my arm and squeezes it, looking at me with unmistakable hero lust in his big doe eyes.

I know what he wants, and I want it too, but the timing is bad. I guess we could go into the back of the Wagoneer on the way to the Tidepool, but our clothes will get messed up. We'll just have to wait.

*Screw that. Want.*

I push Logon against the back window of the Jeep and lean against him as he flattens the palms of his hands against the glass. The curve of his ass fits my crotch perfectly and the curve of his neck begs for my kiss. I let my fangs sink in, and I suck, the warm liquid filling me with a fierce euphoria. To the whooping encouragement of the gearheads, who either don't know or don't care that Logon's not a girl, I hump his round butt while he humps the Wagoneer's tailgate. My problem with public performance seems to have disappeared; I'm as hard as astrophysics and set to pop at any second. I slide my hand down the front of Logon's pants and grab his dick, and he goes off like a Titan missile leaving the launch pad. Vinnie blows the horn as I blow my load. This makes me laugh for some insane reason. Whatever. I got mine.

"Damn," Vinnie says as me and Logon get in the backseat. "Does the phrase 'get a room' mean anything to you?"

"Do forgive me if I held up the expedition, Miss Goodbody," Logon says, and I give him a hug for being extra cute.

"Ha-ha," Vinnie says, but I can see her smile in the rearview mirror. It makes me happy that my peeps have a truce. I used to think it would be cool to have two people fighting over me, but the reality is as ugly as prejudice.

THE Tidepool.... It's like someone took a basement blues bar from Bourbon Street and dropped it down on the east side of the Gulf between two warehouses. In front is an eat-in/takeout seafood shack complete with newspapers on picnic tables. From the smell, I assume it's as authentic as the sign claims. In back of the restaurant is a smoky, sweaty lounge that manages to give the impression that it's underground. Syrupy-slow blues riffs slink around the brick walls like stray cats. Yeah, I hear ya. I slipped into Analogy Boy mode again.

As soon as we walk into the place, two things happen. Bon Tom says, "He's here," and everyone turns to look at us.

I feel like I'm in a scene from that eighties movie, *Crossroads*. It's about an old blues man who breaks out of a nursing home with the janitor. If you haven't seen it, I'll just say that it ends with a guitar duel between Satan and the Karate Kid. I'm not making this up.

When I was little and Aunt Bootsy would come for one of her long visits, her and Mom always spent Sundays in their pajamas watching eighties movies. I have a more than fair working knowledge of gems like *Fast Times at Ridgemont High*, *Say Anything*, *Risky Business*, and of course, the queen mother, *The Breakfast Club* by Grandmaster John Hughes. But enough digression. As if there could ever be enough digression.

"He's here now?" Vinnie's saying.

"Sorry, false alarm," Bon Tom says. "He were here, but he gone."

"Can you follow him?" I ask.

"I can try, cher."

"Where do we start?"

Bon Tom crosses the room, weaving between people and tables like he's made of fog. Well hell, if he can do it, I should be able to. Holding on to Logon's hand, I follow Bon Tom. Vinnie does a sultry slide in our wake and the crowd parts for her. We should've put her out front.

"There's a vampire in here." Bon Tom stops in front of a door labeled *Employee's Only*. I'm so wired that I don't even bitch about the misplaced and superfluous apostrophe on the sign.

What would be the best plan of action here?

Bon Tom opens the door. He doesn't even knock. Who does things like that?

"Come right in." The voice that invites us in is deep and mellow, like one of those actors who read for audiobooks.

Bon Tom steps aside.

*What, me first?* Better get my vamp face on.

"Come on in, young'un." A large black man stands up from behind a big desk. "You and your friends. Shut the door behind you, please."

To the right of the desk sits a vampire. Now that I see him, I'd never mistake him for anything else. Everything about him is just exquisitely perfect. Each curl of his auburn mane looks like it was carved out of mahogany and polished to a high gloss. His complexion is amazingly smooth, not a wrinkle or blemish in sight. And his eyes.... They're a bright, clear green like the water in pictures of tropical islands. I can't look away, and I feel kind of funny. Not *ha-ha* funny. Weird funny. I can sense that he's way older and a lot more powerful than me. That he knows so much more than I do. I'm a child next to him. I should just get on my knees right now.

"Hello, young one," the vampire says in a plummy British accent that snaps me out of my trance.

*Whoa!* That was scary. Is that what people feel when they look into my eyes? Nah, probably not. I imagine that's something that comes with age and experience. I really hope I look as good as he does though. He's definitely from the Wattahawti tribe.

"Hi," I say. "I'm Vlad."

"Surely not."

"I haven't had time to come up with a good name yet."

The vampire raises fox-colored eyebrows. "Let me wish you luck with that. I'm Simon Bonesteel, by the way."

"That's an awesome name," Logon says.

"My parents were satisfied with it." Simon doesn't look at Logon as he speaks. In fact, he ignores everyone but me. "I don't know you, *Vlad*, which means you're very young. Tell me who's been careless enough to add another predator to the ecosystem."

"His name's Troy." Damn! How did Simon do that? I didn't intend to answer him right away, but I did. I obeyed him without thinking about it.

"Troy." Simon says the name like it's a particularly insidious drug and gives the black man a sharp look. "Do you mean to say he was in the area and didn't visit me? Very rude, I call that."

"I think he's still here, not right here, but in the area. Anyway, I'm looking for him. He was rude to me too."

"And who are you? The accidental by-product of a frenzy-feeder with no restraint. Keep to your place and be thankful you're not a rotting corpse awaiting burial."

*Smackdown!* Okay, I get that this Simon guy is my superior and all, but he doesn't have to be a dick about it. "I'd still like to find him, if it's all the same to you," I say. I get super-polite when I'm being condescended to.

"What if it isn't all the same to me?" Simon stands up, and he's like six two or three, and though I'm five-eleven, he's kind of looming over me now, and it's not a pleasant feeling.

"Let's talk about that, shall we?" Where am I getting the balls to talk to him like this? I guess if I'm going down in flames, I might as well do it with style.

"I'm not the sort to be impressed by spunk, my lad. You've shown proper respect in presenting yourself to me. Don't ruin the impression by peeing on the carpet."

Oh. Kay. Another approach. I've had experience with management types with delusions of power. "Now that we've met, sir, do you mind if I look for Troy in your territory?"

"At least you have manners... when you're reminded to use them." Simon adjusts the perfect knot of his lavender tie. "You were Turned young, and the young these days have no knowledge of how to behave courteously."

Damn. How could such a smokin' hot guy be such a massive turn-off? I swear he's giving me a throbbing soft-on.

"'Scuse me, Lord Bonesteel," says the guy behind the desk. "If you got private business, my office is yours."

"Stay or go, depending on what pleases you, Cedrick." Simon looks none too pleased by the interruption. "And since my money finances this club, I assume that this office and everything else in the building is mine to do with as I please."

Cedrick sits back down. Simon's 'tude is now officially on my nerves. And he's so obviously not going to do anything to help me, so screw him.

"So you're like a loan shark?" I ask.

"I own this property and several others throughout the city."

"Oh, so you're a slumlord."

Simon fiddles with a cufflink before he answers. "I overlook your lack of respect because you don't know how things work yet."

"If the way things work has anything to do with turning a vampire into a profit-driven leech, I don't want to know about it."

"Leech," Cedrick says under his breath. "Ain't that the truth."

Vampires have ears like bats. "Have you already forgotten what it's like to be in my black books?" Simon asks Cedrick.

To my surprise, Cedrick answers. "Look here, I know you bad, but you squeezin' too hard now. I send you a cut of the profit and all the warm bodies you want, but I respectfully request that you ease up on me."

"Right on, brother," Vinnie says. "Don't accept subhuman status."

Simon chuckles. "I'm not treating him as subhuman. I'm simply treating him as human."

"You have to respect everyone's dignity." I'm shocked to find myself quoting my mom.

Simon's chuckle is louder this time. "Don't be ridiculous. It's not as if we're equals."

"That's not the point."

"You're reaching the point where youth cannot excuse your cheek. If you expect to be accepted into vampire society, you'll have to mend your ways." Simon brushes phantom dust from the lapels of his off-white suit.

"I've never wanted to be accepted, and your society sounds boring." Spoken like an eighth grader sulking over not getting picked for the team.

"You are a prime example of why I oppose the Turning of anyone less than thirty years of age."

Oh no he didn't! I'm tempted to give him the *chronological age is no indicator of emotional maturity* speech that my mom gave to at least one of my teachers every year during my brief stretch in public school. But that would be a waste of my nonexistent breath. And if this pompous ass doesn't know where Troy is, staying here is a waste of my time.

"Whatever," I say. "I didn't come here for the purpose of rebelling against your rules or anything like that. I'm just looking for the smeg that sucked me dry and left me in an alley."

Simon sits back down and makes a big deal out of thinking things over. "Troy knows the consequences of misbehaving on my territory," he says. "You have permission to hunt him, but you must bring him to me for judgment."

"Any idea where he might be?"

"Someone at Eyrie will know." Simon smiles a really smug smile that I want to remove with a scouring pad. "But you wouldn't know about Eyrie, would you?"

"No, of course not, 'cause I could never be as cool as you," I say.

Either Simon misses my sarcasm or chooses to ignore it. "That's right," he says. "I shouldn't tell you about it, but imagining the look of surprise...." Simon beckons with a bone-white, perfectly tapered forefinger, and I lean toward him. "I'll tell you how to find Eyrie, but first you owe me a tithe as your lord."

"What kind of tithe?"

"Blood, of course. You can offer me your consort. He's on the scrawny side, but he looks as sweet as a jam tart. I see by your expression that this is not palatable to you. Your other option is to let me drink your blood."

Am I the only one sensing a trap here? I turn and look at Cedrick. "Do I have to let him drink my blood?" I ask.

"What?" Cedrick looks up from his magazine, genuinely shocked. Not a good sign.

"What are you trying to pull?" I ask Simon.

Simon leaves off giving Cedrick the death glare and turns it on me.

"What's going on?" Logon asks me.

"Simon here wants some blood before he'll tell me where this Eyrie place is."

"Shoot, I can tell you that," Cedrick says.

"One more word, Cedrick, and you'll be attending several funerals in the near future. You still have a surplus of relatives."

"You suck!" Yeah, that was a pretty lame thing to say. Oh well, too late now. Just keep talking. "When I walked in here, I thought you were supercool, but you're a supertool."

"And you're very naïve," Simon says.

"Yeah, I've heard your opinion on the subject. If my ignorance bugs you so much, educate me."

"I'm afraid I haven't the time or inclination to take on a protégé. Even if you are as beautiful as ink strokes on rice paper. You'll find Eyrie on St. Andrews Drive in Belleair. Drive past the resort and onto the island. There are approximately twenty homes on the loop, but you'll have no trouble finding the one you want. There's a stone arch at the entrance to the drive, and the house is the only one that's set back from the road. Park on the lawn and go to the front door. You'll be admitted." Simon gives me that smirk again. "And you'll be on your own."

"No he won't," Logon says. Have I mentioned that I adore him?

"Damn right, he won't," Vinnie says. Actually, she kind of growls. I'm so proud of my new crew right now. My eyes are getting kind of watery. I wonder if my tears are pink like my cum.

"I be watchin' he back too," Bon Tom says.

"That reminds me." Simon's upper lip curdles into a sneer when he finally looks at Bon Tom. "If you ever come back here, leave your dog at home."

"He's not my dog," I say. "I mean I don't really know him. He's kind of tagging along."

"Really?" The look on Simon's face is the definition of enigmatic. "And he just offered to put his life at risk for you. How curious. Either you're a liar or an ingrate. Either way, you have no idea what sort of creature you've taken in."

"Could you be a just a teensy bit more condescending? Because I think you've almost got the world record in the bag."

"Isn't adolescent humor a little beneath you? You're a member of a superior breed now. Try and rise above the schoolyard."

"Yeah, I'd say that cinched it. All vampires aren't like you, are they? Please say no, because you have a fun factor of zero."

"You think being a vampire is about having fun?" Simon actually throws back his head and laughs. Asshole looks *good* doing it too. "After I conclude my business, I look forward to seeing what's become of you."

"Let's go," I say and lead my peeps back into the club. Once again heads turn, but this time I stalk to the nearest exit and I own the room. I have to say that the swaying snake-charmer number the band is playing makes for a nice soundtrack.

Now, do we drive up to Belleair tonight, or wait until tomorrow?

"If it can wait, I've got clients tomorrow," Vinnie says. "I should get a little sleep so they don't think they're subbing for someone's grandmother."

"You could never look like a granny, cher," Bon Tom says.

"Let's go home then." I cut Bon Tom off before he can elaborate. "Tomorrow night... Eyrie."

# CHAPTER FIVE

"YOU'RE in so much trouble," is the greeting we receive as we walk off the elevator.

"Petie!" Vinnie's mouth drops open at the sight of her baby sister curled up in the birdcage chair. "What are you doing here?"

"You planning on missing Frankie's baby shower, airhead?"

"Meep!" Vinnie makes a noise like the Roadrunner about to go into hyperdrive.

"Exactly," Petie says, uncoiling from the chair.

Petronia Testardo is five foot ten and a half inches of coltish girl-child with thick honey-brown hair that hangs to the middle of her back. She's wearing worn jeans, a gray hoodie with an *Orlando Magic* logo, and a pair of moccasins. I'm trying to calculate how old she is now. *Failing.*

"Damn," Petie says, looking me up and down. "Nosebleed!"

"Petie, don't anoint my guests with your drool," Vinnie says. "How'd you get in?"

"Wasn't locked. That's an awesome dress."

"Thanks. Why are you dressed like you just got your period?"

Petie blushes.

"Want a heating pad and a muscle relaxer?"

Petie nods.

"Excuse us," Vinnie says and pulls Petie away. "Girl talk."

"I suppose the two of you wanna be alone," Bon Tom says when Logon and I look at each other. "I'm goin' back out."

"Um, thanks for saying you'd watch my back."

"I like you, cher. You didn't know that?" Bon Tom laughs as he goes back to the elevator.

"What a freak," Logon says as Bon Tom sinks out of sight.

"I can't figure him out. We've met a lot of unique people recently, but he's a real mystery."

"A mystery freak."

"Why so harsh, angel?"

"You did *not* just call me angel."

"Why not?"

"Angels are all sky-blue and fluffy and vanilla and lace."

"That's not what I meant. And I think you're thinking about the Care Bears."

"What *did* you mean then?" Logon moves in close, standing about a millimeter away, not being confrontational, just *front*ational. What a tease.

"Just that you're *my* angel." I've never been what you'd call a lover-boy. I've had the normal amount of sex for a guy my age—judging from magazine articles and conversations with my peers—but I'm no smooth stud. Most of my romantic encounters have occurred in alleys, cars, and cluttered bedrooms at friends' parties. Rarely have I enjoyed the luxury of sleeping all night with a lover without the stress of wondering who's going to walk in.

It's different with Logon. I don't worry about what he's going to think of me if I'm awkward when I kiss him. There's no fumbling around, no inadvertent jabbing of tender spots, no apprehension about performance. My fingers know just how to touch him. His body fits seamlessly with mine. There's no anxiety about what to do next or whether it will be greeted with a groan of pleasure or disgust. It's exactly how I imagined sex would be before I ever had any experience.

"Would an angel do this?" Logon grabs my junk.

"Mine would." I take his glasses off and put them in my breast pocket. "You're happy, right? I mean… it's okay with you that Vinnie tapped you to—"

"The day she introduced me to you was the best day of my life."

"Does it seem weird that you'd take so completely to someone you'd never met before?"

"I guess so, but I don't care. I've never felt this good in my entire life, and I don't ever want it to end." Logon squeezes my stiffening dick. He knows just how to touch me too.

"How do you feel?" If I was still breathing, I'd be breathing hard.

"Like everything is right." Logon's lips are moving on mine as he finishes his sentence.

"Yeah, me too." I want to talk some more, but Logon wants me to sex him up.


WOW, I need a shower. But first, where the hell is Logon? He should be right here beside me, partially draped over my chest, breathing on my neck, but he's not.

*This is not good.*

Here are my clothes, right outside the closet, but Logon's are gone. Wait, I can hear his voice coming from the living room.

"Mornin', cher." Bon Tom is sitting on the oatmeal-colored divan with Logon.

Logon puts down his coffee cup, jumps up, and runs over to hug me. The world is right again.

"Vinnie left you a note," he says.

"I'm starving." I nuzzle his earlobe suggestively.

"Don't mind me," Bon Tom says.

"I won't." How does he always manage to make me sound bratty? Who cares? Logon's head is tilted to the side, baring his neck. The blood soothes my hunger pangs, nothing sexual about it for me, though Logon is clearly having a different experience. His skin is flushed. His eyelids are at half-mast, and he's grinding his pelvis against mine. "Go get in the shower," I say. "I'll be there in a couple of minutes."

"The note right here." Bon Tom points to an hourglass-shaped end table covered in stingray hide.

Vinnie's purple-inked prose informs me that she's making an emergency house call at her parents' home and that she'll most likely be gone for a couple of days. I have her cell number and permission to call at any hour. *Really?* She's abandoning me on the eve of a visit to what sounds like a den of vampires? Vinnie wouldn't want to miss that. Petie must have laid an obscene amount of guilt on her big sister.

"Queenie didn't look thrilled to be goin'," Bon Tom says. "Keys to the truck are in that little bowl that looks like it's made outta bug shells."

"Carapaces."

"There's that big vocabulary again." Bon Tom sounds more amused than impressed.

"I'm going to take a shower."

"Fine with me. Any other announcements you wanna make 'bout your bodily functions?"

"Piss off," I suggest.

Logon is in the shower, which is an entire room separate from the toilet and sink. The floor is slate, and the walls are made of the kind of rocks you'd find around a waterfall. Sunk into the floor on one side is a Jacuzzi tub big enough for half a dozen people. In the opposite corner, several water jets are set in the rocks at varying heights. I like the ferns growing here and there. I also like naked Logon with shampoo in his hair. I know he knows I'm there and that he's taking his time so I can get a good look. It's worth the time. His skin is all wet and shiny, and I like the way the lather slides down his back and over his butt as he rinses his hair. He has a great ass, if I haven't mentioned it, convex without being a complete bubble, smooth with a downy drift of tiny blond hairs in the cleft. Garsh, he makes me all poetical and stuff.

Logon drops the soap. "Stupid gravity," he mutters as he bends over.

*Vamp warp speed!*

"*Mae govannen*," Logon says in Elvish as he straightens up to find me right behind him. My hard-on fits perfectly in the groove of his ass. *Perfectly.* "Welcome to Rivendell, my lord." He pushes back against my crotch.

Ooh! Role-playing! I love this shit! It's not hard to figure out that Logon is an Elven warrior prince, but who am I? A Prince of Gondor? A raggedy Ranger? Another Elf? A *dark* Elf, perhaps? Just give me a clue, boo. I really *love* this stuff.

"Tomorrow we set out for Mordor and some of us will not return," Logon says with his voice all full of doom.

Okay, I got it now. Time to make Middle-Earth move for my forbidden lover. "Then let me love you as I've always dreamed."

Logon rubs his butt harder against my dick. I know I've mentioned how well those two things fit together. I put my arms around him and run my hands over his chest and abs down to his groin. He says, "I wish for that also, Estel."

*Estel?* The way Logon's soapy butt cheeks feel sliding against my hard-on is making it hard to think. Estel. Estel. Oh yeah. Now I remember. Estel is Aragorn's Elvish name. Okay. I'm in the saddle now, figuratively and literally, as Logon bends over, braces his hands on the lip of the huge planter, and invites me in. He's framed by the miniature rain forest in the planter, and it's not hard to imagine him as one of Peter Jackson's gorgeous tree-dwelling Elves. Our lovemaking is passionate, sincere, and poignant. Epic. I'd be happy making love to him for the rest of my life... or death, as the case may be.

Damn! Now the whole *immortal in love with a mortal* angst-a-thon is on again. What a buzzkill! I'm holding Logon and savoring my climax and now *this*. What a colossal drag. And he feels my mood change, of course.

"Why sad?" he asks.

"Well, you know, you'll get old and die. That's sad."

"So Turn me into a vampire."

For some reason, this idea isn't as appealing as it should be. I have a feeling that if we're both vampires, something essential about our relationship will change. Not sure I want that.

"Is that what you want?" I ask.

"I don't know. I like the whole idea of vampires, but I'm not sure I'm meant to be one."

"Then why did you ask me to Turn you?"

"I didn't. I was just trying to make you feel better. If you don't want me to die, make me a vampire, that's all I'm saying."

"Let's keep that option open."

"Suits me."

"You're amazing."

"No, *you're* amazing."

"Let's see if we can get our amazing selves dressed without Vinnie's help."

"I'm missing so many classes. I should just drop out," Logon says in the middle of reconstructing his ensemble from last night.

"I have so much to learn about you. What are you studying? Computer science?"

"No. I learned computers from a friend, and I keep up with the new stuff in my online groups. I'm a history major."

"Yeah, I can picture that. Cool." I kiss the top of Logon's head as he tucks my gloves into the pocket of my suit coat. "Guess we've kept Bon Tom waiting long enough."

"I don't think he cares. He just goes into idle mode and conserves his energy."

"Like an android?"

"More like a cheetah."

Logon's hair smells wonderful as I follow him out to the front room. He's pulled it back into a ponytail, and I have the recurring urge to take hold of it. I'm a little vague on what happens after that, but my fingers are itching to wrap around the thick ponytail and tug on it.

Bon Tom stands up when he see us and gives me a look that says he knows what I was thinking and that I'm a naughty little boy. His face is amazingly expressive.

"Ready to ramble?" he asks.

"PRETTY work," I say as Logon drives the Wagoneer through the stone archway Bonesteel described. The drive is hemmed in by trees on both sides, making a tunnel in the headlights. At the end of the narrow road is a three-story house fronted by broad lawns. The lawns are filled with rows of cars.

"This place needs a vampire valet," Logon says as he parks at the end of one of the rows.

There isn't much light from the mansion, just chinks here and there where I'm guessing a heavy curtain isn't closed all the way. This suggests that there are things going on inside that the occupants don't want anyone to see. This is definitely the right place.

The double doors open as we step onto the porch. A little light sprinkles the broad shoulders of the figure that greets us.

"Welcome, sir," says the tall man in the very proper Victorian butler's uniform. "You and your consort may enter, but sir's pet must remain outdoors."

Bon Tom doesn't look offended. "I'll catch you later," he says.

The butler guy stands aside. I'm feeling this weird bad premonition kind of vibe, but why wouldn't I when I'm standing in the doorway of a house full of vampires? Um, because *I'm* a vampire *too*? Nope, doesn't work. I'm still anxious. I actually wish Bon Tom was with me. He's got the aura of a real ass-kicker.

Logon actually crosses the threshold first, eager to see more vampires. Since he's holding my hand, I go with him. Inside, it's all gloom and candelabras, velvet and shadows, antique gold fixtures, and ivory skin. Standing and sitting around are some of the most beautiful people I've ever seen in real life. Like Troy and Simon, they have flawless skin, glowing eyes, glossy hair, and buff bodies. Beauty might not be more than skin deep, but it sure fills the eye and mind. And if I need justification for my shallowness, I offer this: as a mammal, I'm hardwired to find symmetrical features attractive because this denotes healthy genes to pass on to offspring that help insure my species' survival. It's a fact. Google it if you don't believe me.

"They started off beautiful, and the Turning enhanced it." A woman speaks beside me, her voice low and carrying hints of an East European accent. She's probably about my height, but since she's wearing boots with four-inch heels, I have to look up to meet her eyes. "It's not a coincidence," she continues. "Most vampires choose attractive prey, and usually it's the most attractive that get Turned."

I could take that as a compliment, couldn't I?

"Of course it's a compliment," she says. She's talking to me, but she's looking at Logon. "I haven't seen you here before."

"I haven't been here before."

"A gentleman should introduce himself first," she says.

"I'm Vlad. My… consort's name is Logon."

"Maybe you aren't as green as you smell." She holds out a red-gloved hand. "I'm Augusta. Welcome to Eyrie."

"Is it a club?"

"More of a salon, if you take my meaning."

"It used to mean a gathering place for like-minded people to appreciate and discuss different aspects of culture," Logon says. "Artists and philosophers and high society mixed together at a tipsy tea party."

My little history major. I'm so proud of him.

"You're so fresh," Augusta says, patting her upswept hairdo. "Allow me to be your guide."

"I'm looking for someone."

"Of course you are."

"His name is Troy Sanger."

"I don't know him," Augusta says too quickly.

"Then if you'll excuse me, I'll go ask someone else."

"Don't be hasty. We do things a certain way around here. Blundering about making inquiries won't win you any allies."

"Allies?"

"Well, you know, *friends*." The way she stresses the word elegantly underlines her sarcasm.

"Well, I think you set some sort of land speed record this time, Gussie. They aren't even out of the foyer yet."

Augusta turns ninety degrees and the temperature drops significantly. "Gordon Dunhill, are you stalking me again, you hound? You really must find a new hobby."

"I was just going to say the same to you." Gordon leans away from Augusta and takes a long look at her red leather catsuit. "You look like one of those comic book superheroes, lass. Are you the Scarlet Woman or the Red Plague?"

"Excuse us," I say.

"Don't go." Gordon bats his eyelashes at me. He has amazingly long, thick lashes and eyes that are somewhere between green and gold. His hair is black and pulled up with combs on the sides so it looks sort of like a Mohawk or one of those Roman horse manes. He's shirtless, so I don't have to wonder about his build, which is outstanding. He looks like he lifts brick houses to warm up for some real exercise. It doesn't surprise me that he has the self-confidence to wear a kilt or that his legs are equally spectacular. I actually put a hand on Logon's arm like I'm afraid my boo will gravitate to this manly man like an iron filing to a magnet. But who's going to hold *me* back?

"Is that what you call flirting?" Augusta says to Gordon. "Why don't you just lie down and hoist your legs in the air?"

"Do you think it would work?"

I like Gordon. Are you surprised? Didn't think so.

"You're new," Gordon says to me. "Are you local or an import?"

"Hometown boy," I say. I'm proud of my casual tone.

"How did you find us?"

"A guy named Bonesteel told me about this place."

Augusta and Gordon cover their reactions but not well enough for my vamp senses. Bonesteel must be a really big deal around here. Maybe I shouldn't have been such a wiseass with him. Nah, fuck it. He was a kick in the crotch.

"If Lord Bonesteel sent you, you *have* to let me show you around," Gordon says. I like the way his speech wavers between modern and something from the not-too-distant past. "I'll give you the VIP tour, and I won't let the less ethical pounce on you." He cuts his eyes at Augusta and winks.

"There are vampire ethics?" I ask as I walk beside Gordon.

"For some. Things were wide open in the South until Lord Bonesteel showed up about forty years ago. Florida was a free-for-all. Vampires came from all over to eat and run—it was like a fast-food counter. After Lord Bonesteel arrived, he started making rules, and he put together a kind of hit squad to make sure he was obeyed. Before long, everyone saw how much better things were with some kind of structure, and he didn't need the commandos anymore."

"Wow, a vampire hit squad," Logon murmurs in awe.

"Oh, they weren't vampires, darling boy. They were rogue shape-shifters that Lord Bonesteel held in thrall, wild things. He kept them chained up unless he needed them. Crazy bastards."

So he's telling me that forty years ago, a vampire lord with a pack of rabid werewolves took over Central Florida like a Mafia don. *Boggle.*

"We'll go straight on upstairs if that's all right with you," Gordon says. "That's where the really interesting things happen."

"So this is just a place where vampires hang out?"

"Lord Bonesteel bought it soon after he arrived and made it into a refuge for our kind. The corporation that owns the estate donates heavily to several political funds to make sure no one ever gets too curious. Here, we can let our hair down, so to speak."

"Cool." Maybe Simon isn't as big a tool as he seems. "Hey, I'm looking for a vampire named Troy. Have you seen him?"

"Oh yes, I've seen Troy, all of him."

"Is he around?"

"It's entirely possible, but you don't want him. He's a rascal, always up to something nasty or underhanded."

"Yeah, I know."

"So it's revenge you're after. I wish you luck. Troy's as slippery as a greased eel."

Out of all the vampires in the world, I had to get bitten by a con artist. Don't get me wrong; I love *The Sting*, great movie. But in real life, I rate con artists a little lower than slug poop. I know the saying that *if it seems too good to be true, it probably isn't,* but come on. Taking Social Security money from elderly people? That's really low.

"I'm pretty clueless here, Gordon. I always thought vampires just kind of spent their time being vampires. Now it looks like they have jobs and stuff just like everyone else."

"It depends on the vampire. Some of us have accumulated enough wealth that we don't have to do anything but be fabulous." Gordon smiles at me and I feel a definite tingle. I also feel like he *gets* me. It's a good feeling. "Now meet my family," he says as he opens a door.

The room is lit by candlelight and has the same opulent furnishings as the rest of the place. And I'm not just throwing around a word like opulent. All the upholstery and drapery fabrics are velvets, brocades, and silk. The furniture looks like it belongs in a castle, and there's an enormous fireplace against the far wall. And it's all real: the wood, the marble, the cloth, nothing synthetic that I can see. That's luxury in my opinion.

The half dozen vampires and a couple of people I assume are consorts are dressed in the same vaguely Victorian style that Simon Bonesteel was wearing. With my black frock coat and Edwardian collar, I fit right in. *Nice.*

"Let me introduce you to everyone," Gordon says as "everyone" eyes me and Logon like we're a late-arriving strippergram. "What do I call you?"

"I prefer to be called Vlad. This is Logon."

"Just one name." Gordon smiles. "Some of the older vampires go by one name. Maybe it'll become a trend again."

"I'm still trying to think of a good vampire name."

Gordon smiles again, but this time he looks indulgent instead of seductive. He leads me to a dark-haired woman in an elaborate gown of tiers of powder-pink satin and creamy ruffles. She breaks off a conversation with a man in a burgundy tailcoat as we approach.

"Vlad, this is Sophia and her consort Alain."

"Good evening," Sophia says. Her eyes are so dark that I can't see the pupils, and I feel lighter when she moves her gaze to Logon.

"This is Logon," I say. "My beloved." I know. Gay, right? Not sure where it came from, but it felt like the right thing to say.

Sophia smiles. "How sweet. Aren't they precious, my heart?"

Alain nods. "Very sweet."

I have to ask. "I don't mean to be rude, Alain, but you're not a vampire, right?"

"No, he isn't," Sophia answers. "If he were Turned, his blood would no longer be sweet for me to drink." Wow, that's quite a euphemism for, "I'd miss the mind-blowing orgasms."

"How long have you been together?"

"Not quite a decade."

"Stop me if I'm being too personal, but what about the aging thing?"

"I'm afraid it's inevitable," Sophia says. "Alain is my fifth companion since my Turning."

I don't like the sound of this. "That sounds really sad to me."

"It's terribly sad. I know I can never replace my first consort. I will never love again as I loved my Gavrail, but he's gone, and it's even sadder to be alone."

I can't look at Alain while she's saying stuff like that. Doesn't she care about his feelings? Is being a consort something he wants so much that he'll put up with this treatment? Am I being a humongous hypocrite? Isn't the reason I haven't Turned Logon because I don't want to give up the rush of drinking his blood? Do I really need to deal with this right now?

"I should introduce Vlad to the others," Gordon says.

Okay, that was depressing, but I learned something. And if these vampires are going to be my peers, I want to know as much about them as I can. So far, they don't seem like the types I'd hang out with for fun, but I'm going to give them a fair trial.

Next up is a group of four: three vampire males and a human woman. Crispian, James, Declan, and Margot. Pleasant exchange of names, then their faces change as Gordon mentions that Sir Simon sent me. Margot's giving Logon the look you'd give an abandoned puppy. What's that all about? Or is that just the way her face is? She's pretty mopey in general, all lank, blonde hair and big melted-chocolate eyes. She belongs to Crispian, who's got the style and the demeanor of one of those mod members of the House of Lords from a sixties movie about swinging London. He's the one who offers me a drink. I catch a flicker of alarm in Margot's eyes, but maybe I'm imagining it.

"That's a good lad," Gordon says to Crispy. "Why don't you fetch Vlad a glass of something warm? I'll have one too."

Crispy doesn't look happy at being treated like a waiter, but he goes away, and Margot follows him. Is it just me, or does she kind of look like Logon? Silky, light blonde hair. Doe eyes. Catlike body. Hmmm....

Another vampire joins our group. "Vlad, this is Valerie," Gordon says.

Gordon isn't being rude by not introducing Logon. I've caught on now that it's customary to let a vampire choose to give out a consort's name or not. "Hi, Valerie," I say. "This is Logon."

Valerie has Persian-cat eyes, rich green and almond-shaped, and her hair is a Marilyn Monroe nest of platinum floss. I'm very taken with her off-the-shoulders, petticoated, violet velvet mini-dress, which makes her look like Marie Antoinette as a cocktail waitress. I swear there's a drag queen inside me screaming to get out. Or a drag duchess at least.

"Hel*lo*, Logon," Valerie purrs. "You look sweet as honey."

"Thanks. You're a major hottie," Logon replies.

Valerie looks a little surprised. Are consorts supposed to be seen and not heard? More and more it occurs to me that I could use a guidebook, or some kind of manual.

"I love meeting young ones," Valerie says. "So thoughtful of Lord Simon to send you."

James chuckles and Gordon gives him an annoyed look, which he ignores. James has the kind of salt and pepper hair that I hope to have when I go gray—I mean if... *if* I go gray. It's just so... wolfish, you know? The rest of James isn't very lupine though—more Dobermanish, if you know what I mean. His eyes are a funny reddish-brown, and he has thick, dark eyebrows that stick out over them. Plus, he has a long nose and a mouthful of sharp-looking teeth. He doesn't look like he'd be easily intimidated. No, he looks like he's used to doing the intimidating. I wonder what he'd think if he knew I was imagining him with a spiked collar. Maybe I should just stop picturing crap like that around mind-reading vamps.

Here comes Crispy with a tray of wineglasses and one tumbler of what looks like ice water. Margot trails him, carrying a highball glass that she sips from. Gordon takes a wineglass and the water and hands them to me. I give the water to Logon and sniff my glass. It's blood, of course, but it's mixed with something else.

"Pinot noir," Valerie says. She lifts her glass. "To the ultimate blended wine."

It's not bad. I'm not a big wine drinker, but I could get used to this. It's already making me a little light-headed. I hope I don't start giggling and attempting my William Shatner impression like I usually do on a red wine buzz.

"Where's Ambrose?" Valerie says like she's just remembered there's one more big present left to open. "Vlad has to meet Ambrose!"

"I'm sure he'll put in an appearance." Crispy has a dry voice, and his accent reminds me of a Monty Python character, which barely makes him tolerable. It's very depressing that most of the vampires I've met are stuck-up bullies. I've been at war with that type for most of my life. The last thing I want is to turn into one of *them*.

"I could swear I heard my name." A young man materializes at Valerie's elbow and plucks the glass from Crispy's hand. "Lovely vintage," he says. "What's the occasion?"

Allow me to describe the exquisite Ambrose. His hair is so blond that it's white, and his eyes are honest-to-gosh purple. He's decked out in meticulous Gibson Guy drag. If you don't know what that is, look up Gibson Girl, and then look at the guy dancing with her. Or don't. It's really a minor detail. The story's the important thing. Let's just say that Ambrose is exquisite, exactly how I imagine Oscar Wilde's Bosie. When I was a sophomore, I read everything I could find about famous gay people, and old Oscar was my favorite. He was just stylin', and he wrote that excellently creepy Dorian Gray book.

"Ambrose, this is Vlad," Valerie says. "Simon sent him."

"Did he now?" Ambrose raises an eyebrow that's improbably dark for someone so blond. It looks like he's had each tiny, individual hair dyed the color of soot.

"Yeah, he did." I might as well join the conversation, since it's about me. "He seemed to think I could find Troy Sanger here."

The laughter of those around me is not reassuring. "So was he wrong? No one here knows where Troy might be?"

"He *might* be in my pocket," Ambrose says. "But it's highly unlikely."

That was kind of prickish, wasn't it? I think Ambrose is pissing all over me. I hate this kind of frat-boy secret-handshake nonsense. Accept me or don't, but don't expect me to play stupid initiation games or put up with your hazing. And please don't subject me to your holier-than-everything smugness. Sure, smug feels good, but only to the smug one, if you catch my drift. Or maybe I'm overreacting. It's possible.

"Nice costumes." Ambrose takes another sip of the wine and looks me up and down. "Why do I feel as if somewhere a Renaissance Fair is missing two village idiots?"

Definitely a prick. And there's something weird about him. Okay, there's something weird about everyone in this place, but he's extra-weird. All the other vampires have a particular "feel" to them. I can't read their minds, but I can get a sense of their ages and how strong-willed they are, but not Ambrose. All I get from him is garbled static, like an underwater radio station. And he doesn't like me. No doubt about that. Unfortunately, he appears to be some kind of rock star around here. Well, SFW. Maybe I should be impressed, but I'm not.

"If someone would just tell me what I came here to find out, I can leave and cease lowering the coolness quotient of the entire neighborhood," I say.

Gordon laughs, and Ambrose attempts to eviscerate him with his eyes.

"Vlad's looking for Troy," Valerie says. She grins expectantly as though she's delivered the punch line of a really good joke.

"So I've heard," Ambrose drawls. "I wish Troy *would* show his traitorous face around here so I could rip it off and show it to him so he knows what a rat looks like."

I'm resisting the urge to roll my eyes at this overblown vampire version of macho posturing. "So you don't have any idea where he is?"

"You really don't have the first clue, do you?" Declan finally speaks.

"No, I don't. That's why I came here." I speak slowly, enunciating each word clearly. At least I'm trying to. My tongue is being uncooperative, insisting on sticking to the roof of my mouth.

"He's on his way," Augusta says loudly as she comes into the room.

It sounds like an announcement. Is there a surprise birthday party in the offing? *Who's* on his way? And why does Augusta have a twin? Wait a sec; everyone has a twin. Weird. I feel dizzy. Where's Logon going?

WHY is my bed so hard? And why can I hear Simon Bonesteel in my dream?

"Open your eyes, Vlad. You really don't want to miss this."

Craptastic. I'm still at Eyrie and Simon is real. Where's Logon?

I can actually feel Simon gloating when he answers. "He's right over there."

At least the double vision is gone. I only see one naked Logon covered in vampires. And I seem to be strapped into this chair.

"Struggle if you must," Simon says. "It will have no effect on the shackles."

Of course I'm struggling. Logon has been turned into a human buffet. There are vampires sucking on various parts of my lover. He doesn't seem to be in pain. In fact, he looks delirious with pleasure. His eyes are glazed over, and a there's a string of drool connecting him to the pillow under his head. His leaking hard-on rests against his lower belly in a slick of cum, sliding lazily whenever one of the vampires shifts him to a more convenient position.

The effect on me is hard to describe adequately. Imagine being shoved outside—wet and naked—in the winter in Antarctica, followed immediately by billions of red-hot needles piercing your skin, muscles, and bones all at once. Imagine having your insides scooped out with a melon baller and the empty cavity packed with steel wool soaked in rubbing alcohol. Being freeze-dried alive couldn't possibly hurt this much. What's happening is so wrong that all my cells are rebelling against it. It's even worse than being seasick.

"Excruciating, isn't it?" Simon's voice is right in my ear.

"Make it stop."

"I suppose I could stop it—my flock is deep in blood-languor by now. But... I don't really want to. I think you've probably learned your lesson about disrespecting me, but frankly, the sight of your consort writhing in unspeakable ecstasy pleases me. It always amazes me how much stamina the scrawny ones have."

"Please." I'll beg. I don't care. It has to *stop*. Logon is *mine*.

"How long are you going to drag this out?" Ambrose appears at Simon's side.

Simon frowns. "You aren't enjoying the show?"

"I admit I've never tasted blood like Logon's. It makes me want to run naked under the moon and mate with someone as swift and beautiful and deadly as I am." Ambrose looks down at me. "But this one is simply boring."

Oh no he *didn't*! Boring? That's the worst insult I can imagine. And I am *not* boring. I started life with my feet in two worlds and it hasn't changed. I'm a fascinating puzzle of dichotomous elements; you can ask my mom.

"You find his anguish boring?" Simon says.

"It's so predictable. If you make a vampire watch his consort being gang-fanged, of course he's going to suffer, and he's going to rage at you. He can't help it. The blood bond compels him." Ambrose sighed. "I'm still waiting for you to show me the wonders you mentioned when you lured me into this life. I was perfectly happy as an American ambassador's son in Zurich."

"You'll be young and beautiful forever. Isn't that a wonder?"

"You just don't get it. What's the point in living forever if I'm bored?"

"High maintenance much?" It isn't easy to talk past the grinding nausea, but I manage it just so I can burn Ambrose.

"I'm worth it," Ambrose replies.

"Indeed you are," Simon says.

Logon whimpers. The leather straps around my wrists cut into my skin, but they don't let go. I'm having the horrible mental image of pulling my hands off.

"Your pain is delicious," Simon says. "Are you regretting every saucy word you said to me?"

"If I say yes, will you let me go?"

"I don't hear the ring of sincerity in his voice, do you, Brosie?"

"Don't call me Brosie in front of others!"

"Forgive me."

"Can I call *you* Brosie's Bitch?" I ask Simon.

"I'm beginning to think you have no control over your tongue," Simon says.

He's about to threaten to cut out my tongue. I know this. I'm not just guessing. *Whoa!* I know what Simon's thinking... a little. It's not like I can read his mind, but I'm definitely picking up emotions and intentions. Maybe only the really strong thoughts get through. I'll have to think more about it later. Simon's leaning over me like he's about to kiss me. *Don't want.*

"Simon, if you French kiss him and bite off his tongue, you can forget about touching me with those lips for a good long time."

I look up at Simon. "Really? Yuck!"

"I know, right?" Ambrose lapses into mall-rat speak. "He's always doing gross crap like that and whatnot. Maybe that shit was cool back in the day, but it's beyond disgusting, if you ask me."

"You're both spoiled." Simon says.

He's thinking that young people today could use a touch of the buggy whip to call attention to their ingratitude. I can't believe I ever wanted to be able to read minds. It's like eavesdropping; you never hear anything good.

Across the room, Logon arches his back as Valerie sinks her fangs into his inner thigh. A few drops of jizz ooze from the tip of Logon's dick. I see each one in slow motion, glistening as it falls. How long has this been going on? They're going to turn my boo into jerky.

"Stamina," Simon says. "Your consort can take much more. I've seen his kind last for days before they're finally drained. And the entire time, they're in a state of sexual arousal so intense that I'm surprised they don't melt."

"You do this for grins?" I say. Simon's right. I can't control my tongue.

"Only when necessary."

"Oh my goolies, you're Ferris Bueller's sister!"

"Who's that?" Simon narrows his eyes.

"Allow me to enlighten you. You don't know how to have fun, so you're going to stop anyone else from having any. Oh man, you're the worst kind of ass-cramp."

"Shut up," Simon says. "I can see there's only one way to deal with you."

Amazing how someone can go from pathetic to scary in a few words. And I know without doubt that this has been his goal all along. He baited me and sent me here to be drugged and bound so he could do whatever he's about to do. The whole scene with Logon is just icing.

"Would you mind telling me why Troy has redheaded stepchild status around here?" I'm panicking, and that's the first thing that pops into my mind.

Simon looks surprised at my question, but he answers it. "He tried to steal from me."

"He seems to steal from a lot of people. Must have been something pretty valuable."

Simon's eyes go to Ambrose. "Very valuable. Priceless."

"No way! He put the moves on Brosie-boy? What a masochist."

Simon frowns. "Troy Sanger is a disgraceful vampire, more like a human really. He thought he could concoct a formula that would increase a consort's life span. I told him that if such a thing were possible, it would already exist."

"Maybe he thought of something no one ever thought of before."

"Troy?" Ambrose laughs. "He's not exactly a genius."

"He was clever enough to fool you," Simon says.

"He did *not* fool me. I met him at that hotel to find out if he was still wooing that Vodou witch doctor freak. That half-and-half whore could be real trouble for you."

"So you say." Simon and Ambrose lock eyes in a battle of wills, and Ambrose caves first.

"You'll believe what you want to believe," he says, but it's a white flag and we all know it.

"You set me up good," I say to Simon. "Letting me think I could find Troy here."

"Well, you're very inexperienced," Simon says. "Though you have a wayward tongue, I think the brain behind it is sharp. You just need guidance."

"Do you know where I can find someone to guide me?" I'm kissing ass like it's going out of style, but I'm succeeding in stalling him, so I'll endure the humiliation. It's not like I expect to suddenly break free, or someone to burst in and rescue us, I'm just trying my best to put off whatever it is he has in mind. Because if Simon wants it, it can't be good. That much I'm sure of. I just don't know how bad yet. Then again, how could it be much worse?

"Once I've taken a little of your blood, I'll be happy to discuss your troubles on the proper footing," Simon says.

I don't know why the thought of him drinking my blood makes me feel like a guillotine is poised over my neck, but it does. I'm an idiot for walking in here like it's a kegger at U of F. And a bigger idiot for bringing Logon along. This isn't cosplay, or any kind of play. It's real, and my panic is rising exponentially by nanoseconds. This is real dread, the feeling that horror movies work so hard to instill, but always fall short of. I've been nervous before, and I've had the crap scared out of me, but I've never felt this sick, numbing, helpless agony of the spirit. I have to keep my cool. If I give in to this pressure, I'll belong to Simon. I'll be his flunky like everyone else in this house. I'll just pretend I'm Han Solo about to be encased in liquid carbonite.

Ambrose turns his back on me and Simon. *Shit*! This is bad.

Simon turns my head to the side and pins it to the back of the chair. He's megastrong. I can't move a millimeter. His lips are on my neck. They feel like raw liver. *Gross*. Even if I wasn't restrained, I wouldn't be able to move. I'm literally paralyzed with horror.

Glass shatters. Simon straightens up and looks around, and I almost piss myself with relief. I hear the *shoosh-floof* of heavy fabric being violently yanked aside. A woman screams—probably Margot. Is that growling? And snarling?

"Kill that thing," Simon says, and no one leaps to obey him. All his vampire buddies are hammered on Logon's blood. By the way, hearing someone yell "kill that thing" while you're strapped down is *not* a good feeling.

"Where you at, cher?"

*Bon Tom!* That's Bon Tom! "I'm over here!"

To my surprise, Simon and Ambrose give ground as Bon Tom comes closer. No wonder. His eyes are glowing like gas flames, his fingers have sprouted three-inch talons, and his wide-open mouth displays a set of choppers that would make a great white weep with envy. And he looks bigger somehow.

"Whoa!" One swipe and Bon Tom's claws shear through the strap on my left wrist. My sleeve and skin are unmarked. Another swipe and my other hand is free. I can deal with the ankle straps myself. "Get Logon out of here," I yell, just like Captain Kirk, or any other hero in this situation. It's amazing how automatically the words come. Maybe there's a good reason why all action-movie dialogue sounds alike.

Bon Tom doesn't hesitate. He bounds across the room and pulls Logon out of the pile of groggy vampires. Simon's flock hisses like a bunch of disturbed geese, but they don't put up a fight. In fact, once they get a look at Bon Tom, they cringe away from him.

"Let's go," I holler.

Bon Tom throws Logon over his shoulder and spins around, coming face-to-face with Ambrose. Ambrose and Bon Tom lock eyes for one of those suspended moments of great significance, and then Bon Tom knocks him across the room with a sweep of his arm.

"How dare you!" Simon says. "How dare you enter this house, you mongrel!"

"I don't go or stay at your word no more." Bon Tom gives Simon a sidewise look.

"If you were still wearing a collar—" That's as far as Simon gets before Bon Tom cuts him off.

"You don't wanna go there."

Bon Tom comes to the broken window, and I take Logon from him. He's set to jump when Gordon runs into the room. I don't know where Gordon was, but he's most definitely *here* now and roaring Bon

Tom's name as he charges at us. Gordon may look like a Bowflex jockey, but his muscles aren't just for show, and they're powered by a vampire's strength and speed.

"Go on, cher. I got this," Bon Tom says as he launches himself at Gordon.

I swear I hear them collide as I look out the window. There's some serious shrubbery below, and none of it looks like cactus. If I hold Logon under the armpits and lean out as far as I can, I think he'll be all right if I drop him. The noises behind me are nasty, and I'm convinced I can feel Simon sneaking up on me. No time to waste.

Logon lands in the bushes and hangs there like a damp beach towel. He's buck nekkid, as we say around here, but I'm not going back to look for his clothes. I feel like a dick for leaving Bon Tom, but Logon is my priority. I have to take care of him, so it's out the window I go to hoist him over my shoulder. He's heavier than he looks, but I'm strong as hell.

*Where the hell is the car?* The damn thing's the size of a Winnebago. Why can't I find it?

"Over here, cher."

Bon Tom's hands are bloody to the elbows and most of the rest of him is splashed with red, but he's moving quickly so he can't be hurt too bad.

"I move the car when you go inside," he says as he gets behind the wheel.

I push through the overgrowth on the passenger side and put Logon on the backseat, climbing in after him. "Whenever you're ready," I say.

Bon Tom punches the gas and throws divots from all four tires. Apparently, it's in four-wheel drive mode. And the need for speed is debatable anyway. As far as I can tell, no one's chasing us. I don't even see anyone looking out the busted window. Time for a reality check.

"Do you see anyone coming after us?" I ask.

"Not likely, cher. I schooled Mr. Gordon, and the rest of 'em are worthless right now." Bon Tom bounces the bus over the berm and onto the drive.

"Yeah, what was up with that?" I pull Logon's head onto my lap. "Simon called it blood-languor."

"Never seen that before 'cept when they mixin' somethin' like opium in they sippin' blood." He makes a funny noise that conveys his contempt for such things.

"Why would Simon let them get so wasted?"

"For one, he don't have as much control as he like to think. For two, he ain't scared a you."

"You know Simon better than you let on."

"Them not happy memories, cher." Bon Tom wrestles the Wagoneer through the arch and we're on pavement.

Logon makes a feeble noise and gremlins yank at my guts with razor-sharp crochet hooks. Something's wrong; I know it. "Do you know what's wrong with Logon?" I ask.

Bon Tom glances over his shoulder. "Overload. You want Bon Tom's advice, we take him to Orisha. Fix him up good."

"Okay." I sit back and stroke Logon's hair. "By the way, I looked up Orisha on the Internet. That can't be a real name. What kind of person calls themself after an entire pantheon of gods?"

"You done met Orisha. What kind of person you call that?"

"You have a point." I pause when Logon moves restlessly. "At least we're not too far away from Indian Rocks."

"Not in distance anyway. Just keep the sweet thang quiet now, and we be there directly, cher."

# CHAPTER SIX

I CARRY Logon in my arms, and he's conscious enough to put his arms around my neck. He's still delirious though, and he feels like he has a fever. If anything happens to him…. The future looks really grim all of a sudden.

Orisha makes a disapproving noise at Logon's condition and points to an afghan-covered bench. I lay Logon down on it.

"Can you help him?" I ask

"Sure 'nough," Orisha answers. "Move out my way." Orisha looks into Logon's eyes and touches their foreheads together. "Poor lamb. Don't fret. We'll get you fixed up real quick."

"Let Orisha work," Bon Tom says. "We walk down to the water."

*I'm not leaving Logon.*

"Better this way, cher. Better for him." Bon Tom nods at Logon.

"I want to stay with Logon."

"I know you do, but if you want me to help him, you leave me be," Orisha says sharply. "Go and wash up now."

I'm covered in blood, and I either trust Orisha or I don't, so I follow Bon Tom across the dark, sloping lawn to the water. The grass gives way to sand and sandspurs, pretty fast, and then to wet sand. The mild surf sounds like a line of semis passing by on a wet road. Bon Tom goes bounding into the water, moving with determination until he's deep enough to dive under. He surfaces and waves to me. Did I mention I can see in the dark now? Yeah. Cool, huh? Damn right, it is. I can see Bon Tom clearly as he gestures for me to come in.

No thanks. I can do without hanging around in wet clothes slowly going stiff with salt as the inescapable sand rubs precious parts of me raw.

"Suit yourself, cher," Bon Tom calls out. "But you got a fair amount of blood on you. Brine's the best thing to wash it off, 'specially this kinda blood."

"Why? What's it going to do to me?"

"Stain your dainty white shirt and make it smell somethin' awful. Werevamp blood the worst."

"Were*vamp*?"

"Come in the water, fool. Bon Tom tell you all 'bout it."

It would just be silly to try and explain my long-term unsatisfactory relationship with the beach. On the one hand, the ocean is majestic and powerful and eternal and all that. On the other hand, it's salty, sandy, and hot as hell most of the time. These are not three of my favorite things. But I can smell a rotten odor that's getting stronger. Imagine the stench of decayed flesh mixed with burnt hair and broccoli farts. The theme from *Jaws* is playing in my head, but this reek is even worse than dumpster water.

"Are you sure it's okay?" I holler. Yes, if you must know, my mom did hold my hand the first day of school, but I have a legitimate concern here. In many vampire films, salt water is like acid on undead flesh, just as bad as holy water, which I'm going to put in a Super Soaker squirt gun for the next time I run into Simon. Swiss cheese, *le fromage suisse*, that's what I'm talkin' 'bout. I don't know how, but I'm going to pay him back for tonight.

Bon waves again. "Yeah it's okay, not even too cold. Only a few shark."

*Asshole*. I remind myself I'm a big bad creature of the night and wade in. I take off my boots first though. Those mothers were *expensive*.

The water is chilly, but it doesn't bother me. I'm waist-deep when I realize I don't see Bon Tom anymore. Crap! Something's got my ankle. *Crap!* I'm being pulled under and— Whoa! I can see just as well underwater as…. Oh my goolies, I forgot that I don't need to breathe. I can stay under as long as I want.

Bon Tom materializes out of the murk, grinning in my face. He shoots off past me. I chase him for the sheer joy of moving underwater like something born there. When I catch him, he jets to the surface, taking me with him. Shaking the water from his hair, he showers my face with salt spray, blinding me for a moment.

"Good exercise, cher," Bon Tom says breathlessly.

"I can stay under as long as I want," I announce.

"I know. Come in real handy sometime, you bet."

I don't speak for a record five seconds as I think about a few million things. "I keep asking who the hell you are, but I still haven't gotten an answer."

"Lord Bonesteel one selfish sucker," Bon Tom says. "It don't matter to him what happen to other people so long as he get what he want."

"That sounds about right." I know I'm being sidetracked, but what can I do about it? I can't make him talk about something if he doesn't want to.

"He done things shouldn't be done."

"Like what?"

"Force a vamp and a shape-shifter to breed. Them two don't mix for a reason."

This is starting to sound really sordid. "Why would he do that?"

"He try to make hisself a perfect bodyguard. Done pretty good. Too bad Gordon stone-crazy… and stone-dead."

"He seemed okay to me. A little flamboyant maybe." My feet don't touch the bottom. I'm bobbing on the small swells, and it's not a bad feeling.

"Well, you left the party before he show his true color, cher. When the wildness come up in him, it ain't a pretty sight."

"I felt bad about leaving you, but—"

"No need to explain."

"You didn't get hurt, did you?"

"Course I did. I was fightin' a werevamp. Good thing Bon Tom know they ways. Good thing Bon Tom quicker than they. Good thing Orisha a healer."

"Seriously, man, that accent…. Oh, never mind. I think you're just screwing with me anyway. I'm going in and check on Logon."

"He be right as rain, cher, don't you worry."

It's easier walking out of the ocean than into it. Bon Tom's beside me, leaping and splashing. This is a side of him I haven't seen. It's kind of weirdly cute, you know?

"Hey, you two." Orisha greets us on the back patio. "All clean now?"

Bon Tom sheds his wet clothes and uses the towel Orisha throws him. Orisha raises an eyebrow at me and offers a towel. I take the towel, but I keep my clothes on.

"How's Logon?" I ask.

"Sleepin' like a baby. You wanna see him, you go right through the door there and into the second room on the left. Best you let him rest now, you hear?"

"He's all right? Those other vampires didn't do anything… nasty to him, did they?"

"Nothin' permanent. If we lucky, he don't remember it at all." Orisha smiles. "You know he got three nipple? Yeah, reckon you do."

"Thank you for helping us. I really appreciate it, and I hope I didn't mess up your prep for your drum ceremony."

"Your mama raised you right, and that's the truth. No charge for you, pretty vampire boy."

"Um, can I ask another favor?"

"Yeah, you can park it here tonight." Orisha laughs. "Just lay right down next to Sugar-Britches. No light gonna get into that room, and ain't nobody gonna mess with you."

"Thank you. I owe you big time."

"I reckon you do. Go on now. I know you itchin' to see him."

I follow directions, but I don't need them. I can feel Logon, glowing like an ember in the dark. My clothes go over a ladder-back chair, and I slide into bed next to him. He's very warm, and he squirms a little when I press my cold body against his, but he doesn't wake up. I'm a little disappointed. Orisha told me to let him sleep, but I'd like to see his eyes just once and hear him tell me he's all right. I'm still shocked that becoming a vampire has made me *more* tenderhearted, instead of heartless, which is what I expected. But Logon is so precious to me that it's scary. Tonight I had a small taste of what it would be like to lose him, and I didn't like it one bit. I'm feeling much better now, but I vividly remember the paralyzing pain and the sickness.

Logon murmurs something. I pull him closer, wrapping an arm around his chest and one around his waist. His hair smells like herbs and smoke and him. I feel a little sleazy, but I need a drink, so I take one. He doesn't stir as my fangs slide in, and I push aside the thought of how many vampires drank from him tonight. The small wounds have all closed, and his skin is unmarked except for a few small bruises like the marks of fingertips dipped in blue ink. He moves a little, pushing his butt against my crotch, but he's just settling in, not trying to turn me on. His sweetness flows into me with the mouthful of his blood and overpowers the ugliness of the night's events. What happened was horrible, but we're both alive—in one form or another—and we're together. If I need revenge, it can wait until tomorrow night.

I HAVE roughly a gajillion messages waiting on my phone, most of them from Vinnie. I'm scrolling through the texts as fast as I can while Logon eats omelets on the patio with Orisha and Bon Tom. The eggs are super fresh; Logon says he watched Orisha take them out from under the hens right after he got up. My clothes feel horrible from the salt dried in them, and they chafe. This is important because I pace when I'm on the phone and my thighs are being sandpapered. Screw the messages. I punch the call button.

"Where the hell have you been?" Vinnie says in my ear.

"Me and Logon and Bon Tom went to a place up in Belleair. We were pretty effed-up when we left, so we stopped at Orisha's. I'm still in Indian Rocks."

"Everything go all right?"

"More or less. No one died. Except one werevamp that Bon Tom killed, or so he says."

"Wait. What? *Werevamp?*"

"Yeah, I know, right?"

"How cool is that?"

"Actually not very, according to Orisha. Apparently, werevamps are all psycho. Bad wiring."

"Sucks."

"Word. So what's new with you?"

Vinnie sighs heavily. "It's great seeing Frankie, even if she does look like she's smuggling a watermelon. Just kidding. She looks really cute enormously pregnant. Hang on—I'm going outside. Mom and Dad bought the lot behind them and they're working on some sort of English garden, they say. I'll go pretend to have a look at it. Okay, I can talk now. Where do I start? Frankie's husband is a douche-nozzle extraordinaire. You know that guy Ross on *Friends*? Bryce is worse."

"Damn."

"Yeah, the mind boggles. I've never heard anyone whine this much, and I worked day care for three years in high school."

"Start agreeing with everything he says."

"What?"

"The next time he complains about something, agree with him. Say yeah, it really *is* too cold in here, or seriously, there's *way* too much salt in this soup, or whatever."

"Won't that just encourage him?"

"Survey says no. You'll be taking attention away from him by sharing the spotlight."

"That actually makes sense. I'll try it. I have at least one more night and day of this guy's overbearing presence. No matter what anyone's doing, he knows a better way to do it. And he's very generous with advice."

"What's Frankie doing procreating with a jerk like that?"

"Oh, you know how love is. She sees a completely different person when she looks at Bryce. She thinks he's brilliant and discerning—her words."

I remembered Frankie fondly as Vinnie's next youngest sister, who usually occupied the passenger seat of Vinnie's secondhand car on parking lot cruises of football and baseball games. Frankie's pretty in a standard little girl face/big girl body kind of way, and she attracted jocks like a porch light attracts bugs. Once, when I was a senior and she was a junior, she flirted with a bully to take his attention away from me. She's that kind of girl.

"Sorry to hear she's in love with such a bite in the ass."

"I haven't even told you what he does for a living."

"I'm ready."

"He's a professional golfer."

"*Merde!*" I swear. "I can be there to pick you up in less than an hour. Be at the curb with your bags."

Vinnie laughs. "Thanks, bro, but if I can't outlast the likes of his neo-Republican ass, I'll have to turn in my big girl panties. And wonder of wonders, I'm actually kind of enjoying being with the fam. Petie even let me do her nails last night, and Mom asked if I'd paint hers, not the same color of course."

"What color?"

"Cyanotic."

"That's such a pretty blue."

"I miss you, Vlad. Are you really doing okay?"

"It would be better if you were here. I still haven't found Troy, and I don't know where to look next."

"Hmmm, well, at least it sounds like you're meeting more vampires."

"True, but they're not exactly what I thought they'd be. Mostly they're just like people, only stronger and faster, and of course there's the blood-drinking thing."

"And the immortality thing."

"And that. Plus they're gorgeous."

"You keep saying *they*."

"I didn't notice. I guess I just don't identify with the vampires I've met so far."

"You're such an Emo kid."

"You take that back."

Vinnie laughs again. "Are you still driving Massey's bus?"

"Yeah, I should probably get it back to him eventually."

"I doubt he's going to send the cops after you."

"It does seem unlikely that he'd want to draw the attention of the *gendarmerie*. Anyway, I should probably get off the phone and see if anyone else has any ideas about what to do next."

"Don't forget that the Internet is the information superhighway."

"It's more like the pornography back alley."

"Thank the Goddess!"

"I miss you too, Vinnie. Have a nice visit and call as soon as you're coming back."

"Aw, I'm all gooey inside now. You know, you might want to think about a visit to *your* mom's."

"That sounds like sugar-buzz talk. How many pieces of your mom's Key lime pie have you consumed today?"

"You remember Mom's Key lime pie?"

"I have a photographic memory for excellent sweets. Bye, Vinnie."

"Bye, Vlad. Keep me posted."

"I will. Bye." I hang up before either of us can speak again and start another half-hour-long ramble. I clear my text messages and go out to the patio. The temperature is perfect, one of those rare, magical Florida intervals where it isn't so hot and muggy you can't breathe, or so dry and cold that your bones hurt. Temperature doesn't seem to affect me as much now that I'm dead, but I'm still aware of it.

Logon pats the bench he's sitting on, and I settle next to him. His plate is clean with his knife and fork neatly crossed over it. There are so many little things about him that I find endearing.

"My omelet had lots of spinach and cilantro," he says in his idea of flirting. "They build up your blood."

"You just ate. The nutrients haven't had time to get into your bloodstream."

"Do you really think this is a good time to be logical, Spock?" Logon looks at me from under his lashes, and I finally have a legitimate use for the word *coy*.

"Go on," Orisha says. "We done had our breakfasts. Have yours. Unless you shy."

She's right. Breakfast is the most important meal of the day, no matter what time your day starts. Logon's tilting his chin in that cute way that invites me to bite him, and I can't think of any reason to be shy, ashamed, or embarrassed about doing it.

For the first time, I'm able to rein in the rampant sexual aspects of feeding. I still feel aroused, but I can resist the compulsion to cover Logon with my body and wallow in pleasure. It's a new feeling to be in control of so much emotion and energy, like holding the leash of a timber wolf.

When I withdraw my fangs, Logon relaxes against my chest with a sigh. I know I can release the restraints whenever I choose, and sometimes it's nice just to have a cuddle. Orisha's looking at me like a proud parent, which confuses me a little, but whatever. I'm happy to have Orisha on my side, and I'm not put off by weird. I like weird. I was the only nine-year-old in my neighborhood that dressed as Cthulhu for Halloween.

"Thanks for feeding Logon," I say.

"Weren't no trouble and he already thank me."

"Well, it's really nice of you."

"You the enemy of my enemy."

"Cool. Do you have any more ideas about where I can look for Troy?"

Orisha watches Bon Tom walking down to the water while she answers. "No, lamb, I don't. Wish I did. If Bon Tom cain't sniff 'im out, he ain't gonna be found."

"What's Bon Tom's story anyway? I know he's something more than human."

"He's a shape-shifter can't shift no more. Nothin' I can do to fix it."

"What happened?"

"Bon Tom was taken away from his people when he was just little, brung up in a cage, fed all kind of thing with drugs in it. He was beat on and trained to kill."

"He was one of Bonesteel's rogue weres." It's clear to me now.

"That's right, child. So-called Lord Bonesteel done somethin' to Bon Tom, and then Bon Tom cain't change all the way no more, only part way."

"That's horrible."

"It a bona fide sin. Poor Bon Tom. All his animal thoughts got mixed up with his people thoughts. He not exactly crazy, but he ain't right. You seen how he is around females."

Yeah, I noticed. "So he escaped from Bonesteel."

"Got lost on a hunt some twenty year ago. I come cross him in Louisiana tryin' to find his way home. He took to me, and we been takin' care of each other ever since."

"Bonesteel's vampires seemed really scared of him."

"Reckon so. Bon Tom is a weapon to kill vampires. His bite never heals, you hear? If he bite but don't kill a vampire, that vampire sure 'nough gonna die anyhow, slow and nasty while the poison eats away at flesh and bone."

"Shit."

"Yeah, shit, Sugar. Bon Tom a weapon designed by an old vampire that know all a vampire's weaknesses. Simon needed him a way to get rid of his enemies, and this his solution. Simon be a shortsighted devil."

I agree. "What an assjack."

"Yeah, he messin' with the arcane eco-system in a very bad way."

"When I met him, he said something to me about Troy being irresponsible for creating another predator, or something like that."

"Mister Pot, meet Mr. Kettle."

"Yeah, seriously." I shift Logon in my arms. He's asleep again, and I'm feeling all mama bear.

Orisha says, "You know Halloween in just a couple days."

"And?"

"I'm thinkin' I throw a big damn party if you ain't found Mister Troy by then. If he around, he gonna come to my throw down."

"That sounds like a good plan. Meanwhile, I'm not sure what I should be doing."

"Go have some fun."

"Huh?"

"Ain't they somebody you want to impress with you bein' a vampire?"

I calculate and realize it's Saturday before Halloween, which is on Monday this year. *Suck.* Normally that would suck, but now that I'm a vampire, I can stay up late whenever I feel like it. And tonight all my usual hangouts will be full of people doing some early celebrating of a geek's favorite holiday. I think a visit to Spacely's is in order. But first, I need fresh clothes or a Laundromat. I haven't been back to my place for almost a week. No pets, but I have some plants that are going to be giving me dirty looks.

"Logon." I give boo a little shake, and he looks up at me. *Mine.* The feeling of possession lances through me with a fierce and joyous ache. "You feel like going out?"

"Where?" Logon yawns, and I want to lick his tonsils. Gross, I know, but just because I'm gay doesn't mean I'm not a guy. I could tell you that I really want to lick his balls too. But I was in the middle of planning my Saturday night.

"I was thinking Spacely's."

"Cool, I can get a mocha frappé." I'm not surprised that he knows Spacely's. I'm only surprised that we never met before.

"I'm also thinking we should drop by my place and change our clothes."

"I like the way you think." Logon kisses the spot where my jaw meets up with my ear and then sticks his tongue in said ear. What a nut. I adore him.

"How about you, Orisha? Want to go out on the town with a couple of studs?"

Orisha laughs. "Not tonight. Why you don't ask Bon Tom?"

"You think he'd go?" I still feel like a turd for leaving him to face a roomful of vamps.

"How I know? I'm not a mindreader."

"Okay, sheesh, I'll ask him myself."

"*I'll* ask him," Logon says, sliding off my lap and walking away.

Just look at him. I love the way his lean muscles flex when he moves.

"You love him," Orisha says.

"Yeah," I sigh. "A lot. I've only known him a few days, but I'd die for him."

"That's good. You take good care of the sweet thang, he take good care of you."

"My mom says something like that. Take care of the people you love, and they'll take care of you."

"Wise woman. She know you a vampire yet?"

"First of all, I'm twenty-one, not twelve. And I haven't had a chance to talk to her since it happened. Damn. Don't give me the evil eye. I just want to take care of this Troy thing first. What if he leaves town?"

"Don't let it slide too long."

"Okay. Okay. I won't. Jeez. What a nag."

"Vlad! Bon Tom wants to go with us." Logon stops beside me. His cheeks are a little flushed from running, and his eyes are sparkling with excitement.

"Cool." I grab his ponytail and pull his head down. I have to kiss him. *Have* to. His lips are soft and warm, and the inside of his mouth is sweet. There's nothing I don't love about him. I give him another kiss in promise of more to come and let him go. It's time to get on the road.

I'M DRIVING this time. It's just easier than trying to tell someone how to get to my place. I live in what used to be a warehouse on a barge canal cut in from the bay. It's cheap to live there because there's still a lot of industry around it, but it's slowly turning into a neighborhood of artists, professors, and such. I don't blame them. The old loading docks that overhang the canal are perfect spots to hang out. The opposite bank is overgrown with papaya, elderberry, and buttonwood, so you have the illusion of privacy even though you're in the city. The problem is that most of the so-called streets around my "neighborhood" are really just alleys between large buildings, so giving directions can be time-consuming.

I pull up to the roll-up door of my warehouse abode and push a button on my key chain. The door goes up, and I drive into my foyer. I rent out part of the space to a metal sculptor who dates one of the guys at Metro Media, but I don't see her around today. The welding torch is hard to miss when she's working.

There's also a disassembled Harley Sportster on a tarp in a corner. The owner pays me a few bucks a month so he can work on it without pissing off his wife. I've seen him exactly twice in eight months, but the checks keep on coming, allowing me to afford my own place *and* pay the power bill. I do have a lurking fear that someday the sculptor chick is going to use the motorcycle parts in a piece of art, but I can live with that, and let's face it, it would be a nobler fate for the Harley than resting in pieces.

"This is it," I say as I get out of the Wagoneer. "Chez Vlad."

"I like it," Bon Tom says. "No inside walls."

Sections of my living quarters are marked off by different colors of carpet sample squares artistically laid out during an afternoon of beer and nachos with the guys from work.

"You could have a primo party in here," Logon says, looking up at the steel beams two stories overhead.

"A party?" I open my laptop and open my browser. My inbox is several pages long.

"Yeah, you know that thing where your friends come over to drink your booze and trash your place."

I hit reply on an email from my boss as I talk to Logon. "Next to the bed you'll find all my clothes in drawers and on hangers. You can wear whatever you want. And see if you can get Bon Tom to put on something else."

Logon takes Bon Tom by the arm and steers him toward the bedroom area. By the time I finish answering a few messages, Logon and Bon Tom are dressed and Logon's giving me the *we're waaai— ting* look. So cute. I close my Mac and check out what Logon and Bon Tom are wearing.

So we're dressing way down tonight. Not a bad idea for Spacely's. It's pretty low-key even though it's very trendy. People who go there save their really extreme ensembles for clubbing. Don't get me wrong: Spacely's is a club, it's just not, like, a *dance* club, you know? You won't see anyone with a pacifier in his/her mouth here. The drug of choice is Corona, not Ecstasy. And to tell the truth, Spacely's probably sells more coffee than alcohol. It's that kind of crowd: hipsters, gamers, and the general geekizens of the area. It used to be called Otaku Pad before Rook bought it.

That's right; I'm on a first-name basis with the owner. You're going to love Rook. He's just so... himself, you know? And he's so genuinely enthusiastic about the things that he likes that you can't help getting caught up in it with him. He's like a big fourth-grader—a big fourth grader who won the lottery. Not kidding. Rook hit a seventy-two million dollar jackpot on a quick-pick at the convenience store by his cousin's house. His aunt sent him down for ice cream, and he bought a ticket with the change. True story. He wasn't even going to go to the party, but his mom guilted him into it. Even after taking care of family, Rook had plenty of bank left over to finance his dream of having an ultimate hangout space.

Anyway, me and Rook bonded in our arcade rat days because we're both half-Asian, even though we're different nationalities. My dad is Korean, like I told you; his mom is Japanese, full-blown. Forget to take your shoes off once at her place, and you could find yourself banished. Rook's real name is Haruki Chester Collins. His dad is Ches Collins, the big-deal orthodontist that sponsors the fun-run marathon every year to promote dental health. Yeah, so what, right? What you want to know is what Logon and Bon Tom are wearing; am I right? Thought so.

My blood boo is resplendent in skinny black jeans and a pink pinstripe shirt with the sleeves rolled up to show a goodly amount of fawn-skinned forearm. Yummy. And I like the way he threw on the vest from my emergency-event three-piece suit. For footwear, he's going with classic high-tops, black Chucks. Sort of a naughty schoolboy vibe. I approve.

Bon Tom's entire presence is transformed by a change of wardrobe. In a pair of my shredded jeans and a tobacco-brown, long-sleeved T-shirt, he looks like one of those models who try to sell you jeans with names like Diesel and True Religion. *My, my, my.*

"You are worthy to be seen with me," I say grandly.

"Good, that's the look I was going for," Logon says. "We're waiting."

"Be right back." I throw on my favorite black T-shirt with the slightly embossed black-on-black Square Enix logo and a pair of jeans in this great maroon color that I call Dried Blood. My olive-green Doc Martens complete the ensemble, if I may call it such. For accessories, I wrap a black bandanna around my left wrist and ask Logon to knot it for me. He unwinds it, twists it, and re-wraps it, tying a knot with perfect little tails. He's amazing. Every new detail I notice about him makes me fall more in love.

It's a lot to deal with, being turned into a vampire and finding the love of my life in twenty-four hours. All I can do is keep moving forward, base my decisions on the sense of ethics developed from the examples of the people that raised and taught me, and hope I don't eff it up too badly. Now let's go have some fun.

IT'S ten thirty on Saturday night and Spacely's is cranking up. By that I mean that it's slowly filling with people who sit or stand around in groups drinking alcohol or caffeine and talking earnestly. The music spectrum is from The Beatles to The Fall to Radiohead, and the coffee bar is just as busy as the *bar* bar. These are my people. They think intelligence, the supernatural, and cartoons are cool, among other things, but those are the three big ones for me. At Spacely's, I can find like-minded individuals who get my sense of humor and fashion—which I find go hand-in-hand much of the time. If clothes can't be fun, why wear them? I mean unless you're in a cosplay contest where you have a chance of winning a date with Wesley Crusher from *Next Generation*—the grown-up actor, not the character.

Another thing about Spacely's is that the people who come here make a point of being blasé about things like race, religion, nationality, or sexual orientation. If asked, most would claim to be bisexual, and you see a lot of boys making out with boys and girls making out with girls, which I don't object to at all, but I think a lot of it's for show. Whatever. If it furthers the cause of equality, I'm for it. And I'm happy to have a place to hang out where I feel comfortable holding my boyfriend's hand.

"Yo, Cyborg," Rook calls out when he spots me coming in the door. Rook spends a lot of time in his "office." His office is an alcove to the left of the entrance to Spacely's and is the closest thing to an external womb I've ever seen. The custom-designed Me-Shell is egg-shaped, and the interior is padded with memory foam upholstered in fleece—as in sheepskin. Surround speakers are built into the casing, as well as a large, very high-definition screen. In front of the seat is a flat surface with an ergonomic keyboard and slots and hooks for gaming consoles, gloves, and goggles. Built into the bench seat are armrests, one of which holds a mini-fridge, and the other, storage for snacks. With the little oval door open, he can see whoever walks into his place. When the door's closed, he's in his own world. If it had a toilet, he'd probably never leave.

I should mention that in direct response to his mother's traditionalism, Rook shuns anything Japanese, which explains his wiggah wardrobe and pimp-daddy attitude. This pose usually makes me snicker in a superior manner, but on Rook, it's cute.

He's dressed down tonight, wearing nothing with more flavor than a white Adidas tracksuit with leprechaun-green stripes and a pair of moon-boot sneakers, loosely laced, of course. The V-shaped expanse of his bare, hairless chest is accented with a couple of medallions on chains—Mercedes and a Rastafarian flag—but nothing like the ghetto-fabulous style he usually favors. He does have a new haircut, shaved really close on the sides, a cornucopia of curls on top. *Very* the artist formerly known as Prince—circa 1986.

"Tight 'do," I say. I can talk the talk when I want to.

"Was time for a change, dawg." Rook gives me the gangstah hug, chin on my shoulder, a hearty slap on the back, pause to keep it real, and... disengage. "Whazzup?"

"Brought some new friends in. Logon and Bon Tom. Actually, Logon's a special friend."

"Mazel tov," Rook says. He's not gay, but he's not threatened by it either. He nods to Logon and Bon Tom. "Welcome to Spacely's."

"I've been here before," Logon says.

"You like it?" Rook asks.

"Yeah. Love the mocha frappé. And the music. Great atmosphere."

Rook holds up a finger and speaks into his Bluetooth. He flashes a smile at Logon. "Mocha frappé is on the house," he says.

"Thanks," Logon says. "That's really nice of you."

"Well, since you gots the good taste to hook up with my nizzle, I figure we gonna be tight. Ain't no point in ownin' a joint if you cain't buy your homies a drink."

Rook raises his fist, and I knock his knuckles with mine. "Righteous," I say.

"Somethin' diff'rent 'bout you, Cyclone, and it ain't your hair." Rook grabs my hand. "Why you so damn cold?"

Because I haven't had any blood to drink in a few hours? That's what I want to say, but I wonder if it's really such a good idea to brag about being a vampire. I used to want to be rich and famous, but since I heard what a hassle that can be, I'm not sure I want torrents of fans. I think I'd rather be rich and vaguely familiar.

Gah! That sounded suspiciously mature. I'm barely twenty-two, or will be in a few days. The second of November, All Soul's Day if anyone's interested. I accept gifts.

"For real," Rook says. "You spacin', my brother."

"I'm in love," I tell him. I can always let him in on the bloodsucking thing later.

Rook nods sagely. "Nothin' changes a man like love or vengeance." I nod back as he continues. "Some of your colleagues here already. Bought a rack when they come in."

"I'll check it out."

"Don't leave without sayin' so long."

"Never."

"Have a good time." Rook shoots us a peace sign and returns to his egg.

"He smells good," Bon Tom says.

I exchange a look with Logon. Why am I suddenly getting the feeling that I've brought a large-breed puppy into a room full of delicate things that smell irresistible? Am I going to have to scold Bon Tom for chewing on random passers-by? I've often wondered what Wolverine was like growing up. I hope I'm not about to find out.

"Follow me," I say. "And don't wander."

The main lounge is moderately crowded, only two empty seats at the bar. There's a fair smattering of people in costumes. I see two Darth Vaders before we reach the nonelectronic game room. A dartboard and three billiard tables. The room is empty except for three guys shooting pool. They're all from my work crew and happy to see me. They all know I'm gay and rag me about it, but they're far from homophobes.

Carlyle's parents are an African-American/Heinz 57 Caucasian Lesbian couple, and I've never met anyone with more tolerance for his fellow mankind, in deed, if not in word, as Aunt Bootsy would say. He's the perfect customer service rep, and tonight he's dressed as Captain Jack Sparrow from those cute Disney pirate movies.

Barge's real name is Joe Allen Moultry, which he thinks makes him sound like a country and western singer, and I can't argue. He got the nickname Barge because he's six three and weighs 265. You can imagine what he looks like in the Metro Media Day-Glo vest. At the moment, he's dressed as horror movie psycho-killer Michael Myers, with his mask pushed up on top of his head and a plastic butcher knife stuck through his belt.

The third guy is Abimelech McGee; we call him Mel. He escaped from an IFB family, and he's still a little twitchy. IFB stands for Independent Fundamentalist Baptist, if you want to know. Don't get me wrong; I support the right of everyone to choose a faith, but it *has* to be a choice. What those people do to their kids…. But I'm not getting into it here; you can look them up and make up your own mind. Just a hint: Abimelech means *my father is king*. BTW, he's not wearing a costume.

"Where's Meevie?" I don't see the female member of our Saturday night league. Her real name is Mary Ellen Victor, and she showed up for orientation at Metro Media in a pink monogrammed sweater, M E V. Carlyle immediately christened her Meevie, and it stuck.

"She's here." Carlyle points toward the library room with his cue. "But she's got a date."

"So?"

"So she's probably afraid, and rightly so, that we'll make utter asses of ourselves and embarrass her in front of the guy."

"She sound like a smart gal," Bon Tom says, his gaze wandering in the direction that Carlyle pointed.

"Enjoying your vacation?" Carlyle asks me, casting a significant glance at Logon and Bon Tom.

"Yeah, it's been outstanding so far. Went out on my own on Tuesday night. Picked up a major hottie at the Inferno, and he Turned me into a vampire. I ran into a friend from high school, Vinnie Testardo, and later, she introduced me to Logon." I pull Logon forward by the hand. "We hooked up, and we've been together since. This guy is Bon Tom. He's from Louisiana." Maybe I shouldn't be breaking my own recently adopted nondisclosure rule, but unless I quit my job, I'll have to work with these guys every day, and the longer I keep it a secret from them, the more hurt they'll be when they do find out. I may snark, but I care about people's feelings.

"And this is the first we're hearing about it?" Carlyle says, all reproachful with puppy dog eyes.

"I've been busy."

"Says the guy with the cell phone surgically attached to his ear." Barge puts the three ball in the side pocket and looks up at me.

"I know. I know. Can you believe I only made one call in three days?"

"Sign of the Apocalypse," Mel says. Everyone chuckles, including Bon Tom.

It's funnier to Mel's friends though, because we know his background. *Interesting digression.* Mel left his church and his family mainly because they believe in strictly following the Bible, never mind that it was written a couple thousand years ago. I mean seriously, now that we know how to avoid trichinosis, there's no reason not to eat pork, just for example.

Anyway, one of the bonneted, fresh-faced lasses of Mel's community shared some special moments with him after Bible study. As the song goes, three months later, she's a gal in trouble. She tells Mel, and he asks her to marry him. Problem solved, right? *Hold on. Not so fast, buster.* Mel tells his parents the joyous news, and they shit themselves. Turns out, they betrothed Mel to a girl in a congregation up near Savannah, only they never told Mel. Woe and calamity. The next thing Mel knows, his mom and dad have gone to the pastor and made a complaint about the girl—Judith—seducing their son. Mel's dad is a big deal in the congregation, and the pastor takes his word for it.

Now, these people have church pretty much every day, and that evening, Judith's parents were told to bring her to church instead of her doing duty in the nursery like usual. Mel says the pastor gave a real loud sermon about carnal sins, and at the end of it, he pointed to Judith and told her to come up to the front. He made her face everyone, and then he tells them she's a sinner and that she's carrying a child conceived out of wedlock. Mel still remembers the words. He tried to go to her, but his dad and his uncles held him in his seat.

At first, Judith's mom defended her and said that Mel was just as much to blame. The pastor said that Mel was a man and there was nothing wrong with men having carnal relations. But there was something wrong with a female luring a young man into procreating to trap him in marriage. After four hours of sobbing while being hammered with questions and criticism, Judith "confessed." She was then subjected to another hour of chastisement. Mel says it was brutal. Not everyone attacked Judith, but the ones who did were vicious, and for the entire four hours, not a single person left the room or said a word in protest.

Judith was packed off to live with another IFB family out on a cow ranch in Lake County. Mel ran away in his dad's truck and tracked her down. She took off with him down I-75, and they ended up in Tampa. Mel got a job waiting tables at Friday's while Judith was falling in love with the bass player in the band that practiced in the apartment under theirs. When the band went on tour, Judith went with them, eight months pregnant in fishnet stockings with her hair dyed pink. Mel is sad that he has a child somewhere that he'll never know, but he's glad Judith is happy. What a guy, huh? That wasn't sarcasm, by the way.

"Hang on," Barge says. "Did you say you were Turned into a vampire?"

"Don't encourage him," Carlyle says as he lines up his shot.

"Okay." Barge folds his arms. "Can we talk about Cy's boyfriend? Or is that off limits too?"

Carlyle misses his shot and gives Barge a look. "Could you talk a little louder the next time I'm shooting?"

"Don't blame your sucky playing on me."

"It's been like this all night," Mel tells me. "Carlyle has never played worse in his life, and Barge has never played better. I'm afraid it's gonna get ugly." He's only half kidding.

"Is this a serious game?" I ask.

"There's no money on it," Carlyle says. "But still…."

"You know Barge didn't make you miss that shot."

Carlyle makes a sheepish little-boy face, sticking out his lower lip and tucking in his chin. "It wasn't me," he says.

"Lame," I say.

"So let's hear about your new lifestyle." Carlyle drops the act, handing his cue stick to Mel and picking up a mug of dark beer. "Wait! Hang on. Pizza's here. Let me pay for this, and we'll listen to your story over snacks."

"I don't eat pizza anymore, and I already told you the story."

"What crap." Carlyle hands the waitress a card. "If you can resist eating a slice of this, I might almost believe you're a vampire."

"Great goolies! What's that stench?"

Logon laughs. "Garlic maybe?"

"Oh hells no!" I wail. I actually wail. I love garlic, and now it smells like burning tires and baby poop.

"Extra extra extra garlic," Carlyle says. "Just the way you like it."

"I'm gonna ralph."

Logon grabs my sleeve and pulls me upwind of the a/c vent. I bury my nose in his hair and inhale. Better.

"That's a good act, Cy," Carlyle says. "But I know you can't say no to Spacely's white with triple-X garlic." He leans toward me and takes a big bite of a slice.

"Get it away from me. Seriously. I'm gonna hurl blood all over you."

"Good one." Carlyle offers the pizza to everyone else. "You've got real will power, Cyberus."

I'd forgotten about that nickname. *Sigh.* Too late. I'm already used to Vlad, and that's how I was introduced to the other vampires, so that's that. Too bad. *Cyberus.* Maybe I can be Vlad Cyberus. That could work. Although, *Count* Cyberus would definitely rock.

"Why screw around, Vlad?" Logon says, tilting his head in that sexy, sexy way. "Surely you could use a drink by now."

My friends are watching me like kids whose mom hired a magician for the birthday party. Okay. Like Logon said, why screw around? There's no one in the room but me and my friends, and I really *could* use a drink.

Logon pulls his hair to hang over one shoulder and bends his neck, arching it for me. I'm amazed my hard-on doesn't rip right through the fabric of my pants. I wrap my hands around his biceps and pull him closer. I've done this enough that it's a fluid action now; I dip my head in a kind of swoop, fasten my lips on his skin, and my fangs penetrate. The blood flows out, and I swallow it down, my tongue moving lazily on his flesh. He sags a little, and I catch him with an arm around his back. He clasps his hands behind my neck and lets out a little moan.

"Damn," Carlyle says reverently, and I can sense the rest of them staring in awe.

I have truly, deeply, and profoundly impressed my friends. Life holds too few perfect moments like this one, and I savor it.

# CHAPTER SEVEN

"MAN, that is the coolest thing ever." Carlyle runs the pad of his thumb over one of my fangs. "Can you retract them?"

"No, they pretty much stay like that." Logon answers for me since I have a thumb in my mouth.

"What's it like being bitten?" Mel asks.

"You know how it feels when you're getting a slow, thorough blow job by someone who loves the taste of dick?"

Mel shakes his head.

"Hm." Logon taps his lips with his forefinger. "I don't think I can describe it to you. But it feels better than the best thing you've ever felt."

"No shit?" Barge looks dubious as he drains his mug. "It doesn't hurt?"

"There's a little sting, but it's over in half a second. After that, everything is orgasmic."

My work crew has completely accepted my boyfriend. It doesn't hurt that Logon is articulate, computer savvy, and just as rabid about gaming cons as they are. After a flurry of fanboy bragging about close encounters with *soi-disant* celebrities, number of Red Bulls and Ramen cups consumed in a twenty-four-hour period, and high game scores, they settle into a Q and A about bloodsucking. *Big surprise.*

"So are you still gonna hang out with us?" Mel asks me.

"Why wouldn't I? Right now, I'm still figuring things out, but I don't see why I can't keep working the evening shift and going out with you guys. Looks like Logon fits right in, and he makes the group an even half dozen. We can play teams at horseshoes again."

"Good," Mel says. "Believe it or don't, but we missed you the last few days."

"Fag," I say.

"I'll be your fag anytime, dick-breath."

For some stupid reason, I'm touched by Mel's juvenile response to my juvenile response. I have extra moisture in my eyes all of a sudden, and my throat feels all tight.

"The boss is gonna shit a brick when he gets a look at you," Barge says as he moves to lean on the pool table closer to me and Mel. Logon and Carlyle have gotten into a discussion about the classic elements of vampire lore, and apparently Barge's lack of detailed knowledge has excluded him from the conversation. Bon Tom disappears through the men's room door as I answer Barge.

"Do I look that different? I can't see myself in mirrors, so...."

"You mean besides the white skin and fangs?"

"Yeah, besides that."

"Well, your hair's always been black, and it still looks like a cat lost a fight with a blender, but now it's more—"

"It's rock star hair," Mel interrupts. "You look famous, Cy."

"Yeah, that's it," Barge agrees. "Good call, Thumper." Before you ask, Thumper is short for Bible-Thumper, which is what we call the kind of Baptists who back up all of their arguments by pointing to the Bible. Barge is ribbing his buddy Mel for his religious upbringing, not referring to him by the name of a Disney rabbit.

"Famous?" I give them the Spock eyebrow, a move I perfected by age twelve.

"Yeah," Carlyle says as he joins the conversation. "Famous. You look like you have a staff of people to maintain your fabulous *I just got out of bed with my gorgeous, sexy lover to appear on your talk show* look."

"Piss off."

"Whatever. You don't look the same."

"I think he looks like the perfect *seme bishie*," Logon says as Meevie comes in. She looks like Peter Pan from the Disney cartoon: red hair, bright green eyes, turned-up nose, freckles.

"Did someone say *bishie*?" I love Meevie's voice. Her accent is kick-ass. Kentuckians sound a lot more Southern than people who live a lot farther south.

"So what kind of costume is this?" I ask as I try to hug her.

She points proudly to the two car-wash-sized sponges in shoeboxes that are harnessed to her chest. "You like? I'm Spongeboobs Squarebra."

"Cute," I say, thankful that Bon Tom sloped off to the john, or he'd be all over her, and I don't want him to get hurt.

"So no costume?" she says.

"Let's talk about something more interesting. Where's the new boyfriend?"

"What business is it of yours?" she answers all sassy.

"I wanted to introduce your new boyfriend to my new boyfriend." I put an arm around Logon.

"I knew I heard someone say *bishie!*" Meevie takes a step back to better admire Logon. "Wow, you look like you stepped right out of a host club anime."

If you don't know the terms *yaoi, bishonen, seme,* or *uke,* you won't get most of Meevie's conversation. But you're probably sitting somewhere near a computer so take a minute to look them up. Or not. It totally depends on your level of curiosity. Anyway, Meevie is devoted to Asian animated series that feature guy-on-guy romance, especially if they're fantasy-based or period pieces. She dearly loves a pretty boy in a puffy shirt. She had a crush on me for a brief, uncomfortable time, but when she realized I really was gay, she moved on, and we went back to being friends. *Yay!*

"He's *really* cute," Meevie whispers as she hugs me. "Hope you're gettin' some."

"You have no idea," I whisper back.

"What are you gonna do with the rest of your vacation?" Carlyle asks me.

"I'm kind of on a mission."

"*Kind of* on a mission?" Barge says. "How does that work?"

"Not very well, so far. I'm looking for the guy that Turned me, but no luck."

"What's the story on that?" Carlyle asks, so I give them the whole sordid tale.

"What a dicksmack," Barge says. "Let me know when you find this Troy douche, and I'll pop off his head for you."

"Barge, he's a vampire," Meevie says. "He'll probably squeeze you like an almost-empty tube of toothpaste. I agree with the dicksmack part though."

"Seriously," Carlyle says. "Say the word, Cy-dog, and we'll hunt this mother down and tattoo your name on his ass with a blowtorch."

"That sounds really painful," I say.

"That's kind of the point," Carlyle says.

Meevie interjects. "Except, as you guys keep forgetting, he's a *vampire*. Maybe he doesn't feel pain."

"Vampires feel pain," I say. "It's more of a mental thing, but it works the same way."

"Can you make me a vampire?" Meevie asks.

*Whoa.* Wasn't expecting that. Well, maybe I was, but not right away.

In some of the books and movies about vampires, the vampires agonize over whether to Turn someone else into a vampire. I always thought that was bogus, self-created drama; why wouldn't someone want to live forever young? But when faced with the choice, I dither too. There's a lot to consider. The whole vulnerability to sunlight thing. The fact that I wouldn't hang out with any of the vamps I've met so far. And you can't see yourself. Maybe I shouldn't do that to someone I care about.

"I guess I could," I tell Meevie. "Why don't we talk about it again later after I learn more about being a vampire? And it'll give you some time to think about it."

"I've been thinking about it since I first heard of vampires."

"It's not how you imagine it. Trust me."

"Okay, we'll talk about it later. Right now, let's talk about finding Mr. Happy-Fangs and extracting justice from his ass."

"Girl, you are *so* bad!" I give her a high-five.

"We just want you to know that we're here if you need us," Barge says.

"Aw, I'm all warm and fuzzy inside," I say.

"Lick my lollipop of love," Carlyle retorts as my phone rings.

I don't recognize the number, but I answer anyway, turning my back on the group. "Hello."

"Vlad?"

"Uh, yeah. What can I do for you?"

"Tell me where you are so I can meet you."

"Who is this?"

"*Am*brose." He says his name like he can't believe I don't already know who he is.

"You want to meet me?"

"Did you bite someone on drugs earlier tonight? Tell me where you are."

"Well, gee, since you ask so nicely… forget it!"

"I can help you find Troy."

He takes me by surprise, and it's a second or two before I answer. "I'm willing to stipulate that," I say, "but why would you help me?"

"You'll have to talk to me to find that out."

"What are we doing right now?"

"Face to face, simpleton."

*Sigh.* "I'm at Spacely's. Figure it out." I hang up.

"Who was that?" Logon asks.

"Ambrose."

"Who?"

It appears as though Logon has no clear memories of what happened at Simon's house, thank the PTB. He remembers going there, and he remembers waking up at Orisha's place, but nothing in between.

"He's a vampire," I say. "One of Simon's."

"What does he want?"

"He wants a meeting."

"When."

"As soon as he gets here."

"Another vampire?" Meevie says. "Sweet!"

"Not really," I say. "He's a conceited jerk."

"Suck-burger. But I should get back to Zach anyway. If I leave him alone for too long, he might wither."

"Tell me you didn't hook up with another mopey butt-puppet in smudged eyeliner."

Meevie smacks me on the shoulder. "Zach is sensitive and has actual thoughts besides how to get into my panties."

"Has he written you a poem yet?"

"Why?" Meevie narrows her eyes at me.

"Just wondering if you could still be saved."

"Up yours sideways." Meevie blows me a kiss. "Logon, it's a real pleasure to meet you. Boys, stop your lyin' and start cryin'—I'm outtie."

"Hey, Meev?"

"Yeah?"

"Don't tell anyone I'm an ampire-vay, okay?"

"No prob." Meevie says as she leaves the billiard room.

"Anyone want to play a game?" Carlyle asks as he racks the balls.

"I'll play," Bon Tom says as he returns to the table.

He's the worst pool player I've ever seen. The rest of my friends are in guy heaven teaching him how to shoot. I'd rather sit on this banquette with Logon on my lap and watch the mayhem.

My senses must be getting sharper with time because I feel Ambrose arrive. His entrance causes a ripple of interest that widens until it touches my perception.

"What's wrong?" Logon gives me a puzzled look.

*Wow.* My whole body tensed up without me realizing it, but Logon felt it. Gently, I slide him off my lap and stand up. For some reason, I want to be on my feet when Ambrose finds me, which I know he will. And the reason is an obvious one. Ambrose is a spoiled snot, but he's also dangerous, and I'm not giving up the high ground to him.

And here's Ambrose. He's wearing old-school pegged pants in black with a white shirt and a totally steampunk tapestry vest with lots of brown leather straps and brass buckles. His elbow-length white-blond hair is gathered in a tail that hangs over his left shoulder. If Meevie was here, her ovaries would explode.

"This is where you like to spend your time?" This is Ambrose's idea of a greeting.

"Something wrong with it?" I ask.

"Not if you're fourteen."

Logon's at my side now, his hand curling around my arm in silent support.

"Ouch," I say. "You've wounded me deeply by pointing out my arrested development. Now what else did you want to talk about?"

Ambrose glances around as my friends gather to stare curiously at him. Haughty must be his middle name. I wish I could convey that much disdain with a subtle flare of my nostrils.

"Can we talk somewhere else?" Ambrose says.

"I guess we could, if my friends will excuse me."

"Bon Tom comin' with you," Bon Tom says.

"Me too." Logon squeezes my arm.

"Fine," Ambrose says.

"You could sit in the booth," Carlyle says. "I'll get rid of the pizza remnants, and we promise not to eavesdrop."

The four of us sit on the semi-circular banquette. The garlic fumes are still hanging around, but after I wave my arm a few times, they dissipate. My friends start another game, keeping their eyes on the balls. *Eyes on the balls. Smirk.*

"Can we talk now?" Ambrose asks snottily.

"So talk," I say to Ambrose. "What brings you here?"

"This is where you are."

"And?"

"I want to help you find Troy."

"Why?"

"Because he Turned you, there are ways that he's vulnerable to you. You could get rid of him."

"I don't know if I want to get rid of him. I was thinking an apology was in order."

"Piker."

"What?"

"You think small."

"So? You want me to think globally or something?"

"Maybe you could just think beyond yourself once."

"Ditto."

"Ditto?"

"Yeah, it means—"

"I know what it means. Why did you say it?"

"You are really the least self-aware person I've ever met."

"I didn't have to come here, you know," Ambrose says.

"You don't have to stay neither, cher," Bon Tom drawls.

"I wasn't talking to you."

"*I* most definitely talkin' to *you.*"

"Well don't. You don't have any right."

"Don't need none."

"Mongrel."

"That sound like Simon talkin'.'"

Ambrose looks supremely offended. He meets my eyes, clearly conveying his opinion that I should control my dog. "Can we get back on topic?" he asks.

"I don't know—can we?" I answer.

Logon snickers, and Ambrose sneers. Bon Tom is watching Ambrose with a complicated look on his face. He reminds me of a dog that's had his nose slapped by a kitten but can't resist trying to get the kitten to play. I might be overthinking it, but Bon Tom seems to be going queer on us. And as every idiot knows, the agenda of every gay person in existence is to turn everyone else gay, so.... *Score!* I know I don't have to tell you I'm kidding.

"It's simple," Ambrose says. "I tell you where Troy is, and you go kill him. Or get your dog to do it if you're squeamish."

"Sheesh, could you stop being a little bitch for just five minutes?"

"What?"

"Never mind." Scratch Haughty as Ambrose's middle name; it's O'Blivious. Funny, he doesn't look Irish. "Why don't you just tell me where Troy is 'cause it's the right thing to do?"

"You're kidding."

"Maybe I squeeze your throat 'til you tell," Bon Tom says.

"Try it." Ambrose doesn't sound nervous. The last time he saw Bon Tom, he was cringing; now, he's lipping off. What the H?

"Oh, I think I will try you, cher." Bon Tom grins. "When the time be right."

Ambrose is quick. Bon Tom is quicker. Bon Tom catches Ambrose's hand by the wrist as it flies toward his face. I'm a little disappointed. I've always wanted to see someone slapped in real life. It's just so dramatic.

"Let go of me." Ambrose's jaw is clenched so hard the tendons are standing out in his neck.

"Cain't risk it. You might try to hit me again."

"Enough foreplay," I say. "Either get busy, or stop flirting like sixth-graders. Come on, Brosie. Just tell me where Troy is."

Bon Tom lets go of Ambrose's wrist and sits back. Ambrose rubs his arm as if he can wipe away Bon Tom's touch.

"Will you at least *think* about killing him?" Ambrose bites his lip. "What am I saying? As Simon says, once you're in Troy's presence, you'll feel an overwhelming compulsion to squash him. And now I think I've wasted enough of my evening."

"You still haven't told us where he is," Logon points out.

Ambrose turns his gaze on Logon. "You look disgustingly healthy," he says. "Putting out for the whole party agrees with you. By the way, you have the most delicious blood."

"What are you talking about?" Logon says.

"Nothing," I say. "He's just trying to get under your skin."

"I've been under his skin," Ambrose says. "And it was sweet."

I swear it's like someone struck a match in my brain. I'm out of my seat in the blink of an eye, hauling Ambrose up by the front of his shirt, and shaking him like a sandy beach towel. I say, "Mention it again, and I'll suck you dry." I mean it too.

Ambrose shivers as I stare into his eyes. I get that feeling again that there's something really strange about him, and I almost bite him just to satisfy my curiosity, but Logon's right here. I'm so not going to be *that* vampire. My intention is to be faithful to Logon, which for me means no sucking of strange necks.

"You'll have to eventually," Ambrose says softly. "No matter how healthy your consort is, he can't produce the volume of blood you need over a long period of time… not as he is."

"Stop reading my mind." I let Ambrose go. "Where's Troy?"

"Sometimes he stays at the home of a record producer in Safety Harbor."

"Directions?" I say as I look at the time on my phone. It's kind of a drag having a curfew again.

Ambrose tells me how to get to Johnny Hot's place—Wateredge off Phillippe Parkway—stressing that it's a compound with a gate. I don't think that will be a problem.

"There'll be a big party going on," Ambrose says. "Once you get to the house, no one will know if you're guests or not."

Of course there's a party; it's Saturday before Halloween. Maybe we should go back to my place and change into something less comfortable. Nah, probably shouldn't take the time. In fact, I should get going.

"Gordon's dead," Ambrose tells Bon Tom as I get to my feet.

"I know, cher. I killed him."

"Simon's really pissed about it."

"Reckon he is. Specimen like Gordon hard to come by."

"You should watch your back."

"Bon Tom don't know no other way to live, but thanks for the warnin'."

"Threat," Ambrose clarifies.

"You got your way of lookin' at it, and I got mine."

"You're absolutely maddening," Ambrose says.

"Word," I say as I take Logon's hand and go to say good-bye to the guys. Of course they want to go with us, but it would be too much hassle. Next time.

Bon Tom goes to get the car while Logon and I say good night to Rook. Rook gives me another hug and winks at Logon.

"Can we drop you somewhere?" I ask Ambrose just because my mother *did* raise me right.

Ambrose looks at the Wagoneer as Bon Tom pulls up to the curb. "Is that Bob Massey's car?"

"He loaned it to me."

"I didn't know you knew him."

"I get around."

Ambrose smiles. "Enjoy the party."

"If this is a trap, I swear—"

"It's not a trap," Ambrose says. "That's not my style."

"See you later, cher," Bon Tom calls out the window.

"What a goof," Ambrose says under his breath.

"Do you want a ride?" I ask again.

"No."

"Okay then." I wait for Logon to slide into the front seat next to Bon Tom before I get in. There's plenty of cheek-room for all three of us. Just because I know it'll annoy Ambrose, I don't glance at him even once as we leave.

"Babe," Logon says as Bon Tom pulls out of the parking lot onto the street.

"Yeah?"

"I want a nickname."

"A nickname?"

"Yeah. You have about a dozen that I've heard so far; I just want one. I thought Brosie was a really cute nickname for Ambrose."

"Hm, that doesn't really work with your name."

"I know that." I can hear a pout in Logon's voice. "I'm just saying I want a nickname. It doesn't have to be like that one."

"I think of you as my blood boo."

"That's fine, but I don't want anyone else calling me that."

"I got nothin'," I say. "Let me think about it."

"You can't get a cool nickname by thinking it up. It has to occur naturally."

*Like Meevie.* "I understand."

"Don't worry, Blondie," Bon Tom says. "You want a nickname bad enough, one gonna come to you. Bon Tom just hope you like it when it show up."


SO THIS record producer guy, Johnny Hot—real name Gianni Hatzipanagis—made a fortune in the early seventies with sun tan oil.

Yeah, believe it or don't, but back in the day, people used to put stuff on their skin to *intensify* the effects of the sun's rays. We know better now, but in 1972, when a University of Florida dropout used his knowledge of chemistry to make a lotion that not only smelled like a piña colada, but tasted like one, people bought it by the gallon.

He used to sponsor a beauty contest every year in Daytona on Spring Break. A bikini-clad Miss Tropic-Glo would be crowned and reign over the massive kegger that followed. For a brief time, Tropic-Glo coconut rum was available for purchase, but that was a long time ago. I only know this stuff 'cause Mom was a runner-up for Miss Tropic-Glo in 1982, the last year of the event. If she'd won, Johnny Hot could have been my father, which is how she always ends the story.

I know Johnny's name as a promoter of local talent. Through hiring bands to play his Tropic-Glo events, he got to know the circuit and decided he wanted to leave the fringes and live the real rock 'n' roll lifestyle. He holds a battle-of-the-bands contest every Fourth of July, and admission is cheap. It's been a tent pole of my summer schedule since I was twelve and allowed to ride the bus downtown by myself. I'll never forget the time Sonny Arjibay tried to ride his skateboard down the rail on the auditorium steps and tore his taint when he fell off. *Good times.*

Driving up to Johnny's place reminds me of Simon's refuge except that the house, the outbuildings, and the grounds are lit up like Times Square. Even the trees and shrubs are covered with lights. The cars parked in the big crushed-shell lot are all Maseratis, Lamborghinis, and stretch Hummers.

"Loud," Bon Tom says as he turns off the engine. He's referring to the phat beats blasting from the house. With no neighbors to annoy, the speakers are cranked to eleven.

"You could stay here, but that would ruin my plan of passing us off as Green Day."

Logon snickers. "Maybe we *should* have a band name ready in case someone asks."

"I've already got one: The Billy Jacks."

"The Billy Jacks?" Logon doesn't look impressed.

"I like it," Bon Tom says.

"I always said if I ever had a band I'd call it The Billy Jacks," I say.

"Fine," Logon says. "It's not like it matters."

Is it possible my sweet baboo doesn't grok the coolness of The Billy Jacks? It's almost as cool as The Lone Rangers. I know; conceited much, right? But I put a lot of thought into the name, and I'm kind of proud of it, especially since I was just thirteen when I thought of it. Maybe Logon's never seen *The Legend of Billy Jack*. Okay, I'm going to stop obsessing over it, and I'm going to stop expecting Logon to be perfectly compatible in every way. What we've got is good. I don't need to look for faults. *Forward... but never straight.*

Judging by the chicklet reeling out of the front door of Johnny's mansion, we're way underdressed for this party. She's in a filmy little Betsy Johnson minidress with gauzy, appliquéd butterflies, and her wispy ribbon-strap sandals are Jimmy Choo or really good knockoffs. She's followed by a flock of downy waifs in semi-transparent slip dresses and raccoon eyeliner. I swear I can see a pastel cloud of glitter around them as they giggle and lean on one another in a mating signal that lets any nearby males know that their judgment has been compromised by drugs and/or alcohol. We stand aside to let them waft by us, unaffected by their kindergarten-call-girl charms. At least me and Logon are unaffected. Bon Tom is quivering like a retriever sighting a covey of quail. I nudge him with my elbow, and we continue up the walk.

The open doorway to the mansion is filled with golden-white light, and we walk into it, and oh my goolies, it's just like every Hollywood party I've ever seen in the movies. You know what I'm talking about. It's a *swingin'* scene. Bon Tom looks anxious, like he desperately needs to pee, and Logon has on his *I am not impressed* face, which seems to be a popular look here. It's a little shock to recognize a vampire over by the walk-in fireplace, but I just nod at her as we pass by. It's big shock to spot Vinnie in the kitchen, looking like Jessica Rabbit dressed as an Andrews Sister. I watch a handsome guy in leather do a body shot off Vinnie's excellent rack before I say hi to her.

"Vlad!" Vinnie squeals. It's something she does when she's excited. It's cute. "Hey, Croft, meet my boss, Vlad the Paler, and his entourage, Logon and Bon Tom." She beams. "Croft is the lead guitar with Swamp Wing. They play old-school Southern rock."

"Love to hear you sometime," I say. I'm lying of course. Here's my opinion on Southern rock: if I never hear *Free Bird* again, I'll have a happy life.

"So what do you call your outfit?" Croft says.

"We're The Billy Jacks," Bon Tom says without hesitation.

"Cool," Croft says. "That's a boss name, dudes."

"Told you," I say to Logon.

"I need to convo with my peeps," Vinnie tells Croft.

"Cool," he says again. "I'll look for you later, beautiful."

Me and Logon and Bon Tom follow Vinnie out the back and around the pool to a quiet area with lawn furniture.

"What are you doing here?" I ask.

"Rockie flew in this morning, and a friend of hers invited her to this party. She asked if I wanted to go with, and here I am."

Rockie is Roxanne Testardo, Vinnie's older sister, the one between Vinnie and Frankie. As Vinnie lets me know, Rockie's in college in Portland, has a girlfriend, and is into making short films with the camera she carries everywhere.

"So where is she?" I look around.

"She's talking to some guy from Guerilla Suit Productions who's deluded himself that he has a chance of getting into her tights. She could get a distribution deal out of this."

"I'll keep my fingers crossed for her."

"What are you doing here, boss?" Vinnie says.

"Think for a minute, Pinky."

"Troy's here?" Vinnie swivels her head like she's being exorcised.

"That's the rumor. Want to help us look for him?"

"Hells yeah!" Vinnie tosses back her rum punch and stands up. "Should we stick together, or fan out and quarter the area?"

"Easy there, G. I. Jane. Since me and Bon Tom know what Troy looks like, we'll split into pairs."

"Okay." Vinnie shrugs and her boobs shift lazily in their warhead bra. "It's a pretty big party though."

"It's hours until dawn," Logon says.

"Okay." Vinnie takes Bon Tom's arm. "Ready, big boy?"

We split up. Bon Tom seems more than happy to be paired with Vinnie, and I know I'm happy paired with Logon. In this crowd of rockers, actors, groupies, and agents, we don't stand out, and it's easy to move from room to room searching the vaguely familiar faces. It's definitely a few tiers above any party I've ever been to, but I remember that I'm an immortal vampire, and it evens the playing field a little.

I see the smarmy weather guy from channel 8, Max Storm—if you can believe that's his real name. I see the insanely tall chick that dances in the background of videos by a local metal band; the rumor is that she's a dude. I see the unfamiliar vampire lady again. I *don't* see Troy.

"Hello, young one," the lady vampire says as Logon and I make it through the west side of the ground floor. She steps from behind a column on the side porch. *Cool entrance.*

"Hi," I say. "I don't mean to be rude, but I'm looking for someone, and I have a time limit."

"When I decided to make the trip from the west coast, I was looking forward to meeting some vampires from the other side of the country, but so far, it's been a real drag."

"I feel you. I'm pretty disappointed myself. Which brings me back to my mission." Oh crap, my good manners are betraying me again. "By the way, I'm Vlad. This is my consort, Logon."

"Claire Mikkels. I'm a casting agent. Thought I might find some fresh faces out here." She eyes Logon. "You're still fully human, and you're *cute*. I know a couple of people that could build a Nickelodeon series around you. Kind of like *Big Bang Theory* but with a gay vibe. Watered down and sprinkled with sugar for the YA crowd, of course. You can play younger than you are, and the time is ripe for a role model for gay kids. What do you say, cookie?"

Logon looks flattered. "I'm not looking for a job," he says. "But thanks."

"Oh, you're really cute," Claire drawls. "Promise you'll think about it."

"Really nice to meet you," I say quickly. "We should get back to our search."

"I understand. Who are you looking for? Maybe I know them."

"Troy Sanger?"

"I've met him, but I haven't seen him tonight." Claire shakes her head. "What a space case. And bo*ring*. He kept going on and on about some formula he's working on. Saint Jerry save me from nutty professors."

"I don't suppose you know where Troy is now?"

"He claimed to have carte blanche at the home of some local millionaire."

"Yeah, been there."

"Guess I can't help you." She pushes some blonde hair behind her ear. "Oh, you probably already know this, but steer clear of a guy who calls himself Lord Bonesteel. He'll try to sell you real estate."

"Met him. He tried to drink my blood."

"Without your permission?" Claire makes the face of someone who's had a roach fly into her mouth. "What a pervert."

"I *knew* it was something bad," I crow. I *love* validation.

"It can give a vampire influence over a weaker one, not to mention the aphrodisiac effects. Unlike Spanish Fly, vampire blood really does enhance pleasure."

"I'm hip, but I'm pretty sure his aim was to control me, not seduce me."

"Did you meet that consort of his?"

"Unfortunately."

"Beautiful, but what a pain. And he spooked me. I couldn't read him at all. He might be a vampire or a human consort for all I know."

"He's a brat, I know that much."

Claire smiles as she takes a card from her sparkly miniature handbag. "If you ever get to the west coast, give me a call."

"Thanks. Hope your visit improves."

"It can't get much worse, but Hollywood's doing more filming in Florida all the time, so I figure it's worth scouting it out. Hey, Vlad, a word of advice? Don't let anyone bite you unless you trust them completely, okay? I've seen young, naïve vampires turned into virtual slaves."

"I'll be careful." What a laugh. When am I ever careful? I blunder down the road of life with my eyes on the carrot *du jour* in the blind faith that I won't get broadsided by the speeding semi truck of fate.

We meet up with Vinnie and Bon Tom out by the gigantic, natural-form pool. They're not having any luck either. It's only an hour until dawn; now it suddenly seems like a good idea to just have fun for what remains of the night. Maybe Troy will stroll by while I'm dancing with Vinnie and Logon. Stranger things have happened; some of them in the last few days. That reminds me of Ambrose, and I tell my crew what Claire said about Simon's consort.

"She couldn't tell if he was mortal or vampire."

"Why you assume he either one?" Bon Tom says.

*Cue ominous music, John Williams-style.*

"We-e-ell." I draw the word out as I lean over to whisper in Bon Tom's ear. "He did drink Logon's blood at Eyrie."

"What you think that mean?"

"Don't get cryptic on me. If you know something, tell me."

"Ambrose ain't the same as when I knowin' him."

I'm so shocked that Bon Tom's talking about his past that I don't know what to ask him first. "How is he different?" is what comes out of my mouth.

"He not a vampire no more, cher."

You want to hit that ominous music switch again?

"Are you saying Ambrose got... cured, or something?" I ask Bon Tom.

"Bon Tom don't know. Just know Brosie not the same. He blood changed."

"Weird," Vinnie says.

"Is that why he wasn't afraid of you tonight?"

"Most likely. If he ain't vampire no more, my bite don't affect him."

"What's the matter?" Logon strokes my forehead. "What's with the frown?"

"There's just so much I don't understand. I'm thrilled to be a creature of the night, but it's like every five minutes some new sitch pops up that I have to deal with completely unprepared."

"*C'est la vie*, cher," Bon Tom says.

"Don't smirk. You're one of the biggest mind-fucks of all." I'm starting to feel twitchy. Dawn must be getting close. Time to go.

Vinnie kisses my cheek and leaves to find Rockie. Me and Logon and Bon Tom get in the Wagoneer and go to Vinnie's apartment because there isn't a single lightproof spot at my place. The spare key wants to stick in the lock, but it cannot defeat my Vamp-Fu.

"That couch is comfortable," I tell Bon Tom as I hustle Logon toward the mobile staircase.

"Rest well, cher," Bon Tom says.

I settle into the blankets and cushions and pull Logon to lie on top of me. We make out for a good while before I do what we both want and drink some of his blood. Logon loves kissing and necking, or petting, or whatever you call it, and I'm more than happy to oblige him. I love the feel of his skin under my hands, the way he rises into my touch, his soft giggles when I find a ticklish spot, the warm wetness of his mouth that puts me in mind of other warm wetness. I didn't intend to have sex when we lay down, but Logon's body beckons and welcomes me so sweetly that I can't resist. And I don't resist when he surprises me by pushing a finger inside me and pulling it out to replace it with his cock. He's a gentle top, and I've done this once or twice. We move easily and deliciously against, over, around, and inside one another. I nip at his wrist as I climax, and he buries himself in me with a long, ecstatic groan, moving slowly in and out until he comes. *Bliss.* And now to fall asleep, warm and sated with my beloved in my arms. Tomorrow is another night.

# CHAPTER EIGHT

I SURFACE, and Claire is in my thoughts—Claire the lady vamp I met at the party last night. I hope I didn't lose her card. It occurs to me that she has knowledge that I want, and she seemed more like someone who'd share her wisdom than the vamps I've met so far. I wish I'd asked when she was leaving Florida, but there's always the phone and the Internet.

Logon isn't here, but he's probably having some of the vile coffee Bon Tom makes. It's thick as Orc blood and just as black. I can't believe it doesn't eat right through the pot. I can only imagine what it does to the lining of your stomach. Gah, I swear I sound more like my mom every day.

If I wasn't so hungry, I'd lie here and think about the plan of attack for the evening, but I'm starting to feel the pins and needles that'll turn into scalpels and ice picks if I wait too long. I'm chilly, but not freezing yet, so I know I have a little time before the cravings start their escalating torture. I'm not thrilled about this feature of vampire life, but it comes with the territory, and I live here now. I'll cope. I hope. Hey, I'm a poet and didn't know it.

No one in the kitchen. No smell of coffee. No noise except from the fountain in the entry. No Logon. No Bon Tom. WTF?

*The elevator clunks.* Okay, they just went out for something, probably another five pounds of coffee or a half ton of sugar. Will I look too needy if I meet them when they get off the lift?

Logon and Bon Tom aren't on the elevator. I can't think of anything to say as Ambrose steps into the loft.

"I hope this isn't a bad time," Ambrose says.

"It's not a good one."

"Oh? Has something happened?"

Bonesteel took my boo. It *has* to be him. Who else? And he sent Ambrose to tell me what the ransom is. "Where's Logon?" I ask.

"Why would I know where your consort is? Don't tell me you've misplaced the little slut."

"Did you come here for an ass-kicking? 'Cause you caught me in the mood."

Ambrose laughs. "I've fed recently, but you look a little puny to me. I think I could take you."

The asshole's right. I feel weak—not for a human, but for a vampire. I could still probably take on three normal people, but Ambrose would own me. Unless he's *not* a vampire.

I make with the tough talk. "What the hell are you doing here?"

"I came to see if you found Troy."

"Why are you so interested?"

"I told you. It's a matter of honor."

"You've never been within sniffing distance of honor." This is a line that Tsellador, my RPG warrior character, used to use a lot. It still comes in handy.

"Honestly, can we stop sniping for a few minutes? It's entertaining and oddly satisfying, but right now, it's a waste of time."

"No, I didn't find Troy." I belatedly realize I'm still naked. "Why don't you sit down over there while I put on some clothes?"

"If you must."

It actually sounds like Ambrose is making an overture of buddiness, but I'm probably imagining it. I leave him on a wet-sand-colored armchair and dress in the clothes I wore last night. Ambrose is looking out the window at the city lights when I come back. *Damn, he's beautiful.* In his gray pullover and black trousers, he looks like an off-duty prince.

"Won't your master be pissed if he finds out you're here?" I ask.

"I do what I want when I want."

"Okay then." I sit down across from Ambrose and try to look nonchalant, though the need for Logon is simmering under my skin. "So I didn't find Troy at the party. Now, in the words of Hannibal Lecter, quid pro quo. You tell me something. Where the hell is Logon?"

"It hurts, doesn't it."

"Don't screw with me."

"Could be fun."

"Don't even go there."

"I know you find me desirable."

"I think you're pretty, but I want more than a nice package."

"I'm just playing with you. Do you really think I'd say something like 'I know you find me desirable' if I wasn't kidding?"

"I don't know. Maybe."

"Well, I wouldn't."

"Simon would."

"Yeah." Ambrose manages to put a world of meaning into a sigh. We have something in common. Neither of us is thrilled with our vampire creator.

"He has Logon, doesn't he?"

"Not to my knowledge. Why are you ignoring the obvious?" Ambrose sighs again, probably at the stupid expression on my face. "Is Logon the only one missing?"

*No.* Bon Tom wouldn't do that. He'd have no reason to for one thing, and for another, I just don't think he would. So there.

"I can see you don't want to believe it, but you can't trust the hound."

"Why not?"

"Oh you know, abusive childhood, that sort of thing. He tries to blend in, but he's a monster."

"Says you."

"You'd prefer to believe a hermaphrodite witch over your own kind?"

"That's not a card you want to play. Simon's the only dirtbag I can think of that would do something like this. Even the Mafia spares wives and children."

"I'll take you to Eyrie if you like, but I really don't think your consort is there."

"I should be able to feel him, but I can't."

"That doesn't mean he's dead. It just means that someone knows how to hide him from you."

"Someone like Simon."

"It's not Simon."

Ambrose sounds so sure that I'm starting to doubt. What if Troy called Orisha and said he'd trade whatever he stole for Logon? Far-fetched? Yeah, it is. Why would Troy want Logon? But my need for him is starting to affect my ability to think clearly.

"Why would Bon Tom take Logon?"

"He snapped and his old training took over."

"In that case, wouldn't he kill me?"

"I can't predict psychotic behavior."

"So basically your theory consists of *let's blame it on the crazy*?"

"There are a thousand and one things the Vodou witch can use Logon's blood for."

"Orisha sacrifices chickens, not people."

"As far as you know."

"Orisha helped us. Orisha *likes* Logon."

"Did she tell you he's special?"

"Yeah. So?"

"You might ask yourself what special means to Orisha."

Screw this. I need help. Vinnie answers on the first ring.

"I need you to drive up to Indian Rocks and see if Logon is with Orisha."

Vinnie picks up on all the subtleties of my request. "How long has he been missing?"

"Don't know. I woke up and he was gone. Bon Tom too."

"Shit. Okay, I'm on it, boss. I'll keep you updated."

"Thanks, Vin. Love you. Mean it."

"Back at ya." Vinnie hangs up.

I dial Carlyle. Voice mail. "Call me as soon as you get this," I tell the recorder.

I dial Barge. He answers. I give him Vinnie's number and tell him to tell her that he's providing backup. Intrigued by the cop-talk, Barge agrees without hearing any more.

"Now let's you and me pay Simon a visit," I say to Ambrose.

"Are you sure you can make it? You look a little shaky to me."

"Your concern is touching. Let's go."

"You need to drink."

"Duh. As soon as we find Logon, I'll do that."

"You don't have to wait."

"Yes, I do."

"You can't rescue Logon if you're too weak to move."

"The subject is closed."

Well, I'll be damned. Ambrose actually shuts up for the length of time it takes to get to street level.

"Where's your car?" I ask.

"I took a cab." Ambrose shrugs. "I don't drive."

It figures. "Of course you don't," I say as I lead the way to the Wagoneer.

HALFWAY to Belleair, I have to pull the bus onto the shoulder and wait for the dizziness to pass. I'm freezing. My stomach is full of razors. The periods of disorientation are getting longer. Can't brain. In fact, it looks like there's zero percent chance of braining. I have to face it; I'm going to wreck the car if I stay behind the wheel.

"I need you to drive," I tell Ambrose.

"I told you. I don't drive."

"This is no time to be snobby. You have to drive."

"I *can't*. Never learned how."

"It's easy."

"No thanks."

"Bitch." I waste a valuable breath to cuss at him.

"All you need is a little blood."

"You're kidding." Apparently, when you're dying, sarcasm is one of the last faculties to go.

"Just drink. You'll feel better."

Ambrose is so close that his thigh touches mine. He's so warm, and I lean into that heat like a man with frostbite. He smells like vanilla, oranges, and cinnamon. My mouth is watering like a fire sprinkler. I just need a swallow or two to give me the strength to go on. That's all.

*No.* I have more willpower than this. I just have to keep the car between the lines.

Ten miles later. Back on the side of the road.

"Drink," Ambrose says. His breath is like honeysuckle. "Do it for Logon."

So I ignore my heart and drink.

He's not Logon. This is immediately apparent, but his blood... his blood is like drinking the end of summer. To put it in perspective, Logon's blood tastes like the first day of spring. Got it now? No? Didn't think so. It's that pesky frame of reference thing again. When I drink blood, I get free-floating impressions, kind of like the visions I imagine an opium smoker sees. With Logon, it's cascading water, vast fields of purple flowers, and that sweet dawn chill. Ambrose is poppies, sunshine that pours down like honey, and endless firefly twilight. I feel the sensuous tug of the mating instinct, but I manage to resist. It helps that we're parked on the side of a moderately busy road with headlights crawling over us every few seconds.

"Thanks," I say. I drank more than I intended, and I find it hard to keep from going back for more. While I don't feel as... fulfilled as I do after drinking Logon's blood, I do feel strong, alert, exhilarated, and grateful.

"It was good for me too," Ambrose says.

Yeah, there's this constant symbiotic loop of feedback between biter and bitten. His responses made it really hard to keep my hands off him.

"Personal question?" I say as I pull back onto the pavement.

"Why not."

"Why do you stay with a butt-munch like Simon?"

"The usual reasons. He's got wealth, status, and a large flock. And of course, he's my Maker."

"So you *are* a vampire. There's been some speculation."

Ambrose doesn't answer for a couple of seconds. "Simon Turned me in 1919. Coincidentally, I was nineteen at the time, just a couple of weeks from my twentieth. He gave me the boilerplate speech about it being a sin to let my beauty fade and so on and so forth."

"So you're like a hundred years old."

"I spent a large amount of time waiting. Simon convinced me to let him put me in a twilight state until he made a place for us in America."

"Why'd he want to come to America?"

"He had no choice really. He's always taken too keen an interest in weres. The shape-shifters in Europe let it be known that they were hunting him for certain... indiscretions, so he had to find a new place, some place where he spoke the language."

"I guess the weres didn't appreciate his interest."

"He was doing breeding experiments."

"Tell me again what attracted you to this guy?"

"I'll be as brief as I can. I was living in Zurich. My father was the American ambassador. I was attending the university, but I didn't spend a lot of time studying. I liked going to parties, and being a diplomat's son made it easy to get invitations. I met Simon at the salon of the French ambassador's mistress. We were introduced, and a medallion he was wearing caught my eye. After a polite interval, I introduced the subject of the occult, and he was very knowledgeable. He claimed to have known Madame Blavatsky, which was very interesting to me because I was a Theosophist. It wasn't hard for him to persuade me. I leapt at the chance for immortality." Ambrose smiles at the windshield. "And he's not unattractive in a physical way."

"He's hot," I admit. "So he showed his true colors later, I assume."

"Vividly. He dotes on me, but he won't tolerate any interference with his obsessions. When he finally brought me over and woke me, I found him living in a hillbilly paradise, to use a colloquialism. He'd found families of shifters in Appalachia and on the bayous of Louisiana, whole clans that knew nothing of their history. He took some of their children, turned them into killers, and eliminated any vampire that stood against him in Florida."

"Why Florida?"

"He's old."

"Fair enough. So when you woke up, Simon had himself a little redneck Riviera and expected you to ooh and ah over it."

"Honestly, you would've thought he'd built the Roman Empire all by himself."

"That's really why you're helping me, isn't it?"

"Partly, but mostly, I want to find Troy Sanger."

"Why?"

"The usual reason: he knows too much."

"About you?"

"And others."

"The night he bit me he was running from Bon Tom."

"He should've expected it. He stole from the witch."

"How do you know Orisha?"

"Orisha? Is that what the oddity calls itself?"

"I think it's a pretty name."

"Rene Gagnier is the name it was born with, according to Troy. They met when Troy was making his way east from California, one scam at a time. I guess the witch was as susceptible to his charm as anyone else. It was Gagnier, or Orisha, if you prefer, who told Troy about the millionaire vampire who ruled Florida."

I'm suddenly feeling very Frodoesque. You know, the ordinary guy who gets plopped down in the middle of something that's been going on for hundreds of years. At least I don't have to carry any cursed jewelry around with me.

"You really don't think Logon's at Eyrie?" I say.

"No, I don't."

"Then where?"

"I told you my theory. The hound took him. Probably to the witch."

"Then Vinnie will tell me that when she calls me in about half an hour."

"Aren't you worried about your mortal friends?"

"Of course, but they know their supernatural laws, and they'd never forgive me if I didn't include them."

"Humans." Ambrose puts another world of meaning into one word, and we're quiet for a couple of minutes.

"You really think Bon Tom took Logon?" I ask.

"Your consort trusts the hound?"

"Yeah, I guess. He called him freaky at first, but he likes him now."

"So it wouldn't be that hard to lure him away, would it?"

"I guess not." I try to think. I used to be good at it. Since I've become a creature of the night, I rely more on feelings than brains.

Maybe I should think about that too. *Sigh.* "What you're saying makes sense, but I just don't feel like Bon Tom would hurt Logon."

"He might not think he's hurting Logon."

I hate it when logic works against me. You just can't fight it. The only people known to make logic-defying a cultural art are the Fundamentalist Baptists, but don't try it at home; the Fundamentalists have blind faith and thick skulls, and they're armed with self-righteousness. But I digress. Probably because my brain wants to explode.

I need to find Logon *now*! I don't know where he is, but I have the feeling I'm driving in the wrong direction. Ambrose's blood surges through me, hot and fierce, urging me to do something, *anything*. All the times I daydreamed about being a vampire mock me now. The angst-level of my life is now approaching Category 5 force.

"Maybe I should turn around."

"No, we're almost to Belleair. Let's at least trade vehicles."

"I'd feel kind of funny leaving Mr. Massey's car somewhere."

"Your consort is in danger, and you're worried about a borrowed car?"

"I was raised to respect other people's property, okay?"

"Here's the turn. Don't miss it."

"I see it. Settle down."

It turns out that Simon, that pig, has three awesome cars, but Ambrose is only interested in the silver Lotus Exige. He leaves me in the garage and goes in to get the keys. He says the keys are hanging in a little cabinet in the back hall, so he should be back by now. I must really be nervous because here he is. I notice he's got on a jacket he didn't have before. It pisses me off that he took the time to change when Logon's in trouble, but I'm actually too worried to bitch.

"At times like this, I miss Gordon," Ambrose says as I start the car.

"He liked sports cars?"

"No, he was our chauffeur."

THERE'S the Indian Rocks Beach sign and Vinnie hasn't called me yet. *Worried. I'm coming, Logon. Hang on.*

I SEE the glow of a large fire as I park on the broad shoulder. Orisha's drive is full of vehicles, and I hear the sound of several voices chanting to the beat of several drums. *Craptastic.* We seem to have arrived in the middle of Orisha's big ceremony.

"Phew! You can practically smell the gumbo," Ambrose says as he levers himself out of the low-slung Italian road sculpture. "Like low tide."

"Is there anything that pleases you?"

"I liked it when you bit me."

"You don't need to go around broadcasting that."

"Especially not to your consort?"

"I see you take my meaning."

"You young ones are so cute. You really believe in soul mates and eternal love, don't you?"

"Don't you?"

"Don't I wish." I think that's what Ambrose says, but we're around the side of the house now, and the drumming drowns him out. A couple of dozen people are swaying, shifting, and singing with the hypnotic rhythm, among them Vinnie and the M Squared crew. Orisha is naked to the waist, a bright length of fabric tied around slim hips flowing and flaring with the steps of the dance. Supple and graceful, Orisha bends and whirls in front of the fire with a rather large snake around her neck.

*Bon Tom!* I spot him beside the brick hearth holding a spray of orchids in one hand and a bottle of rum in the other. I can barely keep from shouting at him. Instead, I tap Ambrose's arm and start making my way around the outside of the circle. If Vinnie or my friends notice me, they don't show any sign. They're caught up in the spell of the music, and the ritual, and—unless someone ran over a skunk—some pretty heavy-duty weed.

The drumming is louder on this side of the circle, and I can hear Orisha's voice over the others. I don't recognize the language, but the longer I listen, the more I feel like I'm starting to understand the words. The snake slithers over Orisha's shoulders and torso, wrapping around her slender waist. Orisha reaches skyward, arms flung wide as if anticipating an embrace.

"Bon Tom," I whisper loudly.

Bon Tom's head turns my way, and he focuses on me. His eyes aren't Bon Tom's eyes. I take a step back and bump into Ambrose.

"Well, now. What do we have here?" Bon Tom's voice is deeper and slower, and his eyes are catching the light like a cat's. He's looking past me at Ambrose. At least, I think he is. Hard to tell with those mirror-eyes.

Ambrose moves around me like a panther around a tree trunk and locks eyes with Bon Tom. There's movement in my peripheral vision, and now Orisha is standing beside me.

"My lord Legba," Orisha says. "You've chosen a vessel."

Bon Tom doesn't look away from Ambrose while he answers Orisha. "Blessings on your people." He raises his hand and shakes it like he's flinging water from his fingers. "Let them know joy," he says.

The tempo of the music speeds up, and the dancers choose partners. The night presses close, soft like dark fur, sliding against skin in a feather-light caress. A light breeze off the water entices the leaves to rub against one another. Everything seems on the point of kindling into flame, but there's no threat in the premonition. This isn't a fire of destruction. It's the fire of passion that leads to creation. I know this as surely as if I'd read it on Wikipedia. When I manage to look away from Bon Tom, I see the dancers disappearing in couples, or just dropping to the lawn and getting busy in groups. I feel their need and their trust that the need will be satisfied under these trees. I feel the trees pulling energy from the air and the earth. I feel the earth turning under my feet. I feel a part of it all, connected, at one with the world around me.

Orisha takes my hand, and the snake slithers down her arm and around mine, linking us. I feel safe and open myself to the experience.

"Is the gate open, Papa?" Orisha says.

"The gate is open," Bon Tom answers in a voice like summer thunder.

"But you still here, and you ain't ridin' *me*."

Bon Tom's glowing eyes shift to Ambrose. "I felt an intriguing presence, and I was curious."

Orisha looks mucho unhappy. "What you want with him? He just a bloodsucker."

"No. He is something else."

"What?"

"I do not know."

Orisha tightens her grip on my hand. "You Legba. You there when Papa Limba split the first people into man and woman. Ain't nothin' you don't know."

Bon Tom leans really close to Ambrose and sniffs. "Lightning powder." He turns his head and looks at Orisha. "Why do I smell lightning powder?"

"Had some stolen from me. Could be this one know the thief. But why Bon Tom don't smell it before now?"

"Because this one is new sort of creature, his scent is unfamiliar. And he is not the only one. Someone is meddling with the nature of these children."

"Tell me what to do," Orisha says.

"Do as you have always done. Stay strong and give help to those that need it."

"You know I will, Papa. What about these *bébés*?"

"Did you take them to raise?"

"No, Papa, but you know how it is. Sweet young things got a way to my heart."

"That is not a bad thing."

"I hear you, Papa." Orisha smiles, and damned if I don't think Orisha's flirting with Legba... who's a god... and not in the figurative sense. I admire Orisha's balls.

Bon Tom puts his palm on Ambrose's cheek in a total grandfather move. "There is nothing to be done about this now. That gate is shut. But whoever is playing around with lives must stop."

"I hear you, Papa," Orisha says again. "I done put my mind to it."

"You're a good child." Bon Tom rests his hand on top of Orisha's dreadlocked mane, compressing the springy mass. "And a good mama. Take my blessings and the blessings of my brothers and sisters with you as you walk this world."

"Thank you." Orisha bows.

"And you are seeking something." Bon Tom focuses on me.

"My... Logon is gone. I need to find him."

"Open yourself. He is calling you. If you tear down all your fences, you will hear him."

"I feel open. Seriously. I feel connected to the plants and the ocean and everyone around me."

"Good. Now make the circle bigger. And then make it bigger. And bigger. Keep on until the circle is big enough to hold Logon."

"How do I do that?"

"First is desire."

"What?"

"You got to want it, cher." Bon Tom's eyes are his own again.

My feeling of being one with the universe drops off by an order of magnitude. "Legba's gone, isn't he?" *I'm the King of Obvious.*

"He gone," Orisha says. "But the congregation gonna feel the effect for a while yet. Let's work on your problem."

I'm thrilled to hear that Orisha's going to help me, but the red and blue lights strobing behind the house are distracting. "I think the cops are here," I say.

"Them heifers next door done called the *po*-lice!" Orisha spits.

"We got to get gone," Bon Tom says.

"Go on." Orisha shoves Bon Tom at me. "Take these *bébés* away from here."

"You come too."

"No, little brother. I got things to take care of. And a couple of biddies need they feathers singed. You go on. I meet up with you by and by."

Bon Tom is clearly reluctant to leave without Orisha, but he does it. All over the landscape, couples and groups of people are jumping to their feet and scrambling into clothes. A few with stronger survival instincts are running bare-assed across the neighboring properties with their clothes in their hands. I spot Vinnie literally hightailing it over a short stone wall, and then I get a glimpse of Barge's bumper as he dodges behind a clump of palm trees. I hope the cops don't get any of my friends. I'll feel like a real dick if they end up in jail because of me, but Bon Tom has quite a grip on my wrist, and he's determined to do as Orisha ordered. With Ambrose right behind us, Bon Tom leads me through the dense growth of elephant ear that nearly fills the space between the house and the one to the east of it. The ground is squishy and tries to suck my boots off with every step. Yeah, I know, I said *suck my boots off.* Go ahead and snicker. I'm not in the mood for levity, as Aunt Bootsy would say.

We slip by the cops—well, we are two vampires and some sort of werewolf after all—and make it to the Lotus. After putting it in neutral, we roll it a fair distance before we get in. Due to space constraints, the top is down and Ambrose is on Bon Tom's lap. I have no idea where we're going, but I'm starting the engine.

"You were wrong," I say to Ambrose.

He doesn't pretend he doesn't know what I'm talking about. "Yes, I was. I admit it."

I let it drop. "Do either of you have a glimmer of a notion where Logon is?"

"Why you don't do what Legba tell you?"

"I'm not sure how."

"Just be open."

"That's easy to say." Now I know how Luke felt when Obi-Wan told him to "stretch out with your feelings." How exactly does one do that?

"You got to be settled. Got to let all the noise go. Got to float like a cloud with no cares."

"Should I be driving when I attempt this?"

"No, cher, I reckon not. Not until you practice some."

"So we need a quiet place. I'm going back to the loft." I glance at Ambrose. "Is that cool with you, or do you need to be somewhere?"

"I'm in this for the duration," Ambrose says. "I'll explain to Simon later."

"Pull over here," Bon Tom says as we approach a rest area.

I pull the car into the empty lot and find a parking space at the opposite end from the bathrooms. Ambrose and Bon Tom get out, and Bon Tom heads straight for the picnic area. Me and Ambrose follow him to the concrete table and benches on a concrete slab under an aluminum pole barn shelter. Bon Tom slaps the table.

"Really?" I feel stupid, but I climb up and lie down.

Bon Tom and Ambrose sit on one of the benches with their backs against the table edge. They're keeping quiet, but the sounds of frogs, cicadas, and the wind in the tall grass fill up the night. I try to tune out individual noises and hear it as a screen of static. There's a kind of rhythm to it, a constant swell and lull like waves at sea. The table is hard and cold, but those perceptions are fading as I fall into the pre-doze state that's been so useful to me in all sorts of waiting rooms. I'd be able to fall asleep if Logon were with me.

My need for him spikes suddenly, seizing my nerve endings with white-hot pain. I miss him so much that it fucks up my thought processes. I'm in the grip of something that holds me so tightly that all I can do is exist and hold onto the hope that it'll eventually end. I've never felt this bad. I can't imagine how it could be worse.

Okay, now it's worse. Whoever's hacking into my skull with a rusty machete needs to stop *now*!

Bon Tom yells, "Holy Snakes!" as he spins around and grabs my head. He flips me over in time to save me from inhaling my spew. Viscous translucent fluid with a reddish tint shoots out of my mouth and splats on the concrete slab. Bon Tom wipes away the strings that cling to my mouth. I must look like King Kong bukkaked on me. But that's not important.

"Logon." My voice sounds like a really old man's, all hoarse and creaky and paper-thin. The pain squeezes me again, but I don't have anything else to throw up.

"You hear 'im, cher?"

"I... feel him."

"Which way?"

I let go of the urge to form thoughts. Something south of here is pulling at me. I resist focusing too hard on the spark at the edge of my senses. It's Logon. I don't doubt it for a nanosecond. He's in pain, and he's calling me.

"That way," I say, looking south as I jump off the table and collapse to the ground. "You might have to carry me to the car."

"Cain't fight evil weak as a kitten." Bon Tom scoops me off the ground and holds me like a baby. "You go on and have a little taste of Bon Tom. Put fire in your belly."

I've already broken my vow by drinking Ambrose's blood, and I need more energy right now. It's not a matter of willpower. If I don't drink, I won't be able to help Logon. That's the cold, hard heart of the matter. I've always said—mostly during role-playing games—that there's always a choice. Now I'm ready and willing to stipulate that there are situations where you don't have a choice; you have to do something you know is wrong, whether you want to or not. I never would have believed it last week, but there are some things more important than your ethics. Would I blow Richard Simmons to save Logon's life? I'd be on my knees in a second. Hell, I'd gobble Dubbya's wrinkled, white worm, and I consider him a somewhat mentally defective son of the devil. Okay, I think I've convinced myself.

Bon Tom's blood is rich and spicy-sweet, like real hot chocolate with a sprinkle of cayenne pepper, a deep, dark river winding under autumn leaves. I can feel my strength coming back with every mouthful I gulp down. And I realize I can feel his heart thudding away in his chest. I also realize that his heartbeat is fading. I don't want to, but I stop sucking.

Bon Tom sets me on my feet and reaches up to touch the wounds on his neck. "Feel better, cher?" he asks.

"Why are we standing around pulling our puds? Let's go get Logon."

I don't give a damn that it's almost dawn.

# CHAPTER NINE

"YOU know where this at, don't you?" Bon Tom says as I pull off the main road.

"This is Bob Massey's neighborhood," Ambrose says.

"And this his house," Bon Tom says as I turn off the lights on the driveway.

"This isn't right. Massey's just a... groupie."

I hear them, but I'm a guided missile now, and I can't talk even if I wanted to. I stalk—yeah, stalk—around to the garage. I get my fingertips between the bottom of the garage door and the pavement and peel it up like the lid of a sardine can. The garage is lit up, but no one's here. I pull the house door off the hinges and toss it aside.

"You badass, cher," Bon Tom drawls as he puts his head in the door and looks around. "You and princess go find the sweet thang. Bon Tom find his own way in."

"Fine." For no reason, I hug Bon Tom. He hugs me back and shoves me away before loping out of the garage. "Freakin' Han Solo," I say.

Ambrose surprises me by replying. "Wait until he finds out the princess is Luke's sister. What? I watch movies. TiVo rocks."

"Cut it out. I'm starting to like you."

A third voice joins in. "And how you feel about me?"

I know that voice. "Hi, Tibbie," I say as I walk into the kitchen.

Tibbie holds up the knife she's using to slice limes. "Don't you hi Tibbie me. Who invited you?"

"No one really."

"Then you can understand why I might think you trespassin' and put some holes in you."

"We're vampires," Ambrose says.

"Well, shit." Tibbie takes a drink of the clear liquid in the glass beside the limes. "Reckon it won't do me no good to call the cops neither."

"Why would you do that?" I ask. "I like you, and I thought you liked me."

"The boss havin' a private party tonight, and I *know* you ain't invited 'cause I'm the hostess."

"Tibbie." This is where I'd take a deep breath if I was still breathing. "Logon's in the basement, and I'm going to go get him. You can do whatever you want, but if you get in my way, I'm going through you."

"Hoo-wee! That's some real man-style talk now," Tibbie says. "What make you think your toot-toot in the basement?"

"I can feel him. Are you going to give me trouble or not?"

"Not." Tibbie puts down the knife and picks up a key. "Here you go," she says as she throws it to me. "Tell you the truth, I don't know what's goin' on in the basement, and I don't want to. But I can see you ain't lyin', and I don't hold with kidnappin'."

"Thanks, Tibbie." I run to the door that leads to the basement. The key works easily and the door swings open. Logon's distress beats at my brain like wings made of daggers. In the coffin room, I find another door and smash through it into a room that looks like a lounge bar. The door in the opposite wall is ajar. I'm through it in a second

Son of a rabid bitch! What the eff is Massey doing? What's with all the bags of blood? And what's he injecting himself with?

Massey sees me and makes an annoyed grimace. He glances at a lighted box in the corner of the ceiling. "How the hell'd you get in here without tripping the alarm? The LoJack on the Wagoneer should have set it off."

"We took my car." Ambrose moves from behind me.

Massey looks at Ambrose and his eyes glaze like Krispy Kreme's finest. If you look in the dictionary under craving, you'll see a picture of him. I'm staggered by the waves of rank lust pouring off him.

"Mr. Cornflower." Massey's got the classic preparing-to-kiss-ass posture.

I look at Ambrose.

"It's my last name," Ambrose says. His expression dares me to find it amusing.

"I just never thought about you having a last name," I say lamely.

"What brings you here?" Massey asks Ambrose. "I've been trying forever to get Lord Bonesteel to accept another invitation."

"Unlike some vampires, Simon prefers not to mingle with humans unless he's hungry. Which brings me to the reason for this visit. Where is Troy?"

"Troy?" Massey says, but he's already looked at the door to his right three times since we came in. I don't think he wants anyone going in there. Interesting.

As soon as I touch the knob, I know Logon's behind the door. His signal kind of cut out when I came down the stairs, but it's back now. I yank the knob assembly out of the door and pull it open.

*I'm going to kill Massey.*

A lifetime of pacifism—barring the virtual violence of video games—negated in an instant. The sight of Logon strapped to a hospital bed with fresh fang marks on his throat dredges up the primal instinct to kill whoever harmed my mate. But first, those restraints are coming off.

"Vlad!" The look in Logon's eyes when he sees me bending over him makes me feel like I could reach up and pluck a star like a flower in a meadow.

"I'll have you loose in a second. Are you okay?"

"He made Troy bite me."

"What?"

"Massey. He forced Troy to drink my blood by starving him. Massey's the inventor, not Troy."

"Get away from there," Massey says behind me. *Is he kidding?*

I pull Logon off the bed into my arms and kiss him. I notice right away that something's different. He's Logon, but he's not the same Logon as when I last saw him.

"What did he do to you?" I demand to know.

"You're going to screw everything up," Massey says.

Why is this douchebag still drawing breath to talk with? Why the hell isn't Ambrose taking care of Massey? I look around. Where the hell is Ambrose?

"Just hold still," Massey says from closer than I thought. "This is for your own good."

A needle sinks into my flesh with a cold sting. Logon's lips are moving, but I think he's speaking Klingon or something. Whoa. I feel really—

"THERE. Now everything is back the way the way it should be. In fact, it's even better." I hear Massey's voice from somewhere behind me.

"Vlad?" Logon's voice sounds strained.

I want to go to him, but I'm as limp as a WASP's linguine. I'm using all my willpower, but I can't even blink. Where the hell did Ambrose go?

"Vlad, are you okay?" Now Logon sounds really worried, and I want to answer him. I want to soothe him and make everything all right for him. I'm such a sap.

"He can't speak," Massey says. "Hang on a second."

Massey's shadow falls over me, and then he sticks a hypo in my neck. In less than two seconds, I can blink, talk, and move my fingers and toes, but that's about it. I manage to turn my head on the flat pillow, and I can see Logon. He's back on the bed where I found him, strapped down like a violent mental patient.

"Sometimes I really wish I had an assistant," Massey says. "But there's nobody I trust enough to help me with this. Not since Troy double-crossed me."

"What's your game, you sick bastard?" It always bugs me in movies when the trussed-up psycho-killer's victim pleads with him. Obviously, the twisted asshole is going to torture and kill you no matter what, so why waste your breath begging? Why not screw with him? Now that I have to put my money where my mouth is, I'm proud I'm not whining. I just have to remember that it doesn't matter what I say. This psycho has an agenda to complete that I can't alter unless I'm free. "And what did you shoot me up with?"

"Oh, I've developed a number of interesting formulas," Massey says. "When you broke in, I was about to inject myself with a mixture that heightens human senses and increases vitality. It has the opposite effect on vampires. Lucky I had that hypo handy, huh?"

"Let Logon go."

"Not a chance. I went through a lot to get him, and he's perfect. As perfect as the other one."

"You mean Ambrose?" I'm guessing, but I think it's a pretty good guess.

"Yes. He's absolutely perfect, but he... he scares me a little, even though I'm the one that made him perfect. Troy may have given him the formula, but I developed it."

"Say what?"

"I don't want to get into a monologue, but I *am* kind of proud of what I've achieved."

"I'm riveted. Please go on." I can lay on the snark when I have to, which probably comes as no surprise this far into my story.

"I should start near the beginning. I won't go back to my childhood, but a little history won't hurt." While Massey talks, he fusses with the sheet that covers Logon. "I met Troy in 1976. He'd lost his consort and been on a seven-year bender when I stumbled over him in a bar in Clearwater. He was trying to pick up one of the golf widows, and I recognized him for what he was right away. As soon as I realized I had a real vampire in my sights, my life changed. Making money used to be my religion; now I make money to support my new life."

"Get to the part where you need to keep my boyfriend in bondage."

"I've always admired vampires, but I don't want to be one. There are just too many drawbacks. What I want is to live as a vampire. I want the immortality, the enhanced body, and the sharper senses. I figured there had to be a way to isolate something in vampire blood that would turn a human into a vampire without the dying and blood drinking part." Massey turns Logon's head to the side and fastens a strap across his forehead. "Troy was very interested. He could see the potential for a consort that would live for centuries. So he let me have some of his blood to work with, and, after twenty-something years, I found the formula. The only thing I can't lick is the aging, but it occurs very, very slowly."

I think about that for a second. Surely it's not a bad thing to want to keep your loved one for as long as possible. Of course, Massey did kidnap my boo. That's definitely a bad thing.

"But you couldn't do it on your own, could you?" I say. "You needed Orisha's help. That's why Troy stole the lightning powder."

"I can see you're trying to piss me off. Don't bother. I'm distilling a new batch—with your blood added to Troy's—and nothing is going to interfere with that. I'm so close to perfecting the elixir." Massey pauses. "If you'll excuse me for a few minutes, I need to check the extractor. Gotta be quick with the other running around loose somewhere."

"Before you go, why do you keep calling Ambrose *the other*?"

"He's a human vampire," Massey says from the doorway. "There are only two."

"What?" I say, but the door closes and Massey is gone. "Logon."

"Yeah?"

"Are you okay?"

"Short or long answer?"

"Just tell me what happened. I've been going crazy worrying about you."

"Really?" Is it me, or does Logon sound a little pleased? "So anyway, Massey found us with the LoJack in the Wagoneer. Bon Tom left right after I got up because he wanted to be at the drum thing at Orisha's. I wanted a mocha latte, and I knew you wouldn't be up for a few minutes, so I went to the Barney's on the next block. Massey grabbed me when I came back. He brought me here, and he's been making Troy drink my blood every couple of hours. He keeps injecting me with something that he says makes my body produce blood faster. Shit. I feel so effing weak."

He sounds weak. I ache all over with the need to hold him.

"It's funny." Logon's voice is a whisper now. "The whole time, I was scared, but not really. I knew you'd come and save me."

"I tried. Didn't turn out too well."

"Maybe we aren't free, but at least we're not alone."

"There is that."

"Don't be a downer."

And I thought I couldn't love him any more than I already do. He's not going the "woe is me" route. He's trying to cheer *me* up. "I love you," I say.

"Love you too. So... Ambrose came with you?"

"Yeah, Bon Tom too. They're around somewhere so don't give up hope."

"I haven't."

"Yeah, I could tell. You're amazing."

"Get bent, fag," Logon says fondly.

The door opens and Bon Tom slinks in.

"We were just talking about you," I say.

"Had to wait 'til Frankie Stein turn he back." Bon Tom slices the straps off Logon like he did with mine at Simon's place. Massey must really trust his potions, because he didn't bother to tie me up.

"Why you layin' there?" Bon Tom asks.

"Massey shot me up with something. I can't move."

"So I got to carry your ass?"

Logon takes a couple of steps toward me and almost loses his balance.

"Easy there, Blondie." Bon Tom catches him and gently pushes him onto my bed.

"You can't carry both of us," I say. "Take Logon out of this hell hole."

"I do that, but I don't leave you with that crazy man."

"Have you seen Ambrose recently?"

"He no help. I think maybe he in on it."

"He thought *you* were in on it."

"Do tell." Bon Tom's eyes have a gleam that doesn't bode well for Ambrose. "What the plan now, boss?"

"Take Logon somewhere safe and come back for me."

"If that what you want." Bon Tom lifts Logon in his arms. "Be back quick as I can."

"Wait!" Logon says. "Just one kiss?"

Bon Tom leans over so Logon can kiss me. Logon's lips are like marshmallows made of silk. It's hard to let him go.

The door opens again and Massey walks in. He sees what's going on and runs back out. Bon Tom starts for the door with Logon, but Massey comes busting back in. This time he has a gun in his hand. Without warning or hesitation, he shoots Bon Tom. Bon Tom goes down, taking Logon with him. This is not good. I need to move.

Massey walks over and lifts Logon onto his bearish shoulder. Without a word, he hurries out of the room. In another minute, I hear his footsteps on the stairs. Son of an F-word! I need to get off my back and go after them.

After an intense effort, I manage to fall out of the bed. Progress! Now that I'm down here, I might as well get crawling. It's not easy. I have to kind of bear down hard on my fingertips and haul my useless body along like a sack of wet cement, sort of like horizontal chin-ups. I've always had good upper-body strength, but damned if this doesn't qualify as grueling. Doesn't matter. I don't care if I wear the skin of my fingertips to the bone. Massey has Logon and is planning to do who knows what to him.

Halfway across the outer room I can see into an open door on my left. At the end of a short corridor is another open door. Framed in that doorway is Troy Sanger. He's strapped down to a bed with tubes running from his veins into bags. His hair and eyes are dull and he looks like a bag of bones. Did you expect that? I didn't think so. Me either.

What an anticlimax, right? I've been looking for him so hard, and now that I find him, he's all broken-looking. Even if I had the strength or the breath, I wouldn't feel like confronting him. He's pathetic. I'm going to concentrate on getting to Logon.

Shiz! The effing stairs. How in blue hell am I going to get up the stairs?

"Look at you, white boy."

If I roll my eyes all the way up, I can see the witchy, pointed toes of Tibbie's stiletto-heeled boots. "Help," I say.

"I hope you don't think little ol' me can drag your butt up them stairs."

"You're smart. Think of something."

"Hmph."

"Please?"

I hear Tibbie's footsteps tapping away on the marble tiles. Fuck me sideways. Okay. Maybe I can lift my hand as high as the first step. Nope. Okay. Try again. *Denied.* Try again. Fail. Try again. Fuck! Fuck! Fuckety-fuck-fuck! I've tried really hard to not to lose my temper, or resort to cuss words, but I'm down to my last nerve.

"Miss Tiburon thinks you might want some help?" Ambrose says from the top of the stairs.

"Get your prissy, piss-gargling butt down here and help me!"

"Since you ask so nicely." Ambrose throws my earlier words to him in my face, but he's coming down the stairs, so I let it pass.

"Massey has Logon," I say. "He shot Bon Tom. Troy's back there."

Ambrose twitches. "The one place I didn't look," he mutters.

"Hey, how about a hand?"

"What do you want me to do?"

"Sweet Jesus," Tibbie says. "Y'all bound and determined to make me break a nail. White boy, just set tight, and I'll come get you. Whiter boy, you get after Bob."

"What about Troy?" Ambrose says.

"I'll see to him," Tibbie answers.

Ambrose is up the stairs so fast I don't see him move. Tibbie comes down and squats beside me. She lifts my arm and hangs it around her neck. With a shoulder in my armpit, Tibbie slowly rises, taking me with her.

"Ain't no earthly way I'm gonna make it up them steps with you," Tibbie says after a few seconds of flailing and fighting for balance.

"Yeah you can. I'll lean against the wall and take the weight off you."

"I got a better idea. Why don't I drag you back in there and you drink Bon Tom's blood? Then you can fly up them steps if you got a mind to."

"Suck a dead guy's blood?"

Tibbie glances through the doorway. "Dead people don't move around."

"The hell they don't."

"Oh yeah, I keep forgettin' you a vampire. Bon Tom ain't dead though."

Despite my bitching, Tibbie half carries me to where Bon Tom lies in a disturbed pool of blood. Those Siberian eyes don't look as bright as usual.

"Look," Tibbie says as she lets me slide to the floor. "Plenty of blood here."

The compulsion to drink is almost overwhelming, but I can't do it. He's wounded, and it just doesn't seem right somehow.

"Go on," Bon Tom says weakly. "Drink."

His white shirt is red, and I can see blood pumping from a group of holes between his chest and shoulder. How in the hell had Massey managed to shoot him there without hitting Logon? *Shudder.*

"Come on, cher. Let Bon Tom be useful one more time."

"Didn't know vamps could cry," Tibbie says. "Look like your eyes bleedin'."

I ignore the comment and crawl closer to Bon Tom. He takes my hand in bloody fingers.

"Don't you feel guilty now. None of this your fault."

"I don't think I can do this."

"You got to if you wanna save the sweet thang."

He's right. I put my mouth on his neck and suck. He's lost a lot of blood, but I don't need much. I can feel it being converted into energy and flowing into every cell. I wouldn't be surprised if I'm emitting a visible glow.

Hey! You know what? Bon Tom doesn't have to be lost. I can Turn him. But I don't have time. I have to go after Logon. But I can't let Bon Tom die like this. Why does it always come down to the hero— well, it is *my* story after all—having to make a choice between a bud and his main squeeze, or his loyal companion and true love, if you prefer. It happened to Luke Skywalker. It happened to Batman. Now it's happening to me.

Did I already say fuck-fuck-fuckety-fuck-fuck? Yeah? Thought so.

"Bon Tom, do you want to go on?" I ask.

"I'm dead, cher."

"I can Turn you."

"No time."

I'm taking that as permission. As fast as I can, I gulp down what little blood is still in his veins. I feel his heart stop, and I do what Troy did to me. I lean in and kiss him, letting blood trickle from my mouth to his, and then I abandon him to his fate.

Well, Tibbie's with him, so at least he's not alone like I was.

Did that sound whiny?

# CHAPTER TEN

NOISES from the garage. A shout of pain. That's Ambrose. *Vamp warp speed, Captain.*

Ambrose is lying on the concrete, something I know he'd never do if he was conscious. Massey is backing the Lincoln out of the accordioned garage door. I don't have to see Logon to know he's in the backseat. Massey looks surprised when I pull the passenger door off the car, and he jams his foot on the gas. The Lincoln's rear bumper hits the bottom of the ruined garage door, but this car's a tank and it starts tearing the door off the tracks. The tires are smoking and leaving rubber on the concrete, and I'm slowly but inevitably being dragged outside.

Did I mention daybreak was a little while ago?

My foot is getting closer and closer to the line of natural light coming under the door. And then the sunlight is creeping up my boot onto my pant leg. It feels warm, but not uncomfortable. Of course, it hasn't touched bare skin yet. I get a grip on the frame and pull myself inside the car. Massey slams on the brakes, opens the driver door, tumbles out, and rolls to his feet like a Weeble. Being flung against the dashboard of a 1963 Lincoln is the definition of bone-jarring, but I don't have time to pass out. What kind of wussy vampire am I?

I crawl out the other side of the car, and the sun on my face goes from warm to hot stove in about three seconds. I can feel it cooking me. I pull my hands inside my sleeves and duck my head, but I can feel the rays burning my scalp. I forget all that as Massey shoulders Logon's limp body and starts down the drive at a heavy trot. *Shit.*

*The car. I can use the car.*

I jump back in the Lincoln and see that Massey has taken the keys with him. Oh well. I pull my shirt up over my head and go after Massey again. He's getting smaller, and I'm getting slower. I've taken a dozen steps when I hit my knees and fall onto my face. No matter how much I want to keep going, the sun is killing me.

"Idiot," Ambrose says as he leans over and lifts me off the ground. "Stay," he says as he puts me in the Lincoln's trunk.

I don't have the strength to answer, but I watch through the crack he left as he runs after Massey. He's a beautiful thing in motion, all long, graceful legs and flowing hair. His skin is starting to smoke as he hits Massey in the middle of the back. Logon goes flying into the shrubs and disappears from sight. No, it's my sight that's fading. It's black around the edges. I can only see what's directly in front of me, which is Ambrose grappling with Massey. *Thank you, Ambrose, you prissy, conceited pain in the ass. Thank you from the bottom of my heart. You're going to end up as a used briquette to give Logon a chance to get away.* I don't know why he's doing it, but I'm grateful. Me, the other piece of charcoal. I'm afraid to move in case lumps of me fall off like pit-roasted pork. Yeah, I know that's gross, but that's what I'm thinking so you get to hear it. Lucky you.

*Great goddess and all the gods of earth and fiction, please let Logon be all right.*

I figure a prayer couldn't hurt, right?

Great goolies, this hurts, and it's getting exponentially worse. If you've ever been badly sunburned, you can multiply that by a googol, and you'll be in roughly the same zip code. Some hero, right? It's the victim that's always found in the trunk of the car.

The pain is making me delirious. I see Massey trundling down the drive dragging Ambrose, and then Vinnie pops up in front of him. She plants her platform boot in his crotch, and he doubles over like he's spotted a hundred-dollar bill on the ground. Barge grabs Massey by the back of the neck and hauls him up so Carlyle can punch him. So glad they're not in jail in my hallucination. And ever so glad they're kicking Massey's ass. *Smackdown*! Told you up front I'd destroy anyone that tried to hurt Logon.

Now I know I'm tripping because that's my Aunt Bootsy talking to Orisha; I'd know that red hair anywhere. Fuck me, I can't believe how bad I hurt. It's not a steady burn now. It flares and dies back in waves, getting worse with each cycle. My vision is really cloudy, and it occurs to me that my eyeballs are poached. Sorry. I can't help it; I have a gruesome mind.

*Logon*! His head is poking out of the shrubbery. He gets to his feet awkwardly because his hands are tied behind him, but he looks okay as far as I can tell. He has leaves in his hair. *My Elf.*

I'm glad he's the last thing I see.

# CHAPTER ELEVEN

A WOMAN stands over me, a redheaded, freckle-speckled woman of medium height with hips slightly wider than her shoulders. It's my Aunt Bootsy, or as she refers to herself, The Spinster. I didn't mention that before? I can't believe I didn't. I think it's a totally cool nickname: The Spinster. Sounds like she'd give Batman a run for his money. I bet she would too.

"What are you doing here?" I look around. "Here" seems to be my old bedroom at my mom's.

"Who do you think hauled your bacon out of the fire?"

"How would I know? I was busy being destroyed by ultraviolet rays."

"Don't whine. It's ugly."

"Yes, ma'am." I sit up a little, hold out my hand, and inspect it. All the brittle black flakes are gone. My skin is smooth, without a single blemish that I can see.

"Relieved?"

"Hell yeah. I was triple extra crispy. I'm surprised to be some version of alive."

"It took a lot of energy from a lot of good people to heal you. You be sure you thank them."

"It would help to know who they are."

"Don't sass me."

"No, ma'am." I can't stand it anymore. "Where's Logon?"

"With your mama."

"Not sure how I feel about that."

"You hush up! What kind of thing is that for a son to say?"

"You know I love Mom, but I like to introduce the idea of her slowly, so my friends get used to the concept before I spring her on them. You know what she's like. A freaking force of nature."

"Damn sure is. And you're her blood and bone."

"You're going to have to explain that one."

"You're from good stock. Hard to kill."

"At least on one side, right?"

"Don't talk bad about your daddy. I know your mama must've told you that Dong-ho Gae never wanted a baby. He never even wanted a wife. He just wanted to be a citizen and a chef. Nothing wrong with that. He didn't try to deceive anyone. So he wanted something and Vix wanted something and they both got it. I'd call that a good bargain."

"I didn't get a dad."

"Whining again? Didn't me and Vix teach you how to throw a baseball and swing a bat? Didn't we shoot hoops with you? Didn't we go to all your soccer practices and games? Didn't we blast aliens with you and build forts and go camping? Didn't we tell you straight up about growing pubes and that something besides pee was going to come out of your pecker?"

"Yeah, you did. I just can't help but wonder though, you know?"

"I know, sweetheart. Truth is everyone has something they wonder about. Mine's a guy named Charlie Farkash. Dated him for a whole skiing season when I worked at Sugarbush. We were crazy about each other, but I was afraid it wouldn't last back in the real world. When he asked me to marry him, I turned him down. It was almost thirty years ago, and I have regrets to this day. I wonder what my life would be like, if I'd have grandchildren...."

"Thanks. That really cheered me up."

"Rascal." Aunt Bootsy tousles my hair. "I'm really glad you weren't lost to us."

"So I guess Mom knows?"

"That you're a vampire? Of course."

"How'd she take it?"

"I was too busy helping her save you to get an opinion."

"Where is she now?"

"With your Logon."

"*My* Logon, huh?"

"Isn't that what he is?"

"Yeah." I grin. And I gush like a fourteen-year-old girl with a crush. I can't help it. "You're really gonna like him. He's amazing."

"I know he is. I've had almost two days to get to know him."

"What?"

"You think burns like yours heal overnight?" Aunt Bootsy shakes her head. "Took two nights." She combs her fingers through my hair. "I'm real proud of you, Cy."

"For what?"

"For being such a good example of a person."

"Thanks but I doubt society agrees with you. I'm not only gay, I'm a gay vampire."

"Screw society. We've always made our own society, haven't we?"

"Yes, ma'am." I'm feeling better by the second, but I don't take anything for granted around my female relatives. "You think I could get up now?"

"You talking about a boner or getting out of bed?"

*I love my Aunt Bootsy.*

"I put some clean clothes for you over here on the chest. Come on out when you're ready. Sun's been down nearly an hour, and you must be curious about what happened after you passed out in Bob Massey's driveway." She shakes her head and makes a little noise with her tongue against her teeth. "Imagine him mixed up in this kind of business."

I let her give me a hand, and then I hug her before she leaves me alone to get dressed.

RESPLENDENT in a pair of Mom's orange overalls and a T-shirt with the message "No Kill Zone" in lime green on pink, I am reunited with my pack, which is what I've decided to start calling my peeps. I thought about calling them my pride, but it doesn't roll off my tongue right. Flock is out because that's Simon's name for his family. Troop has a nice sound, but too many military connotations, not to mention the whole baboon thing. Crew and posse are too trendy, so I settled on pack. It's not very original, but you can't go wrong with a classic. Besides, when I Googled it on my phone, I couldn't find a definitive name for a group of dragons. They were all good names—clan, flight, rage of dragons—but I don't like the fact that people can't agree on one that's most correct. Yeah, anal, I know, but that's how I roll.

Aunt Bootsy hadn't mentioned it, so I was a little surprised to see Ambrose in the living room of my mom's ranch house. He's sitting on the afghan-covered couch next to Bon Tom, and I can't detect even a single drop of condescension between them. Vinnie is in the comfy armchair directly across the coffee table from the sofa, talking while the guys listen. I knew Logon wasn't here before I came in, but I'm still let down. Why isn't he at my side?

"Hey, boss!" Vinnie springs up and hugs me tight. As I sink into her cleavage, I reflect on the blessing of having a friend who took my new lifestyle in stride and stood by me with a loyalty I haven't really earned yet. "You look good as new."

"Glad to hear it." Especially since I *still* don't have a reflection. I wonder if there could be some kind of potion for that. *Yikes!* This is probably how Troy got involved with Massey. "Thanks." I'm sure she knows I'm thanking her for more than the hug. "Wish I could see myself."

"Why don't you get someone to draw you?" Vinnie says.

Damn, she's brilliant. Why didn't I think of that?

Ambrose and Bon Tom are on their feet and patting my shoulders. I feel absurdly touched.

"Where's Logon?" I ask.

Vinnie takes my hand. "He said to tell you to relax and he'd see you when he's finished talking with your mom. She's just as cool as I remember."

I have a cool mom. I know that now, but when I was little having a cool mom wasn't always a good thing. Sometimes it meant that you were "the weirdo's kid." But that was a long time ago. I'm over it. No, really, I am. *Shut up.*

I want to go look for Logon, but if he wants me to wait, I guess I should respect that. It's not *all* about me. "Okay, I want to hear everything that happened after the garage. So we'll start with you, Ambrose."

"Massey turned a portable sun lamp on me. Can you imagine? I'm not a total vampire anymore, but it hit me like I'd run full tilt into a brick wall."

"He was a cunning asshole. I have to give him that."

"After the police found all that blood in his basement, they took a hard look at Bob Massey," Vinnie says. "He's going away for a long time, and I have a feeling the other convicts are going to think he's weird. Might be hard for him to make friends."

"I'll cry later. What about the Metro crew? Everyone all right?"

"Yeah. They had a blast, but they had to be at work, so…."

"Excellent. Remind me to do something nice for them. And Ambrose, I owe you a big thanks for stopping Massey. I'd sure hate to lose Logon."

"I'll think of a way for you to pay me back."

"Could you think of something now? The suspense would kill me otherwise."

"There might be something you could do for me. I've broken it off with Simon, but I'm not cut out for a single life. I need an alpha, and no rule says you can't have two consorts, or as many as you want."

My expression is exceedingly amusing, to judge by the laughter of my friends.

"I'm playing with you," Ambrose says. "Though I wouldn't say no to a partnership with you."

"I only need one consort."

"Relax. I already have someone."

"You do?" I look at Bon Tom.

"Of course he does." Vinnie says. "Duh, Vlad. Have you forgotten Troy?"

"Troy?"

"You know. The guy you've been chasing to hell and back?"

I give Vinnie the look I save for customers who ask me where to find Britney's new CD. "Why is everyone disrespecting me now?"

"Mostly to see the look on you face, cher," Bon Tom says.

"Some minions you are." I reach over and pat Ambrose's hand. "I'm glad you're going to be okay," I say. "And I'm glad you don't look like you got burned too badly."

"I have more resistance to sunlight than a full vampire."

"How's that work anyway?"

"I'm partly human again, thanks to Massey and Troy's formula. My blood is nourishing, and I can walk in daylight, among other things denied to a full vampire."

"Well, slap my ass and call me Sally. It worked?"

"Beautifully. What a pity the police have taken everything from Massey's laboratory."

"Yeah. A pity. So you're what Massey called a human vampire."

"A rather unique creature," Ambrose says. "Though our Bon Tom can claim the same."

"You're a human vampire too?" I bug my eyes at Bon Tom a little. It's childish, but I can't break myself of the habit.

"Hell no, cher. I'm what Bonesteel try to make when he Turn Gordon. Bon Tom a werevamp."

"So I guess there's some sort of rule against doing that?"

"Bon Tom don't grow up with the Law, but he learn 'bout it. Both peoples, vampire and were, say in the beginning they don't Turn each other."

"Why?"

Ambrose answers. "Because when it's done right, it creates a being so powerful that he or she could subjugate all others."

"Oops." I look at Bon Tom. "So when do you take over the world?"

"Don't want the world, cher."

"Fortunately, Bon Tom doesn't have an aggressive nature. He only fights when he has to, not for dominance." Ambrose gives Bon Tom the kind of smile you save for people you love and respect. *Well, well, Troy better watch his step or he could find himself on his own.*

"Where's Troy now?"

"In the spare bedroom," Aunt Bootsy says as she comes in from the kitchen. "He's going to need some time before he's a hundred percent again."

"I'm thinking about taking him to Switzerland," Ambrose says. "A few months of rest, mountain air, and my blood, and he'll be healed."

"I'd kind of like to talk to him," I say.

"He's very weak," Ambrose says, but I can translate. What he's really saying is "please don't hurt him."

"You really love him?" I feel like I have the right to ask.

"We don't have what you have with Logon, but I hope that we will. We each fill a need in the other, and that's not a bad beginning, I think."

"You said he lost his consort."

"They were together for fifteen years when Dewayne developed diabetes. The condition made things very difficult for them, but they stayed together. Even when Troy had to find... other sources of blood. Then Dewayne went blind and lost circulation in his limbs. He developed pneumonia in a hospital and died within a few hours."

I can't think of any adequate words, so I don't say anything.

"Troy changed, as you can imagine. For a long time, he didn't care about anything. And then he met Massey."

"You're making it really hard for me to hate him," I say.

"He was desperate when he found you. Bon Tom was on his heels and he panicked. He sensed the potency of your blood, and he didn't stop to think about what he was doing. He needed your blood very badly, but he didn't mean to drain you."

"Well," I say, and then because I have chronic foot-in-mouth disease, I continue. "Why did you want me to kill Troy if you like him so much?"

"I didn't want you to kill him."

"You said—"

"I know what I said. I had to pretend I hated him to keep Simon from killing him. I couldn't look for him myself, and I thought if you had a good enough reason, you'd find him for me. Barring that, I could at least misdirect you and those who followed your trail. I never imagined that Massey was holding Troy prisoner. A human holding a vampire captive…. No, I would never have thought it possible."

"How did…?"

"Troy requested an audience with Simon. When I saw him, I knew I was going to cheat on Simon. It was a new feeling, a little bit scary, not boring at all. In a matter of days, I was meeting him at a hotel. It was wonderful, but it wasn't enough. I wanted to be his, not Simon's, and I saw a way for his potions to give us a lord/consort bond."

"He made your blood mortal again."

Ambrose nods. "And then he bit me."

Before I can say anything, Aunt Bootsy speaks up. "If you're interested," she says, "Your mom and Logon are coming in from the barn. You can go meet them if you want."

"Excuse me," I say as I bolt for the door.

I'm so jazzed I don't realize Ambrose is with me until I stop by the honeysuckle trellis to watch the two people I love most in the world walking toward me. The yard lights are on, hundreds of strands of tiny white Christmas tree lights woven through the trees, fences, and hedges. Mom's fairyland. Her coppery hair and his pale blondness catch the light like nets of silk. I guess it's true that love makes poets of us all, no matter how bad our poems are.

"Not all of Massey's actions resulted in evil," Ambrose whispers in my ear. "He used Logon for his own ends, but he gave Logon something in exchange."

"What are you talking about?"

"He's like me now. He's a human vampire, but a perfect hybrid. I'm a vampire who was returned to a half humanity, but he's a mortal granted an immortal's strengths." Ambrose continues speaking as I watch Logon come closer. "He's more aware now, faster, and he heals more quickly. He'll age so slowly that one hundred years will be like one. And you can still share the drinking of blood."

"Does that mean what I think it does?"

"Yes. The feelings will still be as intense when you drink from him, even deeper actually."

"Yowzah," I say softly.

"Yowzah, indeed. It wasn't easy for me to leave Troy in Massey's dungeon to go after Logon, but I had to."

"Why?"

"Because I know what it feels like to love someone that much. I'm going to find Bon Tom now and coax him to hunt with me. I hope you have a pleasant evening."

And he's gone like a tomcat when the front door opens. I misjudged him, but then again, he wanted me to, so…. I can hear Mom and Logon's voices.

I move from behind the thick vines, and Logon sees me. He says something to my mom and starts sprinting toward me. *Vamp warp speed.* My arms go around Logon, savoring the sweet, solid weight of him, his warmth, and his scent. I want a kiss, but I don't want to change my position, which we might as well call "the starfish." I'm wrapped around Logon, clamped onto him, absorbing the unique vibe that he radiates, the one that says I'm not alone: I'm loved.

"Can I get some of that?"

"Mom." I manage to peel myself off Logon long enough to hug my mom. "Are you losing weight?" I say. Mom and Aunt Bootsy, the Crittenden girls, are shaped exactly the same, and both fluctuate between 110 and 130 pounds. Mom appears to be on a slim cycle. It sort of points up how long it's been since I saw her. "Sorry I haven't been by in a while."

"We'll talk about that later, puddin'. I think we have more important things on the table right now. First, I know you know this, but I want to say it. I'll never be ashamed of you for what you are, and I'll always love you."

"Great. Now you're making me cry in front of my boyfriend."

"As if he cares."

"I know, right? Isn't he amazing?"

"He surely is." Mom smiles at Logon.

"I can't believe how lucky I am that Vinnie picked him. Love at first bite."

Logon and my mom groan loudly, almost in harmony.

"Lame," Logon pronounces.

"And do you really think it was luck?" Mom says.

"I'm guessing you're going to go with destiny for a thousand," I say.

"Of course. There's no other explanation for why the two of you would find each other. The stars were in just the right places, mark my words."

"So do I sacrifice a goat or what? I don't want destiny to think I'm not grateful."

"Smart-ass. You better not let the goats hear you."

"The pens are too far away."

"I can't believe all the animals you have here." Logon adroitly changes the subject.

"Someone has to look after the unwanted," Mom says.

When I was two, Mom took the money from selling the patents to a couple of her inventions—like the collapsible ring lawn and leaf plastic bag stand—and turned the farm she inherited into a refuge. She eventually had to hire a full-time, qualified staff, which wasn't cheap, and then there was the food. So instead of growing up as a spoiled rich kid who got everything he wanted, I grew up as a child who got everything he needed and a few things that could never be bought with money.

Sure, my childhood was weird by normal standards. I had no dad, and I literally lived in a zoo. But I had a mom with a heart so big that she used her wealth to rescue discarded animals instead of living in a mansion. With servants. And a really big pool. And shopping sprees. You know, that actually sounds pretty good. Just kidding. Sort of.

"What did you see?" I ask Logon as I put my arm around his shoulders. He slips his arm around my waist and the world is a very fine place.

"Oh man. Let's see: llamas, alpacas, a cougar, emus, horses, donkeys, sheep, goats, dogs, and about a million cats. You're so lucky you got to grow up here."

"Yeah. You're right." I smile at my mom. "It's pretty special."

"That touches me, puddin', but if you ever go after someone like Simon Bonesteel or Bob Massey again without talking to me first, I'll tan your hide."

"It honestly didn't occur to me. Are you going to tell me how Aunt Bootsy knew to show up at Massey's place?"

"Do you think an entity like Legba can pay a visit to Central Florida without me or Bootsy feeling it and doing a little checking?"

"I don't know."

"Son, what do you think me and Bootsy mean when we say we're witches?"

"You follow Wicca, right? It's like being outside naked and praying to trees?"

"I blame myself for your ignorance. If you want, you can come and learn alongside Logon."

"What?"

"Witchcraft. What do you think we're talking about?"

"I don't know, Mom. I get fidgety during rituals."

"Magic is nothing more than focusing the will in tune with the forces of nature, but the will must be honed and taught to coax the desired response." Mom smiles at Logon again. "And it helps to be born with the soul of a reincarnated witch."

"So you're telling me magic is real?"

"What? Vampires are real but magic isn't?"

"Good point." I lean over and kiss my mom's forehead. "Thanks for fixing me, by the way."

"Bootsy gets a lot of the credit. And Logon, of course."

I kiss Logon's forehead. "Thanks, babe," I say.

"My first act of magic," Logon says proudly.

"Excuse me?"

"Did you really not catch on yet that Logon's a witch?"

"Warlock," I correct her automatically.

"Actually, in the grove my coven is part of, we just call ourselves witches, whether we're male or female. It's more equal that way."

I look into Logon's eyes. They don't look any different. They're still dark and velvety like the eyes of a deer that stares at you for a long time before it decides to go bounding off.

"A witch? Really?"

"You didn't notice the extra nipple?" Mom says.

"Well, yeah, I did. So?"

"There are some things that witches don't talk about, the kinds of things we've managed to convince people are just folklore."

"Like what? I swear if you tell me you can fly on a broom, I'll... I don't know what I'll do."

"Don't be silly. Come on, let's go inside. I'm starving, and I'll bet the two of you are hungry too."

"Logon and I might need some alone time," I say.

"I had an idea you might. Tell you what. Why don't I go on ahead?"

"Yeah, good idea. It's really nice out tonight."

"See you at the house," Mom says as she walks away. "By the way, I *do* worship naked, or skyclad, as I prefer to call it."

"Thanks for the visual," I call after her. "So," I say, as I pull Logon close, inhaling that scent that's as intoxicating as booze used to be. "What's on the menu?"

# CHAPTER TWELVE

HEY, you're back. Cool. It's been a while, exactly a year and a day since I woke up at Mom's and found out everything had turned out all right for everyone... well, almost everyone.

Bob Massey won't be back on TV anytime soon. After the prosecutors finally figured out what to charge him with, he was swiftly convicted and sentenced. Vinnie said it looked like the judge threw up in her mouth a little when the multiple charges were read. All his assets were seized, and control of them went to an illegitimate daughter no one knew he had. She sold the porno side of the business to a cartel of former employees headed by Tiburon Alou. I heard the daughter used the money to go study voles in the Andes. Pretty neat, huh?

Vinnie started her own business. She's a wedding planner now, and she caters to brides that want something a little different from the usual poufy white dress and the traditional stroll down the aisle. She has packages with names like Sweet Steampunk and Nightmare Bride. Or she'll custom design whatever you want. I'm definitely hiring her when me and Logon get married. I totally want a Transylvanian wedding, and Logon's into it.

I know you want to hear about Vinnie's love life. She's currently auditioning daddies because she figures the later she waits, the more complicated it gets being pregnant. So anyway, she has a steady stream of assorted men showing up to take her out and show her a good time. She hasn't found the right combination of brains, beauty, and good health yet, but she's confident. It helps that she isn't particularly interested in getting married, just knocked up. Personally, I think she's holding out for Bon Tom.

Yikes! Look at the time. Sorry I can't stop and talk; you'll have to come with me. It's a big day at the No-Kill Ranch. Logon's getting initiated later. He's been studying all year, and tonight Mom is hosting the ceremony where he goes from novice to initiate. He's so serious about it. It's really hard not to tease him. But I don't 'cause I'm really proud of him.

So what am I doing walking around when it's still a good hour until sunset? After a year of drinking Logon's "enhanced" blood, I'm slowly building a tolerance to sunlight, and I'm waking up earlier. Ambrose and Troy were baffled when I e-mailed them about it. Drinking Ambrose's blood isn't having any effects but the usual ones on Troy. Ambrose thinks it's because he's a human vampire and Logon's an immortal human. Mom says it's because there's magic in Logon's witch blood. Anything's possible. Trust me; I know.

So who do you want to hear about while I change clothes? Bon Tom? He worked on the No-Kill Ranch for a while, but he's been in Louisiana for about five months now. Orisha's there with him, and they're looking for Bon Tom's family, so they spend a lot of time traveling around the bayous. I wish he could be here tonight, but I don't blame him for wanting to find his people. Seriously, I sincerely hope there's a great big clan of were-whatevers out there eating filet gumbo, floating pirogues, and whooping it up on Mardi Gras. I really do.

I mentioned Ambrose and Troy. They're still together, and Ambrose likes Europe, so he and Troy are living there. They met a bunch of stylishly nihilistic Russian vamps in Paris that call themselves the Volki, and they joined up with them. A match made in hell.

Ambrose left Simon—obviously—which was fairly complicated since Simon was the vampire that Turned Ambrose. Troy released me from the blood bond without me even asking, but Simon was a little less accommodating. More like a divorce lawyer with a personal stake in the proceedings. I was there for the negotiation, so I got to hear Ambrose drop the discreet hint that he'd reveal one of Simon's anatomical shortcomings if Simon continued to be unreasonable. So I guess size *does* matter, even to powerful, ancient vampire lords. Simon lost all credibility over the affair, and his power, as they say, waned. I heard someone reported his whereabouts to the weres hunting him. I didn't forget what he did to Logon. But I was making disparaging allusions to Simon's unit when I got sidetracked.

I haven't talked much about *my* unit, which is strange for a guy, I guess, but I don't really have a lot to say about it. Do you really want to know that it's six inches at rest, but a grower? That my pediatrician was an artist at circumcisions? That I refer to it as my pink ninja, but named it Sebastian for no good reason? See? It's just embarrassing, really. Of course, I've always been a fairly modest type; the type that gets teased for keeping his underwear on in the locker room, but accepts a blow job behind a bar. Jim Morrison was right—people are strange—and I'm a people... more or less, depending on who you talk to.

Anyway, Ambrose and Troy visit every now and then, taking night flights across the Atlantic to hang out for a while. It's never for long though, even though we've fixed up a vampire-friendly guest room. Florida's just not sophisticated enough for Ambrose, or at least, not sophisticated in the right way. He likes towns where the buildings have been standing around for at least three hundred years. We don't have anything like that here. Except maybe St. Augustine, but it's Dullsville for someone like Ambrose. He's the kind of gem that should always be set in antique gold and lit by candlelight.

That description is in a poem I wrote about him. Yeah, I know. How gay can I get, right? Pretty damned gay as it turns out. I've always thought of myself as a fairly average guy with a few out-of-the-ordinary traits. Just a half-white, all-American boy who loves pizza, movies, and all things related to sci-fi. Okay, I was always fashion-conscious, but not in a runway model kind of way, and hey, haven't you ever heard of metrosexuals?

Oh yeah, the Metro Media gang deserves a mention. They're all still working at the store on Bearss Avenue, which we of course refer to as Bare-ass Avenue. Carlyle's a supervisor now and taking management training courses at night. Barge is managing a team in an amateur women's roller derby league in his spare time. Mel is engaged to a chick that works with dolphins at Sea World, and her family has practically adopted him. They just can't believe that guys like Mel still exist in modern America. They say he reminds them of a guy named John-Boy from an old TV show called *The Waldens* or something like that. Meevie moved to Portland with a widower and his two kids—who are both under two years old. Meevie and... damn, I have a really hard time remembering his name. It's one of those like Ian or Liam or Ewan. Anyway, he's in a band called The Stickies. The last time I talked to Meevie, she got mad 'cause I said he should've called the band The Cumwads—because, you know, what's stickier than a wad of cum? I was joking, and there was a time when she would have laughed her ass off, but she didn't this time, so I guess she really loves this guy. Hell, she must *really* love him if she's willing to play mommy to his kids. The maternal instinct is not strong in that one.

What else can I tell you? Let's see. Me and Logon still hang out at Spacely's. Logon still gets his mocha frappé on the house because Rook likes him and Rook still owns the place. Rook was recently discovered by this super-smart black Jewish chick that owns three nail salons and is as rabid about gaming as he is. Word is they're shopping for a console built for two. His mom is currently under sedation and a doctor's care.

Yeah, I know. Nothing more boring than hearing details about people you don't know and will probably never meet. I'm just shooting the breeze. If there's something in particular you want to know—the poetry? Yikes. I was kind of hoping to gloss over that.

Okay, since I became a vampire, it's like I feel things on a deeper level than I used to. They say that when you have a near-death experience, you gain a new appreciation for life. I say it's true, even if your death experience is so near that you actually die. Arguably, I'm not completely dead, but I don't breathe, so....

Anyway, these deep feelings were coming up in me, and Aunt Bootsy told me I should write them down. I started a half-assed journal, but I kept forgetting to write in it before I went to bed. I blame it on Logon. It's *so* much more fun to fool around with him than try to capture my day in words. Of course, there's nothing I'd rather do than him.

This one night, Logon fell asleep just before dawn, but I was awake for a while. He was face down on my chest, one leg thrown over my thigh, a hand on my shoulder. I was running my fingers through his hair—which I beg him not to cut at least once a day—and words started coming to me. After a bit, I thought maybe I should get up and write them down. Of course that's when I went out like a light. But the words were still there the next night, and I did write them down. A lot later, I showed them to Logon.

He cried, and I panicked, thinking I'd hurt his feelings. He told me to stop being a fuckwit and that he thought the poem was really good, and he loved me more than he could say. *Score!* That was my best Valentine's Day ever. Well, Valentine's Night, but you know what I mean.

Logon showed the poem to Mom, who went apeshit. I had to beg her not to send it to the local newspaper. *God, the humiliation!* It was almost enough to keep me from writing another one.

But I did.

And it was also, as they say, well-received.

I wrote some more whenever the urge hit me, and I started carrying the journal around to have it handy if I was inspired. To cut to the chase, Logon e-mailed Claire, the west coast vamp I met at Jack Hot's party. Apparently, he found her card in a drawer when he was looking for a scrunchy for his hair. That's his story, and he's sticking to it. I was pretty cheesed when I found out he'd sent her one of my poems, but to be fair, it was the one I gave him, which technically belongs to him. By the time I got over the gross breach of trust and heinous invasion of privacy—which took an entire bath time—Claire had shown the poem to a friend with a friend in the publishing business.

And that's how I ended up with a book of poems called "Blood-Red Ink" that sold moderately well. Enough to encourage me to write more. As if Logon's cheerleading wasn't enough.

*Crap*! I'm supposed to be putting on my robe. No, I don't mind wearing the robe; I just don't want to be late. Did I mention that this is a big day/night for Logon? I'll have to catch you later.

WOW, that was amazing. Sorry you couldn't be there, but the ritual is private. You have to be a member of the coven. Me? Yeah, I'm a Wiccan. I expect I'll be a permanent novice, but I get to share something important to Logon, and that's what I care about: my hipster-nerd Elf-witch. I tried making an acronym of it, and it has the letters to make the word *when*, but then it stands for witch-hipster Elf-nerd, which doesn't really work, does it?

Anyway, my boo is an official witch now. How cool is that? He gets to learn more spells and whatnot, and he's really hot to learn all he can about herbs. Mom says he'll make a good healer. And I always add: like Lassie. Neither of them ever laughs.

But damn, Logon looks good in his white silk robe, especially since I know he's bare-ass under there, and he's glowing like a lightning bug with all the positive energy he absorbed in the circle. As soon as this feast is over, I'm jumping him. Hell, if Mom's friends don't leave soon, they're going to get a free live sex show. He's radiating pure love for the universe, but narcissist that I am, I insist on believing it's being beamed directly at me and only me. On an intellectual level I'll accept that Logon's an autonomous being with likes and dislikes, loves and hates, and things that belong to him alone, but emotionally, it's more like *mine mine mine*!

Apparently, the bond between me and Logon is even stronger than the usual one between a vampire and his consort. Most vampires choose their companions by a combination of several factors. First is attraction, of course; desire always comes in first. The quality of blood is second. Blood is not just food to a vampire. It's more like wine, to pick an obvious metaphor, but it's so much more. It doesn't just nourish a vampire physically. Something of the person's essence is transferred with the blood, and depending on how it meshes with the vamp's essence, the experience can range anywhere from celestial fireworks to kissing an ashtray. And every now and then, you get lightning in a bottle—these are all Troy's words, by the way.

Anyway, because Logon's a witch, his blood is different; you'd have to get Troy, or one of his doctor friends, to explain the chemistry. And even beyond the chemical reaction, and the changes that took place when Massey's potion interacted with Logon's witch blood, there's something that happens between us that has nothing to do with physics. Call it a soul if you want, but something in me reaches out to something in him, and when those things meet and merge, it's all I need to know about Heaven.

*Damn, aren't these people ever going to leave?*

What was I saying? Oh yeah. Me and Logon have this kick-ass hookup that makes us both pretty special... from a paranormal point of view anyway. I thought Logon was pretty special even before I found out about all the witchy stuff, but Mom, Aunt Bootsy, and their friends are all pretty excited about him. Also, they're making a big deal out of the fact that I drank blood from Bon Tom and now have were-essence running barefoot through my system. They reckon we're going to do something big someday. I hope we don't let them down, but to be honest, I'd be happy spending the rest of my undead life just hanging out with Logon and sexing him up as often as he'll let me. But if there's something I'm supposed to do, I'll give it my best shot just as soon as I find out what it is.

*Craptastic. Mom just brought out another crock of her homemade mead. This party could go until dawn, and I won't get any for at least twenty-four hours. But damn it, just look at Logon spinning with his hair flying around and his robe clinging like a second skin.*

Excuse me again. I suddenly feel like dancing.


HOURS later. At least two before I can get Logon away from the crowd.

"It's so bright," Logon says as he turns in a circle to take in the mini Zen garden behind the main house.

It really is bright. The moonlight reflects off the white gravel, and there aren't any big trees here to cast shadows. I'm happy to see the moon hasn't started to set. Plenty of time to show my boo how much I love him. "I'm proud of you," I say.

Logon beams at me. "Thanks. Your opinion is the most important one to me." He strokes the rough surface of a trilithon, just like the ones at Stonehenge but a quarter of their size. It's an *eclectic* Zen garden. "I kind of wish my folks would get behind it though."

He came out to his stereotypical WASP parents, and they accept that he's gay. His dad is clearly adopting a virtue, but I think his mom is secretly happy she doesn't have to compete with a wife for her son's love. But they just can't get used to the idea that he's learning to use magic. They think he's schizo at the least.

I put my arms around him from behind and pull him close. "We'll work on them," I say.

"You're the perfect boyfriend."

"No, you're the perfect boyfriend."

"Copycat."

"Yeah, but I'm *your* copycat." Logon has the softest, silkiest patch of skin that runs from behind his earlobe to the hinge of his jaw. I never get tired of nuzzling and licking it. And I love the way it makes him shiver. I also love that he's wearing the earring I gave him for Christmas. It's a little silver cross on a short chain. It's shiny and dangly and it makes him laugh when I flick it with my tongue.

Oh, did I mention that a cross has absolutely no effect on a vampire unless he believes it will? I didn't, but it's true. I even went into a church when Vinnie's sister Rockie married her girlfriend, who's a forward on a pro basketball team. They had the wedding at night just so I could attend. Rockie told her parents she'd always wanted a candlelight service, and no one questioned it. So I witnessed the nuptials of Roxanne Odile Testardo and Sha'nade Leaundra Little, and not one lightning bolt struck the building. Silver is no big deal either. I always wear a silver chain that Logon gave me. A lot of the other traditional stuff is true though. The smallest whiff of garlic makes me want to hurl, damn it. Sunlight is very damaging, but as I said, I'm gaining some resistance to it. I'm never going to have a tan, but then again, I don't want one so….

Logon turns in my arms and tilts his face, which is his charming way of saying "kiss me, stupid." I'd be stupid if I didn't.

I *know* I've told you how much I love kissing Logon. I love the feel of his lips moving on mine, the way he opens them at just the right moment, and the slick, sensuous slide of his tongue as it curls around mine. I lean into him, backing him up until he's against one of the standing stones. I wonder if we can do it right here, maybe on the altar. We've done it in so many positions—almost all of them, I think. Super vamp strength is really handy for a standing fuck. Look, we're not sex maniacs; we're just two young guys in love. Okay, yeah, now that you mention it, that is the definition of sex maniac.

"Vlad?"

"What? Am I going too fast?"

"No. Never. I just feel so good and so happy. I'm so full of good stuff that I want to share it."

"You're doing an awesome job, babe."

"I meant with someone besides you."

"Wha?" I stop trying to get the hem of his robe up to his neck and look into his eyes.

"Not that, you possessive freak. I don't want to sleep with other people. I just want to make them happy."

"Sleeping with you sure makes me happy."

"Ass."

"Yes, I'd love some, please."

"Seriously."

"Okay. What is it you want to do? You're already studying to be a healer."

"I feel like I want to travel around and kind of tell other people about how your mom does things, you know, the natural way."

Mom has a disciple. Cool.

"If you want to travel, we'll hit the road," I say. "But wouldn't it be easier if you had like a TV show or something?"

Logon's giving me the look that says he's considering fitting me for a straitjacket. "The way your mind works is a wonder to me," he says.

"But you like it, right?"

"Goddess help me, I do." Logon kisses me. Just a little pressure of his lips before he pulls back.

"You're not sorry, are you?" *God, the insecurity, when will I outgrow it?*

"What? Of course not. How many times do I have to tell you I love you?"

"Once every five minutes should do it."

"I really do love you, you know." Logon takes one of my hands between both of his and holds it against his chest. "Maybe it was random, or maybe it was destiny, but when I saw you standing there in the coffee shop, I knew you were the one. Even if you'd just been pretending to be a vampire, I would've wanted you. We'd probably be walking around a gamer-con right now in our World of Warcraft T-shirts, feeling all daring 'cause we're holding hands."

"You really think so?"

"Well, they might be HALO T-shirts, but yes, I really do. You and me are meant to be together. Believe that if you don't believe anything else."

"Whoa." The tone of his last few words kind of shocks me. "I believe in stuff."

"You just don't seem to take anything seriously is all I'm saying."

"*Seem* is the operative word in that sentence."

"Okay. I'm not trying to start a fight. I guess I'm just being a little insecure."

"About what?" My voice is sharp because I'm surprised. Logon is perfect. What's he got to be insecure about?

"Well." Logon sighs. "Sometimes I think that you think my stuff isn't as important as yours or something. But I don't really know what I'm saying. Just forget it."

"If anything, I think what you do is infinitely more important than anything I do. I guess I just don't know how to show it. Baby, I'm so proud of you, and I love you so much that—"

Logon puts a finger on my lips. "Okay. That's good. I need to hear it too. Maybe not every five minutes, but at least once a day."

"I tell you that I love you all the time."

"Sometimes on every other thrust."

Finally the light bulb comes on in my brain. "Do I only say it when we're doing it?"

"Pretty much."

"Okay. Noted."

"Look, I'm not trying to change you, I'm just.... I don't know what I am, but tonight I feel like I could be whatever I want. And all I really want is to be yours."

"Me too."

"Then I guess neither of us really has anything to complain about," Logon says.

"Well... it is taking a long time to get down to business tonight."

"You're hopeless. I give up."

"Finally." I grab him in a tight hug and kiss him, trying hard to show him how I feel about him. He appears to get the message and replies favorably. I get the robe up to his neck. Do I need to tell you Logon was helpful in getting it the rest of the way off? Didn't think so.

But I will if you want me to. It's not like we're prudes, and making love is a beautiful, natural thing after all. Especially when it's done outside in the moonlight. Things are half-hidden and mysterious and take on the quality of a ritual.

I toss Logon's robe over the flat-topped altar stone and lift him to sit on the edge. Logon leans back on his elbows and relaxes. Gently, focusing on Logon's pleasure, I prepare him. He moans and pumps his hips as I suck his hard cock and ease my spit-slippery finger in and out of him. I go down on him until he comes with my name on his lips. Wasting no time, I pull him to the edge and enter him, pushing my length into his tight heat.

"Wow, I almost came again." Logon lets out a long breath. "I love it when you give me the whole eight inches all at once."

I stop my forward motion and draw back a couple of inches. Folding Logon's legs, I rest my palms on the back of my boo's thighs and rock into him in slow, shallow strokes. Logon grasps his legs behind the knees and holds them back for me. Now I can stroke his cock. Pumping Logon's hard-on with one hand, I toy with his nipples with the other, while I thrust slowly.

"Goddess," Logon gasps. "You know what I like. Give it to me."

"You just love ordering me around, don't you," I say as I increase the speed and depth of my stroke. "Hang on to your hat."

"I love you," Logon says.

He moans as I do several of his favorite things at the same time and comes with a hoarse cry of release. I smirk and raise my hand to my mouth and lick it clean of Logon's cum. I have to love the multiorgasmic side effect of Massey's formula.

"Who's your daddy?" I tease, smacking Logon's ass.

"Shut up, I'll be in therapy for years." Logon grins.

I'm still pushing into Logon, and he bears down on my dick. Gazing tenderly at me, he's doing his best to give me as much pleasure as possible. "That feels incredible!" I gasp. "What the hell are you—? Oh shit, Logon! Logon! Shit! Oh! Oh! Oh, don't stop!"

I come so hard I see spots and I forget to breathe as my cum unspools deep inside Logon. Head canting slightly to one side, eyes softly closed, thick lashes brushing his cheekbones, a Mona Lisa smile curving his sculpted lips, Logon is so beautiful he hurts my heart.

Logon wraps his legs around me as he rises to a semi-sitting position. "You are so fucking beautiful when you come," he says, his voice grainy with spent lust.

I pull him as close as I can without disengaging. "It's a beautiful feeling. I'm thankful I have you."

"I think we've proven we're in it for the long haul," Logon says. "And I know you love me, no matter what you don't say."

I nuzzle Logon's neck as I gently withdraw from the sweetest place I know. I don't know what's next for us, but I know it'll be good as long as we're together.

# CHAPTER THIRTEEN

I LOVE the lazy waking up after falling asleep from a truly earth-shattering session of sweet love. There's nothing better than slowly becoming aware with Logon still asleep in my arms. I like to lie here for a while before I open my eyes. But I've done that and now I want to look at my boo.

*What the hell is that?*

It looks like a small, chubby cat, but I've never seen a cat with ears that long, almost as long as a rabbit's ears. And I've never seen a cat that color either. Its fur looks more like down than hair, and it's kind of freckled black and white, like those really hyper sheepherding dogs. It has eyes as big as a nocturnal jungle animal's, and they're a weird milky green like jade. Did I mention that it's hovering in the air in front of Logon's face with its fluffy raccoon tail curled into a question mark? Well it is.

"Mom!" I holler, reverting to a four-year-old with a nightmare.

Logon jumps and sits up, bumping the back of his skull on the headboard.

The door flies open. "What's wrong?" Mom asks as she looks around the room. She's holding a wooden spoon like a fly swatter, and Aunt Bootsy is right on her heels.

"What is that?" I ask, pointing to the fuzzy.

Mom has seen *it* and is staring at it with big eyes. "Well, I'll be jiggered. It's a familiar," she says softly. "I haven't seen one in.... Elizabeth, how long's it been since we saw Cousin Claudia?"

I know Mom's excited because she never calls Aunt Bootsy by her real name, just like Aunt Bootsy never calls Mom by hers. They've been Bootsy and Vix since they could talk, or so they tell me. Did I mention they're twins? Didn't think so. I hardly ever do. Once people hear the word twins, they have all kinds of preconceived notions. But they're identical twins. Aunt Bootsy's just a couple of minutes older, as she likes to remind my mom from time to time.

Aunt Bootsy looks over Mom's shoulder, and for a second, it's like Mom's got two heads. Kind of creepy and kind of cool. "Aw, it's a real cute one," Bootsy says. "You're really lucky, Logon. And it's been a good twenty years since we saw Claudia, Vix."

"Shhh," Mom says as the bunny-cat-thing floats closer to Logon. "Just stay calm, honey-boy, and put out welcome vibes."

The speckled bunny-cat's fluffy tail curls up over the thing's back like one of those noisemakers you blow on New Year's. It stretches its neck and touches its moist, pink nose to the tip of Logon's nose. Its mouth doesn't move, but it makes a little trilling, inquisitive noise. Logon smiles, and holds out his arms, and the thing descends to light on the palm of his hand.

"Wonderful," Mom says.

"I can't believe I'm seeing this," Aunt Bootsy says.

"Whoa!" I say as the thing scampers up Logon's arm on its dainty feet. From Logon's shoulder, it stares at me as if it's wondering if my eyeballs taste good.

"Beezle, this is Vlad. We love him," Logon says.

The bunny-cat blinks and raises a paw. Feeling all kinds of foolish, I high-five the thing with a finger. As soon as I do, it slinks down the front of Logon's robe and curls up on his lap, where it's now a large lump covered in white, somewhat sex-sullied, silk.

"Hey!" Logon exclaims as the lump moves. "That tickles. Hey!" He gasps. "Oh my God and Goddess! That feels...." Logon's voice trails off in a groan.

"Are you okay? What's that thing doing?"

"*That thing* has a name," Mom says. "Beezle is a very rare, very magical being. You two made love last night, didn't you?"

"Jeez, Mom."

"Yeah, we did." Logon's voice has that breathless edge it gets when I'm going down on him. *What the eff is going on?* "We do it just about every night."

"I'd be surprised if you didn't."

"Jeez, Mom!"

Aunt Bootsy is laughing at me. I give her the sad puppy look, and she laughs harder. Why is my mortification so amusing? It's bad enough that my mom and my aunt are in my bedroom while I'm in bed with my lover, but it's turning into a roundtable discussion, and I'm not in the mood. I just want a few answers.

"He's got that look, Vix," Aunt Bootsy says.

"Yeah, I reckon we'd better humor him."

I hate it when they go all twinsy on me and talk to each other like I'm not there. And if I act like it bugs me, they get worse and talk in some made-up language. They swear I learned it when I was a baby, but I forgot as I got older. I think they're feeding me a load of woonga. Screw it. I lift the hem of Logon's robe and look under it.

Ohhhhh...kaaaaay.

"What the hell, Mom?"

"Well, what did you think the third nipple was for?"

"Not for feeding a tubby cat-rabbit thing... named Beezle."

"What's wrong?" Logon asks. He's talking like a stoner, all slow and drawly.

"You're... breast-feeding that... Beezle thing. Suckling. Giving suck."

"And?"

I catch his tone and dial back my reaction. "It's just… unexpected. I need a few minutes to get used to the idea that my boyfriend has a Pokémon pet feeding on him." *Hey, wait a minute.* "What's Beezle sucking out of Logon anyway?" I look up at Mom.

"Nothing tangible," Aunt Bootsy says. "Familiars get their sustenance from emotions."

"And that's why this precious one came to Logon," Mom says. "You two made love under the moon last night while Logon was filled with the forces of creation. Your love for each other is so big and bright that Beezle was drawn to it and popped into our dimension."

"Are you telling me I'm a baby daddy?"

"Why are vampires so damn smart-mouthed?" Aunt Bootsy says.

"I don't know," Mom says. "But they are. Every last one of them."

"I'm right here," I say. "And I'm not deaf."

"Of course you aren't, puddin'," Aunt Bootsy says. "We should probably leave you three alone to get used to each other."

"You're right," Mom says, leaning her head against Aunt Bootsy's. "Aren't they sweet though?"

"Hold on. Two things. If this Beezle lives on emotions, why does it have to suck on Logon? And *popped into this dimension*? Who are you? Rod Serling?"

"Puddin', I've still got chores before I go to bed, and you need to support Logon while he bonds with Beezle. As for the suckling? My theory is that there's no stronger bond than the one between mother and child, but who knows? That's just how it works. And Logon gets something out of it too. Look how serene he is."

She's right. By the look on his face, my boo has achieved Nirvana. I've seen that look before, but usually it's after I make him come. *Don't like.* That's *my* look, and I'm the only one who should be able to make Logon smile like that. Serene, my ass—that's afterglow.

Logon reads me like a comic book. He takes my hand and kisses my fingers. "It's not like that, babe," he says.

And just like that, it's okay. He puts my hand on the bulge under his robe—try to be mature about it, like me—and I feel Beezle's soft little body vibrating like a purring cat. You know, this is kind of nice, soothing even. Why do I have to move my hand? Oh. Logon pulls his robe up, and Beezle lifts his head, making a mewling noise. The familiar's little mouth opens in a pink yawn, and he blinks several times. BTW: I have no idea if Beezle is a girl or a boy, but I can't keep saying "it," so I'm going to say "he," okay?

I have to admit, the little critter is awful cute. He's rubbing his face like a sleepy toddler and swishing his fluffy tail slowly back and forth, tickling Logon's tummy. I notice the shininess of Logon's wet nipple, and I can't resist. I rub my fingertip playfully around the nub and over it.

Great goolies! Okay. No reason to panic. I've just got a familiar running up my arm.

"Beezle likes you!" Logon sounds so happy. I guess it wouldn't kill me to pretend the furball doesn't make me want to run and hide in the hamper.

"Hey, Bee, what up?" I say. I'm doing my best not to drop my eyes while Beezle stares solemnly at me. "Is Logon the business or what?"

Beezle smiles. I shit you not. Then he nods, just once, before he ducks his head and rubs the top of it against the underside of my chin. Warm. Silky. Lovey. Gah. I swear I'm growing ovaries, but I don't care. The weird little furbag is irresistible after all. And I figure he'll be good practice in case we want a real kid someday. Adopted, of course. What did you think I meant? Logon's a witch, but he can't twitch his nose and actually grow a female reproductive system. But there are lots of kids out there that need homes, unfortunately. So many that they even let gay couples adopt them.

I scootch back to lean against the headboard and pull Logon into my arms. Beezle curls up on my right shoulder and wraps his tail around Logon's neck, linking the three of us. Outside the door, I can hear Mom and Aunt Bootsy laughing and clanging cast-iron pans in the kitchen. But in our room, the sounds are muted: Logon's breath,

Beezle's adorable snoring, and the rustling of the sheets when one of us moves slightly. I think this is called a reverie, and it's so peaceful that I'm not even surprised when I realize I know what Logon's thinking.

Wow, this is so cool! And so much faster than talking. I guess the furball does have his uses if he can connect us like this. It's really *sweet*, not like sugar, but like *bitchin'*.

I'm going to stay here for a while, just drifting with Logon while we think about our future together. I've never been much of a planner—unless you count mapping out the logistics of attending a week-long sci-fi con on an extremely limited budget—and my plan mostly consists of being with Logon as much as possible. If I can help him do what he needs to do, I will. Even if it means being cool with him nursing a transdimensional teddy bear. He's worth it, and I want to live my extremely long life with him, so I'm willing to bend a little... if he is.

Yeah, I know that was a lame double entendre. And it sounded even more juvenile because I was sounding all mature just a second ago. It's true I'm a lot less of a smart-ass than I used to be, but I'm still a bad boy.

Stop smirking.

You know what? Maybe it's time for you to scamper. I'd like to get back to the drifting thing, and this story already has more endings than the *Return of the King* movie. Don't mean to be rude, but after all, you *are* in my bedroom, so buh-bye. Go on now. Shoo. I know you all got lives and stuff, maybe not as cool as mine, but still pretty cool, so go do whatever it is you do the best way you know how.

It's not about playing a role or being cool. Sometimes things aren't what you think, and sometimes they're exactly what you think, but you don't know which they are until later. So treat the people you love like gold, and give the others the benefit of the doubt.

Just don't be a dick. That's all I'm saying.

*Peace.*

MALTHEA neither reveals her birth date nor admits to a last name. She does bow to the necessity for a physical location, which currently goes by the name Gainesville, Florida, though once it was known as Alachua—which Malthea prefers as infinitely more melodic. It was here that she attended college, never managing—or indeed trying—to fit in with the football-centric student body that proudly performed something called the Gator Chomp at every game. It wasn't easy being apathetic in the heart of rah-rah country or dressing in head-to-toe black every day when temperatures could and did reach triple digits, but Malthea credits surviving this ordeal with giving her the perseverance necessary to finish her first book.

Malthea has been fascinated by vampires since she first learned of their existence and has spent many, many hours reading about them or watching them on film. She also loves *Blackadder*, Emma Thompson, and salted caramel lattes. She lives a few blocks from the Hippodrome and used to hang out at the Hardback Café. These days she tends to stay in and get things done… if you count making up stories as getting things done. Malthea does. And she has the unconditional love and unwavering support of a small black Manx named Lirazel and a cardboard standup of Brandon Lee as Eric Draven in *The Crow*. She'd like to travel to places with lower temperatures and more cloud cover.